TWIN FLAME

THE FATE & FLAME DUET
BOOK TWO

LIZ HAMBLETON

EDITED BY
BETH HUDSON INK

COVER DESIGN BY
K.B. BARRETT DESIGNS

LIZHAMBLETONBOOKSLLC

CONTENTS

CONTENT WARNING

Before you read...

The Fate & Flame duet contains mature subject matter that may not be for everyone. If you are not comfortable reading detailed, explicit, on-page romance, this book is not for you.

There are mentions of kidnapping, medical torment, and therapy. Although not described in great detail, there is mention of others taking their life or undergoing trauma.

Please be mindful when you read.

CHAPTER 1

EMRY

I'm fourteen.

The age when girls find themselves on the verge of becoming women, so close to their body and mind coming together into one whole person. It's a transition filled with hormones and anxiety, but beyond all of that, there's a future ready and waiting, full of what-ifs.

What if I become a scientist?

What if I'm beautiful?

What if I find my bonded?

I'm thinking of all the what-ifs as I'm standing in an endless line with my mother. She's nervous, looking up at the big black numbers displayed on the wall. Her eyes are trans-fixed, begging the clock to move faster.

The words, *give your kids the edge and test,* blink above the

1

clock in gold script. We shuffle forward along with hundreds of others, maybe thousands. I crane my neck to see the line that weaves and stretches throughout the cold building. Everyone stands and waits for hours to get our blood drawn — waiting to see if some magic alarm sounds when the red liquid fills the vial, alerting us that something inside is the key to the bond.

My mother is waiting for a check.

It's a small payment, but it's something, and she's run out of her government stipend for the month and it's only the fifth. There was a reception she insisted on attending, sure that it would give her a bonded. Instead, she blew all of our money on a fizzer. That's what people call the receptions where all your hopes and dreams fizzle into nothing.

We need this money to get food. I don't argue the plan because my stomach growls while we inch forward. It's imperative I find a grocery store before she gets another reception booked. I have a few hours to figure out that trick. Maybe I could hide her phone or drop it. Buying a new phone and groceries is still far less expensive than a reception.

She doesn't ask if I want my blood drawn and DNA sampled for testing, but even if we had the cash to burn, I don't think I'd mind. I want to know if I have a bonded. That would take me away from here — away from her.

I bet my bonded would make sure we always have enough food. He would cook delicious meals for me that we both love, and we could eat together with big glasses of wine.

Another hour passes, and she lets out a heavy sigh, raking her hands through her hair to tie it into a ponytail. The icy room gets hotter as we make it further inside, and the hair on the back of her neck is slicked with sweat.

She complains this is taking forever, and she doesn't like the way one of the men in lab coats looks at me. What she means to say is she doesn't like that he isn't looking at her.

The other way my mother makes money is by using men, promising she'll settle with them or co-parent, taking their dollars until they catch on to her plan. She sells herself, but it's getting harder. Younger women catch the eyes of her targets these days. Because I refuse to help her exploit people, I'm competition instead of an asset. The only way I can help her get money is by standing in this line.

New employees enter the room, taking their turn to touch us all, and I flinch. There are no fireworks for anyone, no tears, or applause for a bonded - only disappointment.

I wish I was normal, like the other girls I've met. They live in one place and keep friends and tell me how jealous they are of my life. I get to travel, meet new people, and they think that gives me a chance to find my bond.

Maybe it does and I should feel gratitude for the woman tapping her toe in impatience and dragging me forward when the line moves an inch.

But I want it to stop.

The parties and the moving and us living out of a duffle bag. I want to go into a school building instead of taking classes through a screen. I want friends more than I've ever wanted a bond.

I'm not normal.

It takes four more hours before we make it to someone who draws my blood without a word. She fills six vials and looks over the form my mother filled out, narrowing her eyes when she gets to the second page. I'm so exhausted I struggle to keep my eyes open, the gnawing at my stomach now a persistent ache I struggle to ignore.

"Ms. Crawford," the nurse says, tapping her finger on the bottom of the page.

"Blaire, please," my mother corrects.

"This date of her first and last period is the same," the nurse says.

My mother raises an eyebrow and crosses her arms in front of her chest. "The ad said ages ten to fourteen. It didn't say anything about having a period. I'm still getting the money you promised."

I sink into my chair, mortified, my cheeks flaring red.

The nurse waves her hand at us. "No, no, that's not why I bring it up. There's someone you might like to meet. A rep from the company, Genome Theory. Have you heard of them?"

My mother shakes her head, and the nurse doesn't bother to look at me. I'm an inanimate object in the room, there purely for payment. That's the purpose of my life. I'm a walking check.

"They're looking for children in this stage of puberty," the nurse explains. "She could be a candidate."

My mother shrugs. "A candidate for what?"

"They're leading the field with breakthrough bonding research." The nurse almost laughs as she says this, as if to mean, what else do you think they would want with your daughter? Everything is about the bond.

"Okay. Do you need me to sign something to share her results?" My mother's eyes light up before she continues. "Does that give us another testing fee?"

The nurse rises, jotting down notes on our paperwork while she walks to the door. "Let me get Gilbert. He can speak to you about it, but yes."

"Yes to what part?" Mother asks.

"Yes, there's payment involved."

Decision made.

My mother doesn't look at me while we wait, but I cross my arms across my chest and stare her down. I'm about to open my mouth and break the silence when another stranger barges into the room without knocking.

Gilbert's a small man, and he lowers the seat before he sits, his short fingers clasping over his crossed legs. He smiles without his eyes and addresses me, introducing himself as he hands my mother a packet with happy adolescents on the cover. They're pictured standing in a field, holding hands in bright white outfits.

Is this a cult?

I bet a cult would feed its members regularly.

"I hear you might be a candidate for our program," he says.

I narrow my gaze at the man, looking him over, noticing how his sleeves are too long for his frame. "I hear my mother gets paid if I am, so how about you tell her where to sign and we can be done?"

"Emry!" my mother scolds, but she doesn't look up from the open packet, flipping through the pages to find the gold at the end of her rainbow.

"You would have to sign, not your mother," he explains.

"I'm only fourteen," I huff. "I know how this works."

Gilbert reaches over, turning the pages of the pamphlet in my mother's lap. He points to a page full of compact writing and taps on a paragraph. "Here. It explains your emancipation."

Emancipation.

"Well, how does that work?" my mother asks.

What she means to ask is how she's going to get paid by the government for her gift to society, a.k.a. me, if I'm no longer her property.

"You would be paid for the remainder of the child-bearing stipends on Emry here, but she would be independent as we would take your place as her caretaker."

My mother relaxes back into her seat.

"And you would be paid as well, a stipend put into an account for when you come of age," Gilbert tells me. "It would set you up well for when you mature out of the program."

"And what's the program?" I ask, my voice still dripping with disdain.

"In the most simple of terms, you live in a community with other children your age and we observe you. There's a lot of blood sampling and some other mildly uncomfortable tests, but our goal is to have data from someone who will hopefully bond. All the information over these critical years could give us the key to nature's most precious gift. You would be a part of that."

I don't want to show my excitement, but it creeps into my veins, forcing the hint of a smile onto my face. One place to live and go to school. Friends that I'll see tomorrow and the next day. Years away from my mother with a paycheck on the other side. It feels too good to be true.

"If you have any interest, I can give you a tour, take you through an information seminar," Gilbert says.

"She's interested," my mother announces, handing a page over to Gilbert. I notice her signature scrawled on the bottom, harsh lines that spell out her permission to give me away.

My heart drops a fraction when he takes the form, but I push my shoulders back and keep my lips from quivering, refusing to show my disappointment. It's possible to love someone and hate them at the same time. My mother is proof of that.

"I'll check it out," I shrug. My words don't show how at peace I feel, knowing I'll walk through whatever doors he'll lead me through to a new life.

What I don't know is the years of torture I'll suffer before I walk out again.

CHAPTER 2

I rip someone's hand from my arm, their nails scratching at the fabric of my shirt, searching for contact. Another stranger's sweaty palms run over the skin of my neck, and I growl.

Sebastian doesn't seem to notice, his boots tromping through the crowd, shoulder-checking everyone in his path. He makes contact with a man holding drinks in both hands who spins in place before tumbling to the ground, a result of Sebastian's force and this crowd's drunkenness.

"Sebastian!" I yell.

A woman misted with sweat, wearing bright red lipstick, steps in my way, her hands wrapping around my neck to bring me in for a kiss. I grab her by the wrists, careful not to hurt her, and slide her off of me. She stumbles back to her friends, laughing in response.

Sebastian's stride is almost twice as long as mine, and he glides ahead, unable to hear me over the music that blasts in our ears. He's a foot taller than the crowd, so I won't lose sight of the man. I push another woman away, keeping my eyes ahead to be sure I won't.

Beams of light blind me every few seconds, sprinting in rapid colors around the open space crammed with bodies. Adherence events are chaotic, but nothing compared to this mayhem. I never partook in receptions like these; parties off the books, and as a result, only a tenth of the standard cost. Hell, I never went to any reception unless work forced me.

I'm used to an attendance list, a limit of people, and air conditioning. This underground reception doesn't abide by any rules, not caring if people get hurt or lost.

Which they will.

The dangers don't stop the massive horde of searchers and partygoers that we are forcing our way through, pushing the strangers aside who ignore our protests.

Sebastian's contact is here, and this person can help us find Emry, so I grit my teeth and bear the torture, following the man willingly.

There's one thing this reception, if you could even call it that, has in common with an Adherence event.

Everyone's naked.

It makes this nightmare worse than normal, especially because Emry is awake and knows everything I see and feel, our minds pinging thoughts back and forth.

She's hidden away in some room, waiting for us to find her. Her mind is open to me, and I don't want to lose our connection, even if she's forced to watch sweaty drunk bodies slide their greasy hands all over my skin, stroking my face, reaching inside my shirt and down my pants. It's no better for Sebastian, and for her sake, I try to focus on the mission, and not the blonde who just jumped on his back, licking his earlobe.

"Come on," Sebastian says, turning back and waving his hand at me. At least, I think that's what he says. It's impossible to tell over the roaring music. The girl falls off his shoulders, one of her heels slipping when she rolls on the floor.

"Heels without clothes? I guess I wouldn't want my feet to touch that floor, either."

Emry's voice in my head is one I can't ignore, but I don't know how to respond to her, so I keep walking.

Sebastian was right to take off his shirt, and I give up, ripping mine off to give the strangers easier access to my skin. They don't recognize me in the dark and don't know that I'm bonded and this charade won't do them any good.

Emry tries to hide her jealousy, but she's getting flashes of both of us in rapid succession, our skin being groped and smacked. Watching the two of us under attack by a thousand people at once, she's found a new low in her own personal hell.

I catch up to Sebastian, but only because he's stopped in front of a mirrored door, a black line down the center that I pry my fingers inside trying to open. It won't budge, and Sebastian shakes his head, mouthing for me to wait.

"Get off!" I scream at some woman who tries to climb me. She's hoping I'll carry her piggyback around the party like so many men seem to enjoy. Her ass hits the floor, and she laughs, dropping her drink and spilling it everywhere. Sebastian looks down at her, and she scrambles up, hoping to throw herself onto him next. He shakes his head no in such a way that stops her and causes her to turn up her lip and flick him off.

"Looking for a co-parent," a naked woman whispers in my ear.

Her friend slides up to Sebastian. "Or just some practice," the other woman says.

"I'm sorry. I need to rest and... I can't take this anymore."

Emry shuts off her mind, and I groan and push the stranger away. She shakes her tits at me, and when I don't turn to look, she tries to press them against my back. I arch away, slamming into Sebastian, who jerks and pushes me by instinct.

I fall onto the wet floor, my back slapping on a puddle of spilled liquor, and groan while Sebastian offers me an apologetic look.

The mirrored doors slide open in the middle, and I get up with a sigh of relief, ready to stop the various assaults on my body. We walk through, guards pushing back the women who try to follow us. The smell of alcohol and sex doesn't fade when the door closes behind us, but the population thins, and I let my shoulders drop a fraction.

The people that pass, also naked, run their hands along our bare skin, but it's bearable compared to outside.

"Why all the clothes, big boy?" a woman pouts to Sebastian.

"We need to talk to Vin," Sebastian says to her.

Someone comes up behind me, sliding a hand up my spine, and I do my best not to shy away. The more normal we act, the sooner we can get our information and get out of here.

Emry's been gone for over twenty-four hours, and Sebastian and I have barely slept, spending every moment searching for her. We didn't come to a decision to search together. It just happened, both of us demanding a car and getting inside.

Jack's concern about our constant proximity faded a few hours after watching us work. We're in sync, understanding our strengths and working together well, both of us focused on finding the person we care most about.

What will happen after we rescue her isn't something we discuss.

One step at a time, I tell myself, but for now, we're getting along.

NeXus has this place surrounded, allowing us to collect information before the man we need to see gets spooked and flees. Sebastian has the personal connection that can get us information, but that's not why we're the ones doing the dirty work.

We don't trust anyone else, but in this, we trust each other.

"You're no fun," the woman pouts, running her fingers over her tits, urging Sebastian to gawk and salivate. There are hundreds of naked women dancing around this reception, every size and shape of breast right at someone's fingertips, and although it's impossible not to look at, we don't care. It's boring and frustrating and not getting us any closer to Emry.

"Vin!" Sebastian barks at her.

"Geez, fine," she tuts, turning on her heel to leave. "I'll go get him, asshole."

We follow her, ensuring she's getting Vin, and she heads up a narrow stairway, trying her best to sway her hips in our faces. It's not appreciated and when she doesn't get the response she wants, maybe a slap on the ass or a remark about her beauty, she stomps her feet the rest of the way. Banging on a wood door when we reach the top, she shouts, "Two assholes are here to see you, Vin."

"Vin, it's Seb," Sebastian yells.

There's still a steady vibration from the music that thuds through the walls and under our feet, but I hear someone rustling inside before the door opens, a man matching Sebastian's size reaching out his palm for a handshake.

"Come in, come in," he says. "Damn, Seb. It's been so long. Too long."

Inside there's a full office with bookshelves and televisions, all of them pointed at various angles of the reception. Vin sits down at his desk, offering us both a seat. It's nice enough in here, but everything has a temporary quality to it, ready to be folded up and transported to the next site at a moment's notice.

"This is my friend, Theo," Sebastian says.

"Friend? I'm surprised you keep the poor bastard standing after what I heard." Vin raises an eyebrow and looks me up and down, plucking a pink feather that lodged itself in my hair. "No offense."

"None taken," I tell Vin. "I'm just as surprised as you."

I shrug and look at Sebastian who, in the light, is covered in pink and gold glitter. My eyes widen, and he looks down at himself to see what draws my attention.

"I'm washing this off in your shower, Vin," he groans.

"Why did you walk through the party, anyway?" Vin asks. "Unless you're looking for…"

"I'm not," Sebastian barks. "You wouldn't pick up your fucking phone or answer emails. You know Emry's missing. Drifter parties keep track of that shit."

Vin raises his hands in apology and takes a seat at his desk, the chair sliding back when he sits. "You know how crazy the planning gets."

"Especially with all the police to pay off and officials to bribe for fake permits," I add.

Vin sucks in a breath, his palms hitting his desk. "Easy for you to judge an affordable reception, isn't it, son?"

I bite the inside of my cheek, unable to refute that I'm bonded, and don't have a say in what those naked, drunk, glitter-happy people want to do with their life.

"A girl named Alison was at an underground reception. She's Emry's best friend, and she was taken," Sebastian says. He describes her, giving Vin enough information to pick her out of a crowd. "We believe it's connected to Emry's disappearance."

"We just set up three hours ago," Vin argues. "It wasn't here. Wasn't mine."

"But you know who ran the one where she disappeared,

and you're going to help me get any recordings they have to a company called Seeker Solutions," Sebastian says.

Vin opens his mouth to object, but Sebastian steps forward, his glittered fist slamming into his open hand and making a slap. "Because you owe me that." His jaw tightens with his words, and I still myself, letting Vin think over his options.

He taps his fingers on the plastic desk, looking over the monitors that showcase the raging party below. "Yeah, I do," he admits.

I want to know why, but I suppose it doesn't matter. Someone like Vin is bound to need favors and lots of them.

"Woman named Misty ran the last one," Vin tells us. "I'll talk to her, let her know why I need it, and get it to the right people. Anything else you need, just tell me." Vin swallows hard and I wait, trying not to brush off the glitter that's floating around and sticking to my skin. "Listen. I am sorry about Emry. I know that girl's been through some shit. I should have called you back."

"We got a tip that someone with a tattoo that looks like this—" Sebastian pulls out his phone, flipping through a few images before he hands it to Vin. "That guy knows something."

Vin pales before he hands the phone back to Sebastian, his expensive watch flickering in the fluorescent lights. Despite the temporary nature of this office, the man himself is expensive. There's money in receptions, but he's dressed in quiet luxury only few can afford. Men like him only get sick if they think they're about to lose money, and Vin looks like he might vomit on his fold-up desk.

"He knows the guy," I say, shoving my hands inside my pockets and stepping over to Sebastian.

"I don't think so," Vin lies. "That tattoo looks familiar, but I don't know."

"Person's a cash cow, whoever it is," I tell Sebastian. "That's why he's lying."

"What the fuck do you know?" Vin hisses, rising from his desk.

"That you can get us to that man."

"Who the fuck are you?" Vin sneers at me. "A home wrecker of the worst kind. You took his wife and now you lost her. You don't know shit."

"I know people," I tell Vin. I'm calm knowing his reaction only confirms my suspicions, and he'll break, giving up the tattooed man. "I know their mannerisms, what makes them tick."

"Oh, yeah, what makes Sebastian tick?" Vin asks.

"Caring for people – for Emry," I say back without thinking twice. I lean forward, placing both palms flat on the desk, my eyes meeting his. I may not have Sebastian's stance, but I know how to intimidate, and we don't have time for Vin to second guess giving us a name and location. "He's a genuine, good fucking person."

"No, I'm not," Sebastian says, grabbing the man by his collar and slamming his head down on the desk.

I laugh because I knew how Sebastian would react. We play off of each other and it's almost too easy to get what we want.

Vin groans, grabbing his jaw and mouth, trickles of blood pouring between his fingers. He curses inaudible words before wiping his lips and spitting a tooth onto the floor. He takes a few stumbling steps back before he begins pacing his office and bleeding everywhere.

"I still think you're a good person," I tell Sebastian while Vin curses.

"Thanks," Sebastian says, crossing his arms and leaning back on his heels.

I walk up to Vin, and he freezes.

"This guy pays you for something," I say. "A lot. For something you know is illegal, but you don't ask questions."

Vin lowers his bloody hand from his face while Sebastian's footsteps grow closer behind me.

"We don't care about that," I admit. "We only care about Emry, and he can help us find her. Take us to him."

Vin's eyes shift from Sebastian to me a few times before he offers a nod in defeat. He leads us out of the office and down a hallway, explaining there's someone next to the stage waiting for a transport and the tattooed man is the transporter. Vin can't bring himself to say *person to transport* or *kidnapper*, but we know what he means.

My vision blurs a few times while we walk, and I wonder if I inhaled some airborne recreational drugs or if I'm simply exhausted to the point I can no longer see straight. We step out to a landing, countless people dancing and touching below the grated pathway under our feet.

Vin points to a man standing apart from the crowd and observing them. We notice the thick lines of the familiar tattoo on the man's neck. Sebastian shoots Vin a look of indignation before reminding him to get the video from Misty, and we descend toward the person.

This is the first tip that might get us closer. It's one of thousands, but she's out there, and someone knows something. I check my watch.

Twenty-five hours.

Emry's mind is closed, but I do my best to reach her.

"We're coming. We'll find you."

CHAPTER 3

THEO

"How are you feeling?" Moira asks, her voice heavy with worry.

"He's fine," Sebastian answers as he speeds down the highway. He's disengaged the auto drive, flying through the streets and around cars, eager to reach our next location.

Another tip leads us further away from our home and NeXus, and we're following it after four days of no sleep in our search for Emry.

The information from the underground reception gave us what to look for, but it wasn't a solid path to Genome, not that I remember everything we were told.

I reach for my head, which suffered not only punches from the tattooed man fighting for his life a few days ago but a solid hit when I fell to the floor, passing out.

The first time of many I've collapsed out of nowhere.

"You should concentrate on driving if you insist on doing it yourself like a maniac," Moira chastises him.

"I'm feeling fine," I tell Moira, tapping the hand she placed on my shoulder. She lets go, relaxing into the back seat with a sigh. I'm glad she's here, insisting that she can't just pace around while her shop is well taken care of and Jack is working.

But I'm not telling her the whole truth.

My heart doesn't beat out of rhythm even though Emry isn't near. That's what she's worried about, so the lie feels like less of a betrayal. Once I'm close to Emry, the rest of me will heal, including this raging headache. If they've done anything to her, my bond will help her as well. I shiver at the thought.

Emry's forever fixed something inside of me, mending the damage cursed upon my heart from birth. The weakness that took my father will never be the end of my life.

That doesn't mean I'm okay.

A dark void burrows deep inside my soul, Emry's sadness forming a pit there that I want to sink into. She speaks to me in a faded whisper that's broken and fragmented, growing weaker each day.

She's scared and alone, trapped somewhere, and traumatized all over again. Every hour that passes, her agony gets worse, and I realize something I'm afraid to admit.

We can't live without each other.

If she dies, my will to live will end.

Even if the will was there, if she dies, I'm not far behind her.

"Anything lately?" Sebastian bites out. He screeches around another car, the driver whipping their head at us in confusion.

"Not since you asked five minutes ago," I tell him. What I mean as a warning to back off instead comes out as a dejected admission. I haven't heard Emry's voice in hours, and I keep projecting to her that we're coming and we'll find her, but she's fading away.

"Let's go through it again," Sebastian says. "Just one more time."

Moira groans and shifts in her seat. "Sebastian, that's enough—"

"It's okay," I say before she continues. Moira doesn't need to protect me from Sebastian. We're on the same side, and I'll do anything to help Emry.

I run my hands down my thighs, pressing into the muscles with a long breath. Once again, I tell Sebastian everything that Emry has whispered to me through the bond.

"She was in darkness in a vehicle, and they gave her something that made her lightheaded and sick. She could hear, but it faded in and out. There were sounds of traffic for maybe twenty or thirty minutes until noises from the city went away and she passed out."

I still curse myself for not timing things better, even though Jack says without the speed of the car she was in, we can't determine how far she traveled. There's also the problem that they drugged her, and that dilutes her recollection.

"The people in the car didn't talk to each other or her," I continue. "It was several hours before she noticed the car stopping. She was hot, and the air was muggy, but she couldn't see. Lots of stairs going down, and then she was locked in a room. They kept the bag on her head the rest of the day."

She could be anywhere, the circle of possibilities is infinitely large, and if she's in a hidden facility, well, that complicates matters even further.

"She's underground within a four-hundred-mile radius," Sebastian repeats.

He's said this fifty times. I swear he says this in his sleep, listing off the towns we've visited, every lead that grows cold making him angrier, more agitated. He's not that way with me, but the shift in him when he speaks to others is so focused on Emry, it's terrifying.

He'll burn down the world to find her.

I'll fan the flames.

"Her room is kept dark most of the time," my voice cracks. I can't stand the thought of her kept in darkness like that until they want her. "When they come to get her, she's blindfolded and drugged."

"Monsters," Moira murmurs from the backseat.

"And they haven't done more than you've said?" Sebastian asks. "You aren't keeping anything from me."

"No, not unless…" I suck in a breath. "Not unless she's keeping it from me."

We both sit in silence at the words unspoken.

What if I don't hear everything?

What if she's keeping the worst parts from me?

So far, they've drawn blood and hooked her up to machines, but there are large sections of time missing. They drug her, and she falls under so deeply, that I can't stay awake, the effects stretching between us both. It makes me another burden for Sebastian to care for, although he hasn't complained.

It made me pass out before I could help him much with the tattooed man. Sebastian handled that just fine alone, but he still had to carry my lifeless body out afterward.

I feel it happening again.

"How much further?" I ask, wanting to stay awake for the next stop.

"Not long, but too long," he huffs. "Have you heard anything from Seeker Solutions?"

"Nothing new," I admit.

Alison was taken by a well-trained and organized group that, even though I can't prove it yet, is tied to Genome Theory.

The trail ran cold, and that's saying something for Seeker Solutions. They're the best in the business, and the thought of Emry going through this torture and then learning her friend is still gone, or dead, destroys me.

I'm not good at closing the wall between our thoughts, scared what I know might slip over to Emry, sending her into a deeper depression. She can lock me out so easily, but that's a skill we don't share. When the door is open between us and she's lucid, I'm so focused on her that the knowledge about Alison's disappearance hasn't entered my mind. She's safe in her ignorance for now.

"Sebastian, I, um," I reach for my throat, rubbing the veins in my neck that beat slower. Emry's not speaking to me, and I know it's because she's unconscious, drugged once again by those monsters. The effects of it take over and make my body grow limp.

Sebastian puts the car back in auto drive, one hand pulling at my sleeve, keeping me upright.

"Stay with me," he says. This has happened nearly a dozen times. They do something to Emry, sending her into a deep trance or sleep, and I can't avoid how I suffer the same fate.

I'm desperate to stay connected to her, reaching out to my bonded. The more I try, the worse the effects of the medications are on me.

"Theo," Sebastian says, turning me towards him. "Stay with me, man." He shakes me a few times, but his head blurs in my focus. They've drugged her with something stronger. It passes through the bond between us, pulling me under. I'm drowning, Sebastian's words growing distant.

"Please don't."

Her words and worry shock me awake.

"She's scared," I tell Sebastian.

Sebastian's face falls and his grip on me loosens, sending

me falling backward into the side door. He reaches out to grab me before my head slams into the window.

"Fuck," he murmurs, cradling the back of my head. "You awake? Theo?"

"Sebastian, maybe we should let him sleep," Moira worries. "It hurts him to stay awake like this."

"Can she hear you?" Sebastian asks, ignoring Moira. "Tell her we're coming for her. Tell her we'll find her."

I nod, my eyes growing heavy. "I always tell her," I slur. I'm fighting the lull of the drugs, forcing myself to keep my eyes open.

"We'll find you, Emry."

"I'm telling her," I say to Sebastian. The car weaves through the traffic effortlessly, and the passing vehicles blur into mists of color.

"What do you see?" Sebastian says. "Focus."

I want to scream at him that I am, that I always do, but I don't have the energy. Whatever they've given Emry, it's hitting her hard today. Whatever I'm feeling, she must be experiencing it ten times worse.

My essence reaches out to hers, forcing me to see through her eyes, but the images aren't clear. There's grey brick and a metal gurney, indistinct voices, and the desire to sleep.

When my head droops, falling to my chest and bobbing, everything goes black. Seconds later, my eyes open, my head jerking upward, and I'm more alert than ever before.

"I'm up. I'm up," I say.

Sebastian's driving again, steering through traffic with no regard for anyone's safety. The car jerks to one side, and my seatbelt catches.

Moira reaches between the front seats and rests her hand on my bicep. "You've been out for two hours," she tells me.

Fuck.

It felt like a second, if that. My head falls back on the seat rest with a groan, and I rub my chest, feeling the ache. A discomfort settled close to my heart ever since Emry went missing, but it's not my sickness. It's her departure that sends an unsettling agony into my soul.

"I'm sorry, I thought I... I thought I was able to stay awake," I admit.

"It's not your fault," Sebastian says. His voice is calm, a stark contrast to his driving. The wheels screech as we pass another car.

"For the love of pizza and kittens, Sebastian, slow the heck down!" Moira yells from the backseat.

Sebastian doesn't respond, but I feel the car pull back slightly, our speed reducing as Sebastian settles into the left lane. He puts on the auto drive and rubs his eyes, waiting for me to give another report. He doesn't have to ask, but I hate to disappoint him.

Closing my eyes, I think back, trying to see if there are images or words, something to give him. It's dark at first, voids of nothing, but there are flashes of when Emry opened her eyes. "Lots of plain cinder block," I say.

Sebastian grunts, listening intently, but exhaustion seeps from him. We must be close to the next tip if I've been out for hours, and I hope he's slept a little while I did. "They wheeled her somewhere. She had tubes in, um, both arms."

I don't have to open my eyes to know Sebastian stiffens next to me in the car, his entire body turning to stone at the sound of Emry succumbing to these tests.

I reach out to her, trying to feel her and assure myself that she's okay. I'm still met with emptiness. When I speak to her, she doesn't respond.

"She's not awake yet," I tell him. "There's nothing there."

"That's okay," Moira says. "Try to relax and when she's awake, tell her how much you two love her."

Sebastian nods along with Moira, and as odd as the sentiment might sound to outsiders' ears, I understand.

Sebastian and I should hate each other, but we don't.

We shouldn't be friends, but we are.

We both love Emry, and she loves us as well.

I close my eyes, reaching out again, hoping I'll find a glimmer of something.

"We love you, Emry. We're coming."

CHAPTER 4

I've been awake for some time. Minutes or maybe hours, it's hard to tell. I refuse to move. They don't have anything hooked onto or into me, so how would they know if I'm conscious?

When I'm awake, someone in a mask and glasses will come in here and ask questions, take vitals, and ignore my pleas to be let go. This is the only thing I can control.

"We love you, Emry."

Theo's words repeat in my mind over and over. I heard them in my drug-induced haze, but when the poison left my body, it felt too late to say them back.

They both love me, and they're together, a recipe for disaster in most circumstances.

It's obvious that the two men in love with me are bonded by a singular mission, and that keeps them peaceful, but there is something different about the way I perceive Theo's feelings toward Sebastian. They seep into me, so similar to my own.

Theo's thoughts about Sebastian are full of respect and

admiration, and when he envisions Sebastian and me together, he's filled with joy. It's so odd, but also magical, and somehow... seems right.

Missing from it all is jealousy. There isn't a hint of it, and that is the only thing that brings me peace while I wait for them inside this hell.

I imagine them both sitting next to one another and looking for me, vowing their love so openly, and neither minding.

Could that be possible?

My chest hurts, and I long to rub it, but I refuse to move my limbs and let anyone here know I'm awake. That ache came back soon after they took me — four, maybe five days ago — and it feels different from before. It's not Theo's heart, but more of a longing, something inside my soul that's broken.

I'm not sure if it's day or night, and no one will tell me. They don't speak to me here, treating me like an object or rather a test subject.

I know what I am without anyone telling me, without ever being here before. It's clear.

I'm a Genome lab rat once again.

A light comes on inside the room, and I fight the urge to squeeze my eyes shut tighter, letting my body remain limp and lifeless. The sounds of footsteps make their way inside, and someone clicks a pen routinely.

"Emry Crawford, gentlemen, as promised," a familiar voice says.

I've heard it a dozen times before, but only when I'm near to losing consciousness. They're buying my fake sleep for the moment, too consumed by their hubris to notice the signs.

"When will she be alert?" someone asks.

"She had ten milligrams of ketamine, so it will be some time," he says. "We'll restrain her before she's due to wake up again. The bond amplifies her strength, and we don't want anyone getting hurt."

Is that a lot of ketamine?

Should I be awake?

"Please, let's take a look," the man says, and all of their eager footsteps draw closer. I feel their presence around my bed, and someone's hot breath on my skin. More clicks of a pen snap next to my ear, a nervous habit as this person looks me over.

I tell myself not to jerk when they touch me because they will soon, and I remind myself that Seb and Theo are coming. Sebastian found me once without the help of a bonded speaking to me telepathically. This won't take long, and at any moment, he'll walk through the door with Theo.

A hand presses on my shoulder, rolling me onto my back. My gown falls open at the front, exposing my breasts, but I don't move to cover myself, waiting as they drone on about the last round of testing.

They did a scope, taking cell samples from various organs, which explains why every part of me feels like it's been stabbed with a rusted knife.

That will be over soon, too, I remind myself. Theo will be close and he'll heal me, make me whole again. Maybe they're closer to finding me if I've been asleep for a while.

"Theo, are you there?"

"This will be groundbreaking," the pen clicker comments. "A specimen before and after bonding."

They all make murmurs of agreement to each other, excited at the possibilities I bring them. I'm Genome Theory's newest toy, and they're taking full advantage of playing with me.

Will they suffer any consequences for doing this if they find what they're after? Bob sits in an office somewhere in NeXus because no matter how much he hurt us, he made a discovery, and that's all that matters to the world.

I'm still a means to an end for everyone.

Everyone but Sebastian and Theo.

"Emry, are you awake?"

Theo's voice almost gives me away. My pulse rises when I hear him.

"Yes, but they don't know. They're in the room, looking over their test subject."

His rage hits me, spreading anger in thick vines around my limbs. If it were possible, Theo would snatch me from this table, carry me through the cement walls, and take me away from them.

There's a pause where he calms himself to tell Sebastian. I imagine my husband, enraged with this knowledge, getting them all killed because he's manually driving a car so he can break every speed limit. They've been on the road for days, hardly getting any sleep, speaking to strangers who don't help liberate us.

All this time, I beg them to search for Alison. She's out there somewhere, and they're only focused on me. Sebastian promises he has an entire crew on her kidnapping, but it's not enough. She's been missing for so long, and she doesn't have something they want, a reason to keep her alive.

"There's someone who's active on Genome Theory message boards. They tracked them to a conversation with your mother before it was removed. We're getting closer."

I fight the tears that threaten to escape. It's not just the fact that they're putting themselves in danger to find me, but it's that my mother did this. She's never been a good person, but this is a low I could never have imagined.

After all this time, I never cut her out, and it's not because Sebastian thought I shouldn't. When I'm honest with myself, I know the truth. It's because I wanted a mother. I kept thinking someday she'll put all the bonding nonsense aside and love me enough.

Love me at all.

"What's next?" the pen clicker asks. "How can we test the bond frequency? Is the device ready?"

"Emry, are you there?"

"Hush, I'm listening."

Theo grows quiet, but I feel his presence crawling inside me, reaching out to feel me and touch me.

"It is, but we mustn't rush," a woman says.

"I agree, but we don't have a choice, Deidre. She's bonded, and if we unlock something where Theo could find her…"

I whisper to Theo, *"I think Deidre from NeXus is here"*, then strain to listen to every word as people speak over one another.

Sounds of agreement come from the group, and I relay everything I can to Theo, hoping it will mean something to the people back home.

"We're getting things prepped now," a man says. Someone rolls me to my side, my limbs slipping toward the edge of the bed. A hand touches my back, and then there's the cold metal of a stethoscope moving along the skin.

"Old school," a woman jokes.

"Her lung capacity is amazing, and her heart is clear as a bell. Ten milligrams of ketamine, you say?" His hands move lower, pushing me to rest on my stomach, and my arm slips off the bed, dangling over the edge.

"Let me have a listen," someone says, their body reaching over mine. He clicks his pen a few times before his lab coat rustles, telling me it's the pen clicker putting his tool away.

More hands run over my back, and I'm sliding, everyone seemingly clueless to the fact. My body slips, falling from the table and hitting the ground in a tangle of limbs. I can't help the grunt that escapes when I fall.

"Look at what you did!" Deidre screams. "It's not like we can get another of her at the store, you idiots."

"That woke her up," someone adds.

"You don't say," Deidre snaps.

Hands pull at me, and I fight them off, but there are too many. In moments, I'm strapped back down to the bed, my wrists and ankles shackled to the corners and a blindfold across my eyes.

Theo's rage intensifies, and he's sputtering promises to me. First, he'll kill everyone in that room, and second, he and Sebastian are close. I shut him out, not because I want to, but because I don't want him making irrational decisions in a rage.

"She didn't see anything," someone says as they exit the room.

"Not that it matters," Deidre says, slamming the heavy door behind her.

I'm alone again in the dark.

They're right, I didn't see much.

But I have something.

I tilt my head to the side and reach my fingers into my hair, feeling the small pen tucked inside.

CHAPTER 5

THEO

We pull into a home share, a smiling couple waving as they swing on the front porch. This town is small, with aging houses spread far apart, and fields that may grow corn or wheat, but currently are barren and full of dust.

"Moira, we're going to drop you off here," I tell her. "Robin's sending over a file of more leads today, and I need you to summarize some emails for me so I can fly through them when we're back."

"She's being awfully nice," Moira says.

"I'm waving my consult fee because she's helping," I admit.

"Oh," Moira huffs and points to the couple. "Well, at least those people look nice."

"Get us situated," Sebastian says. "But we may be leaving tomorrow morning."

"I know the drill," Moira remarks, unloading a few necessary things from the car.

We all know it after almost a week of chasing leads. I

thought we would have her by now, but we won't stop. Not ever.

Sebastian's fists are swollen from hits given, and my head strains from constantly reconstructing our data, fishing for anything we might have missed, and constantly passing out without notice. I carry our suitcases to the rooms and rush back out. Sebastian's speeding off toward our next stop the second my door closes.

"Should we wait for the backup?" I ask him. "This guy's house is only three minutes south. We don't want to give ourselves away."

Sebastian grips the steering wheel, his knuckles turning white, and avoids my gaze. He got about three hours of sleep last night, which is double what I got, so I'm not in the mood to argue. He steers the ship, so I accept his silence and stare out the window for signs of anything out of the ordinary. A billboard appears on our right.

Find love in the one of your choosing.

I scoff at the irony of it when another appears seconds later, a smiling family in one giant hug.

The bond distracts us from what really matters.

This town is a settling community, which is curious if this lead pans out to be a part of Emry's disappearance. Does this person hate the bond? Would they hurt her?

Sebastian drives for another minute before I prod him again, and he pulls off on the side of the road.

"How close are they?" I ask.

"I didn't tell them about this lead," Sebastian admits. "And I removed the tracker from the car and your bag."

I jolt forward in my seat. "What and what?"

"They're fucking up the investigation, more concerned with finding their own wrongdoers than Emry. We need to focus on finding her."

He's right that the information about Deidre's involvement took NeXus by surprise, sending them scrambling over their potential liability and other employees who could be guilty of a manner of sins. It's made them overbearing the past few days. It's also why we enlisted Robin. She's faster and can get us information by any means necessary.

Sebastian says Deidre fits the bill of a psychopath, ready and willing to kill if it gets her recognition. She's not after the bond. Deidre wants money, and NeXus pays massive amounts for published bond research. There hasn't been anything new in a decade.

It's in NeXus's best interest to keep Deidre in the dark until they finish their investigation. Emry telling us she's there isn't enough proof for them. They'll only keep a watch on her until we find Emry or they can question Deidre without compromising our search.

"They put a tracker on me?" I question.

"You're an asset to NeXus, so they asked I keep us on the map," Sebastian tells me. "I agreed until now. You and I will finish this. We're close."

I sit back in my seat, shrugging my shoulders. Sebastian's the expert, and I trust him. We care about Emry, and as the days go on, the two of us are getting closer. I'm on his side, on Emry's side, and everyone else can go to hell.

I run my hands down my face and look out at the dilapidated grey home in the distance. This town has some touches of government money, but it's nowhere close to swimming in funds. That's what happens to settler towns. They die from poverty.

"Shit, okay. So, what's your plan?" I ask.

"If this guy has anything to do with taking Emry, and for the record, I think he fucking does, he'll try to run." Sebastian glares at the dirty front door, craning his neck around the house.

"I'm fast," I say. "But there's a wheat field back there, and unlike the rest of them, it's not dead. If he gets in it, we're screwed."

"You go to the front door, get yourself inside if you can," Sebastian orders.

"This bond doesn't give me superpowers. How am I supposed to do that without him running?"

Sebastian puts the car in drive and creeps up, parking on the side of the house. "Think on your feet. If he bolts, chase him." Sebastian's out of the car seconds later, a flash that sprints toward the back of the house.

I step out, shielding my eyes from the sun, and weigh my options. I'm dressed in jeans, so I can't be an inspector of any kind. Maybe I start with a version of the truth. Tell him he's surrounded, even though it's just the two of us. I don't have a weapon, but this guy might, so charging him is a mistake. Emry can't heal me from here.

It strikes me that Sebastian has more faith in me than I do, and that gives me confidence. He wouldn't set me up to fail, not when it comes to something as important as this.

Strolling up the crumbling steps, I feel the pull of Emry. She's awake, the beating of her heart matching mine, but she isn't speaking to me.

"Emry. We're coming."

I take the rest of the stairs, feeling her reach out to me with the foggy dullness of exhaustion. She's still trying with every-thing she has, trusting we will find her. I want her to sleep now and when she opens her eyes, have us standing there to greet her. Pushing the vision to her, I hope she'll see what I imagine.

"I know you'll find me."

Her words force me to knock on the door, dust flying off the wood from my steady *thump thump thump*.

There's movement inside, and I step to the side of the porch, looking through the thin curtains that fray at the edges. The place looks almost bare, with one large chair in the center of the living room. I can see the kitchen, and there are holes where appliances once sat.

"Hello," I call out, hitting a glass pane with my knuckles a few times. The movement stills, and I go back to the front door, banging on the wood again. Sebastian is nowhere in sight, but he's lurking around, making sure this suspect doesn't sprint off into those fields.

I hit the door harder this time.

Bang. Bang. Bang.

"I'm not leaving until you open up, and I have nowhere else to be, so..."

The door unlatches, cracking open a few inches with a metal chain keeping it locked. Someone's beady eyes stare into mine, the chain covering their mouth and my skin grows cold.

"What the fuck do you want?" he seethes.

The man at the door has a week's worth of beard, and it's been that long since he showered from what I can smell. He's wearing pants with grease stains and no shirt, and thick glasses sit crooked on his nose.

"Isaac Simmons?" I'm not asking, but I'm not sure.

He doesn't nod or respond, his eyes narrowing over my form. "You're not from here," he says.

"No shit," I sneer.

This guy could have the whereabouts of Emry, and I'm not in the mood to play nice. A few things start to click into place, going all the way back to the man with the neck tattoo. Lines of people hand off the kidnapped, careful to keep enough distance between them all so no one person can give away Genome's secrets, but I'm seeing the trail as we work backward.

Isaac Simmons is where it started.

I lean into the open doorway, fighting the urge to vomit at his stench. "You can let me in, or talk to me on the porch, but we will talk."

"We're talking now," Isaac seethes.

The sole of my boot kicks the door before I think better of it, the frustration taking over and forcing me to act. I know this asshole is one of our last stops. There's a sense between us that I can't pinpoint, and when the chain snaps, the door flying open, I know with everything in me that Isaac deserves what's coming to him.

The coward that he is, Isaac runs instead of facing me, not that I gave him much choice. It doesn't matter now as I sprint after him through the dilapidated house.

He's through the back door when I hear the smack, and his body crumbles to the ground, sending a bloom of dust from the earth around him and inside the house.

Sebastian was standing there, ready to strike. He steps inside, his boots falling heavy on the crumbling floor, and he gets a look at what's left of the front door. It hangs on the bottom hinges with the broken metal chain swinging in the air.

"Well, you got inside," he says. "I'm impressed."

Isaac groans from the ground, and I pick him up by his ankles, Sebastian turning back to grab his arms. We don't have handcuffs, but we carry around industrial tape, and he's strapped to a chair before coming back to consciousness.

He doesn't fight for his life, screaming and carrying on,

asking why we're doing this, and that's what tells me he's guilty of something. Innocent men don't just sit there, asking for a sip of beer when they're taped to a chair by two strangers that broke down their front door and then punched them in the jaw.

"This beer is shit," Sebastian says, holding a lukewarm can to his lips.

I crack another can, offering Isaac a sip. He takes a long pull, smacking and licking his lips when he's done. "It's all I got unless you're going to get me some of that fancy city shit you drink," he says.

"How do you know we're from the city?" I ask, knowing anyone can see we don't belong. I want to hear his disdain and understand what drives this man to kidnap innocent women.

"Look at you," Isaac answers. "It's all over the both of ya."

"Wrong answer," Sebastian shakes his head. He crushes the beer can in one hand and tosses it next to an overflowing trash can. "You know who we are. You've seen our faces — our pictures."

Isaac pauses, his eyes darting back and forth between the both of us.

Sebastian leans forward and whispers. "Now isn't the time to lie."

Even though we're on the same side, sometimes when Sebastian speaks, I'm nervous. It chills my spine, and I'm not Sebastian's target. I envision the man taped to the chair urinating on himself before Sebastian lays a finger on him, and Sebastian *will* hurt Isaac. It's inevitable because this man is the key to finding Emry.

I feel it.

I know it.

"You know me, and who I am, what I can do," Sebastian

hisses. "You know why I'm here, but you thought you could hide, pretend you didn't take the one thing I'll kill for."

I haven't heard from Emry, and I hope she's fallen back asleep and doesn't see what will happen next. It wouldn't change anything, though.

This man's fate is sealed.

Isaac stretches the best he can while strapped to the seat, the tape pulling at his skin. He shakes his head and then drops his chin to his chest.

"I don't know why you came here," he lies.

Sebastian pulls out his phone, scrolls through a few things with his thumb, and then shows Isaac the screen. Isaac's face goes pale, and I think he might get sick before he starts sputtering explanations.

"That's just bullshit talk," he explains.

I grab the phone from Sebastian, realizing I hadn't read the message boards in full, curious about what it says.

"Freethebond6969," I say to Isaac. "That you?"

He nods without looking up at me, and I scroll through the recovered dialogue.

"BCsearcher9371 is Blaire," Sebastian adds.

The post is titled:

My family member was part of Genome Theory, and now she's bonded. Could that be a coincidence?

There are thousands of comments, and most of them are the standard opinion about the bond or Genome Theory, not anything substantial. Hidden in the dialogue is what our last interrogation brought to our attention.

Freethebond6969: It's not and I have proof
BCsearcher9371: I don't think so either. It can't be!

BCsearcher9371: NeXus took all the data and she's there.

Freethebond6969: She?

BCsearcher9371: This could be the big break.

Freethebond6969: Not from what I've heard.

BCsearcher9371: What do you mean? She's cooperating.

Freethebond6969: I've heard she's trying to get them to break the bond so she can bed down with her husband.

BCsearcher9371: You don't know what you're talking about.

Freethebond6969: She's not helping the rest of us. That's for sure. She made her choice and she gets bonded? That's bullshit. What about the rest of us?

BCsearcher9371: She could be bonded because of Genome Theory but they're gone now.

Freethebond6969: Are they?

BCsearcher9371: Yes.

Freethebond6969: Message me on this server.

I hand the phone to Sebastian, form a fist, and hit Isaac on the other side of his face. He won't be able to see out of both eyes tomorrow.

"Let's speed ahead to what you talked about on the private server," I insist. "You tell her that Genome Theory is alive and well, happy to help pieces of shit like you. But they need help, like a bonded who they've collected data on since she was a child, to crack the code."

Isaac spits on the floor, saliva mixed with blood, and takes a few rough coughs.

"Don't you both act so high and mighty," he says. He looks up at me, his face contorted in anger. "You'd be dead if it wasn't for the bond."

Sebastian kicks the leg of his chair, a warning to stop talking to me, and Isaac turns back to him.

"You both stand there in your expensive clothes, drove up

here in that fancy car," Isaac continues. "You know what happens to small towns like this, ones that don't have enough of a population to get the government's attention? They die. We're dying out here. We can barely get enough money together to send one person to a reception. We can't qualify for assistance to have a kid because we don't have a long enough work history, if any. And then it's a bunch of city boys that get bonded because you can afford all that shit."

Sebastian stands, placing his hands behind his back and nodding. "Okay," he says. "I see your point."

"You what?" I bark at him.

"His motivations," Sebastian corrects himself. "I see his motivations. How much money?"

Isaac looks back at me, his eyes wild with confusion.

"It's... it's gone," Isaac stutters. "It was only twenty thousand—"

"Not how much money did some fuckwit at Genome pay you," Sebastian seethes. "How much money do you want to tell us where Emry is?"

"I don't know where she is," Isaac sputters. "I-I swear I don't."

Sebastian's fist flies from behind his back like a bolt of lightning, hitting the side of Isaac's face and sending a few teeth to the floor. I don't know Sebastian as well as others do, but before this, my impressions of him were that of a controlled man, calm in every action. He didn't seem unreasonable or violent, and the bulky demeanor that scares off most people was unjustified.

I was wrong.

He'll kill this man and take his time about it if it gets us closer to Emry.

I've always liked Sebastian, my heart softening to his

struggle and respecting how mature he's been about our bonding.

After this week, I might love the guy.

"I don't care about your cause or this poor pathetic little town," Sebastian admits. "I don't care about you. I want my wife, and you're going to tell me everything you know and help me find her. We can use money or fists. I don't care either way."

"You're the one that's pathetic. Running around as their third wheel." He juts his chin to me. "And you're taking leftovers."

Sebastian taps him on the knee a few times and Isaac jolts, expecting another hit. "My relationships are not your concern. Your concern is how many teeth you'll have left when we're finished." He rises, stepping into the kitchen, the sound of drawers opening and being dumped onto the floor.

"He'll murder you and get away with it," I tell Isaac.

"And you won't be my first kill," Sebastian yells from the kitchen. "Ah. Perfect."

He stomps back over to us, a pair of pliers in his hands, and then places his knee between Isaacs's legs and grabs him by the throat.

"I've already knocked out one of your front teeth," he says. "Let's make it even. I like symmetry."

"Fuck off," Isaac spits with a slight lisp from his swollen gums and mouth full of blood.

He struggles, but it's pointless. The pliers are in Isaac's mouth, hooking onto one tooth with precision, and I can't look away. Sebastian pulls, Isaac squealing like a pig and shaking as best he can strapped down in his chair until the tooth slides across the floor, stopping at the toe of my boot.

It took longer than I thought for Isaac to urinate himself, but it happens.

"Don't let him kill more people."

Emry's warning catches me off guard, and I want to appease her and promise her I won't.

Except I can't lie to her.

"We'll kill everyone we have to. Slowly. We're close."

CHAPTER 6

"Still no sign of anyone," I tell Sebastian, putting the curtains back and stepping over to the pool of blood, piss, and puke in front of Isaac.

"And he has almost all of his teeth left," Sebastian says.

"And his life, which is good," I add.

Isaac is bawling in the chair. "It's not fair," he cries.

"Don't lecture us about not fair," Sebastian mocks him. He opens up a knife and begins cutting the tape free. "Don't go doing anything stupid, or I'll murder you."

It's not a threat, but a calm promise of what's to come if Isaac steps out of line.

"You worried about untying him?" I ask, realizing how stupid my question is once it's out of my mouth.

"He can't even stand up right now," Sebastian huffs. "And I'm not setting him totally free, just putting him in a cleaner spot."

He tapes Isaac against the open plumbing in the kitchen

and then sets a glass of water on the floor next to him. After giving him the warning again, he pats me on the shoulder, signaling it's time we leave.

"We'll call someone to get you when we're done, Isaac," he calls out as he leaves the room.

We know two things after torturing Isaac, and it's enough to get us to Emry.

Genome Theory is alive and well. Isaac ran security for them while they housed themselves in an underground food storage facility in this town. He worked there, doubling as a lookout with a large paycheck. The money is gone, and so is Genome Theory.

They move around, never staying in one spot for more than six months and finding new test subjects as they go. Isaac didn't know how they acquired the test subjects, but we do.

They're the women stolen from receptions by men like the one with the tattoo, runaways that never come home, and all of it's covered up by companies that don't want dips in attendance.

It's my fault.

I work for these places and companies that support their product, making them more money and helping their image. I look the other way, telling myself they weren't careful. Somehow the victim was to blame in my mind, but that's not what happened.

Genome Theory was lurking around and waiting for a moment to strike, and we all let it happen. We all pretended it was a sufficient price to pay to keep living our lives in ignorance.

The second thing we know from Isaac is the name of the transporter, the person who took Emry to the current facility, Caleb Wright.

Sebastian knows a little something that connects all the dots.

It's enough to create a plan.

I'm on the phone with Robin, ordering a trace before we leave Isaac's house with him blubbering inside. I'd feel bad for the loser if I didn't hate him so much.

He's right about this town. It's dying, and I see it everywhere we look. Every billboard points to settling, and that kills a place on the outskirts of the city. The system doesn't reward those who pick someone of their choosing. It sure didn't help Sebastian any.

"Robin, I need you to run a trace on Deidre Samuels and her partner she co-parents with, Caleb Wright, and all vehicles they own," I say into the phone.

We should have done this yesterday, but we only have so many resources and favors from Robin. I thought NeXus would have more proof of Deidre's involvement, but it works in our favor that they don't.

Deidre will lead us right to Genome's front door.

The call connects to the car when Sebastian roars the engine to life, screeching out of the driveway in a plume of dust. "Sebastian's with me and you're on speaker."

"Have Moira send an email to Witherspoon," Robin orders. "He's putting in a bid for the company, but he wants you to review it."

"I will."

"When?"

"Fucking hell, Robin!" Sebastian barks. He's speeding back to Moira, leaving tire tracks on the road with every turn. "We are a minute from his goddamn laptop. Will you just put on the trace?"

The latch has been broken on Sebastian's control, and he's a loose cannon. I really do love this guy. Robin types in silence as we pull up to the house, the same couple rocking on the front porch. Sebastian leans back in his seat, calming down a moment, and I text Moira to bring my laptop out to us.

The couple waves, and I do as well, hoping I'm a good actor. We don't need them looking at me like I'm someone who I took part in ripping out a man's teeth a few minutes ago.

"Deidre Witherspoon, age thirty-five, daughter of Adam and Regina, co-parents, both deceased. Caleb Wright, age forty-one, no immediate information on genealogy," Robin says.

"I don't care who his daddy is, Robin," I grumble. "I just need a trace. One or both of them will be heading to Genome."

"I don't need to know," Robin adds. She's her typical robotic self. "And I expect to be copied on that email within twenty minutes."

"Not a problem," I say before Sebastian has a chance to speak. "What else?"

"Caleb works for a shell corporation with a generic title. Could be a cover," she adds. "I'll send you their internet history, oh, and here's something else. Looks like Deidre has recently acquired a vacation property. It's in a business name that she is the sole owner of. That's smart of her. Smarter than the wires those security buffoons at NeXus received."

"I can't believe I didn't see this with her," Sebastian rages, punching the dashboard of the car. The couple on the porch quit rocking, Moira rushing by them with my laptop.

I place a hand on the back of Sebastian's neck, his pulse racing against my fingertips. "One step at a time, man. You knew NeXus had rats in their halls. We both knew this. You need to get with them and make sure they don't let on she's been found out."

The moment Emry said Deidre's name, I knew this would get ugly. It's difficult to be betrayed by someone you know, especially when you always sensed something was off about the person. Sebastian had the strongest *I knew it* moment when I told him about Deidre.

Sebastian clenches and unclenches his fists, resting his head back with closed eyes, doing everything possible to calm himself. I take my laptop through the window along with a notepad of Moira's summaries, extremely helpful considering Robin's holding me hostage to work before she offers her resources.

"I have my laptop, Robin," I say. "Looking at the emails now."

"I'm sending the last known address," Robin adds. "Get a portable tracker from NeXus, something undetectable, and put it on her. Use that Moira woman."

Moira curls her lip at the sound of Robin calling her such an endearing term.

"We're going to talk to her—" Sebastian hisses, "—and find out where Emry is."

"An erred plan, Sebastian," Robin says. "Your choice, but it's the wrong one."

"She's right," I say, releasing Sebastian's neck and letting my fingers fly over the keyboard.

"I know," Robin deadpans.

Sebastian shoots me a look. "I know I'm just the muscle here, but enlighten me."

"One of them will lead us straight to Emry," I say. "Easier to follow the blinking dot than rip teeth out of a woman. I don't think even you could do that."

He takes a breath, looks up at Moira's cocked eyebrow, and then buries his face in his hands. "It will take us half a day to get back to NeXus," he grumbles.

"Do it. I'm not going anywhere."

"Emry says it's okay," I say out loud, relieved she's awake

and with me. It's more sporadic today than ever before, a steady reminder we're running out of time. "We don't have a choice either way."

"Get in the car, Moira," Sebastian orders, putting it in reverse. She rushes around to the back seat, barely sliding inside before he speeds away.

Moira yells out at the couple to lock our doors, and we'll be back. They both look at us with their jaws slack, but they wave goodbye and nod.

"Emry, love, are you okay?"

I realize too late I've used the word love, but I can't take it back.

I won't take it back.

This is love between us, and in case everything goes south, I need her to know.

"I'm a little stressed, getting bits and pieces of what you two are up to."

"Emry's up. She's worried about what we're doing to get to her," I tell Sebastian. "But I'll burn down this entire world if I have to. I know you feel the same way."

Moira lets out a small gasp, and Sebastian smiles. I know what he's thinking, just as I do. It doesn't take a bond for us to move as one, both of us doing whatever is necessary to find her. She's ours.

"I am. Both of yours."

I exhale at the sound of her words, resting my hand on my chest that aches for her.

"What did she say?" Sebastian asks.

I turn my head, looking the man over. I can't pinpoint my feelings for him. It's more than friendship, not that I've had a lot of friends to compare my feelings. A brother, maybe, but the link between us feels stronger than family. It's a shadow of the bond with Emry, but it grows every day.

"She said that she belongs to us," I answer. "Both…"

I trail off in a sudden moment of panic at what I just said. This man breaks bones and rips out teeth, and I just granted myself co-ownership of his wife like she's some damn piece of property.

Sebastian's lips rise in a slight smile, and he nods. "Both of us," he says. His words are faint, but they hit me hard, pinning me to my seat.

"Yeah," he agrees with himself a moment later, as if he just came to some conclusion. "She is ours. She belongs to us."

CHAPTER 7

The next person who comes in covers my head with black cloth, and this time I'm grateful. It encases the pen I hide inside my hair, and I laugh a little to myself. It's not a knife or a gun, but it's better than what I had before, which was nothing.

Nothing but the promise that Sebastian and Theo are coming. I need to do my part and fight when the opportunity arises.

When my shackles were released in the night, I crawled onto the concrete floor and hovered over the plastic pen while I shaved it to a point. My fingers throb, worn down from the constant motion. The rest of me already hurts from whatever they're doing when I'm knocked out.

I tell Theo what I have, but that I don't know how I plan to use it. He warns me not to do anything, and the worry that passes through feels different — stronger. They're closer, the tether between us gripping me tight.

I sense Sebastian, too, but that can't be right.

Yesterday I said that I belong to them. I don't know if I was crazy or delirious, maybe both.

When Theo said it back, and Sebastian agreed, something changed inside me. The thought of a future where we're all happy came to mind, but I didn't linger on the idea. I have to get out of here first.

It sounds so simple yet so complicated, and they've kept me too exhausted or drugged out to keep thinking about what it means.

Is it a promise made because they're scared for me, and they don't want me worrying about my relationship status on top of everything else?

I think back to that first day at NeXus when they asked me endless questions, and there was only one I couldn't answer.

Would you agree to hormone therapy for Sebastian Owens? Sebastian would cease to have romantic attachments toward you.

Could I do that, still? Would it be better to live our lives together, the three of us, rather than to set Sebastian free?

Maybe it was said in passing because they're working together to find me.

I can't belong to two men.

Can I?

Hands grab at my ankles and shoulders, moving me to a hard metal surface, another gurney. I hear the door open, and I'm wheeled out of the room, but I can't see where. I tell Theo everything, relaying every word that is spoken and every noise that I hear. Deidre's nowhere yet, and she's the woman they think will lead them to me.

When the cloth over my eyes is removed, I'm alone in another room, this one sparkling white with medical equipment and machines. I arch my back, reaching up to grab the pen from the back of my hair, sliding it down to sit in the gap of my spine.

They're watching me, but they're arrogant, unable to imagine what I'm capable of and what I'm doing right before their eyes.

A voice comes in over the speaker. "We need you to remain lucid with the next few tests. So you'll need to comply, and follow along with our prompts."

"You need to go fuck yourself," I bite back.

There's a small laugh in the speaker before the voice comes back. "We thought you might be difficult, so we've added some incentive."

The speaker cuts off again for a few minutes, my mind racing with the possibilities. When it's back, someone is crying into the microphone, their shuddered breaths making it hard to understand what is being said. It hits me like a brick, and the sob that escapes my throat is unrecognizable, wracked with panic and fear.

"Alison!" I scream. "Alison, is that you?"

"Y-yes," she sniffles into the speaker.

She's gone, taken somewhere with a sharp cry when the voice speaks again. "Will you comply?"

"Yes, yes. I'll do whatever the fuck you want," I say, feeling the sharp plastic in between my shoulder blades, now at odds with my plans for escape. "Just don't touch her. Don't hurt her."

Theo hears this on the other side, his rage making my heart pound, and I see a flash of the man they had tied to the chair, pliers in his mouth while Sebastian tortures information from him.

They'll make them suffer for this.

"That's wonderful," the voice coos.

A door opens, and I turn my head to look at the man walking through. He's older, wearing a crisp lab coat that looks too big for him. The sleeves cover his hands, and the tails reach past his knees. There's a familiarity with the man, his short stature, the way he carries himself as he strides over.

"You've grown into such a beautiful young woman," he says. "So lovely to see you again."

I can't deny who I'm seeing, even if I don't want to believe my eyes. "It's not good to see you, Gilbert," I bite out, forcing myself to stay flat on the table and not grab my makeshift weapon and stab him in the throat.

He shrugs, unbothered by the starved and exhausted woman attempting to insult him, and ushers someone over who holds an odd-looking metal helmet. It's familiar to the one in NeXus, but amateur somehow. The wires strapped to the sides aren't hooked on with precision, and it's clunky, with straps hanging from the bottom.

"We don't want to sedate you for this, so I'm glad we're in agreement," Gilbert says.

Everything about him disgusts me. The way he fiddles with his hands and how he never looks me in the eye. It's all reminiscent of a past I tried to forget.

"Where is Alison? What are you doing with her?"

Gilbert fidgets with the sleeves of his lab coat, rolling them up on his arms. "She's fine. Sleeping. She's a guest as long as you are, but not one that can help us find the bond."

"So you won't be playing your games with her?"

They slide the helmet on my head, strapping it under my chin and securing a strap that reaches under my armpits and around my shoulders, then wraps around my neck.

It feels like my airway is restricted, not choked for air, but enough to cause me to feel the push against my throat. I hate the sensation, and I slow my breath, already struggling to remain calm.

"What is this?" I ask.

"Something you agreed to," Gilbert hisses. "Remain still."

I pull at the neck strap, wanting it off.

"Do I need to get Alison for this?" he warns.

"No!" I shout and lower my hands to the table, pressing my palms into the metal.

Gilbert gives a wave to the mirror in the corner, a gesture telling someone to go ahead. I brace myself for a shock of electricity to the brain or some sort of physical punishment. That's all they know how to do — hurt their little lab rats.

There's a slight buzz when something in the helmet turns on, but then nothing. I look at the mirror, wondering if Deidre's on the other side watching me.

"Speak to your bonded again," Gilbert says.

My eyes shift to Gilbert in confusion. "What?"

"You know what I said." He slaps his hand down on the metal table, sending a sharp ring reverberating throughout the room. "You're an intelligent professor, and you understand me clearly. No more games. Talk to Theodore. Call for him."

"Theo, Gilbert is here. He took me into the Genome Theory when I was fourteen."

"Talk to him!" Gilbert roars.

"I am!" I scream back.

The door opens, and another stranger glides through, unbothered by this show and holding a tablet in his hands. "The signal is up, but the transmission looks different." He gives Gilbert the tablet.

"Again," Gilbert orders. "Talk to him again. Tell him to respond."

"Theo, where are you? Have you found Alison?"

He doesn't say anything, but maybe he's sleeping. No, that doesn't make sense. He's awoken in his sleep before when I spoke to him.

An evil smile appears on Gilbert's lips. "Turn it off," he

says. Something stops inside the clunky helmet, the vibration inside coming to a halt.

He snaps his fingers in my face. "Again, Emry."

"Theo, can you hear me?"

Gilbert gasps and snaps at the man holding the tablet. "On. On," he demands.

"Yes, love. How are you? We've found—"

The helmet buzzes to life, cutting off Theo's words. Tears escape when I realize what they've done, and I have no way to warn Theo and Sebastian that they're silent to me.

"Wonderful," Gilbert sneers. "Now that we can take it away, let's see if we can harness it."

CHAPTER 8

"Something's wrong," I tell Sebastian. "Very, very wrong."

After thirty minutes of no response from Emry, I'm panicked. It's not only that she won't answer. There's an emptiness between us.

When I reach for her, there isn't a wall that I hit. There's nothing. She's lost to me, and a sick feeling enters my stomach, my heart filling with dread.

Sebastian sits up in his seat and grabs me by the elbow. We've been sitting outside Deidre's apartment for hours, waiting for her to leave. Moira's at a coffee shop across the street, her phone face up on the table and waiting for our text.

"Talk to me," he orders.

I'm holding my head in my hands, trying to reach Emry.

"Love, are you there?"

"Please wake up."

"Tell us you're alright."

I only get silence in return, and I turn to Sebastian. The fear in his eyes mirrors my own, terrified something's happened that we can't fix.

"I can't reach her," I tell Sebastian. "Worse, I can't feel her. It's like she's gone, disappeared off the face of the earth."

Sebastian's breath catches. "Is she... drugged again?"

I shake my head. "No, man. I would be out too if that was the case. It's different. I can always extend myself out to her in a way. Touch her, but with something not physical. Suddenly it's empty — nothing."

Sebastian slumps back in his seat, his mouth opening and closing with the question he wants to ask but can't bring himself to say out loud.

"She's not dead," I tell him.

"How... how do you know?" he begs. The crack in his voice kills me, but I'm sure she's alive, and I need him to believe me.

"I would know that. It would hurt me somehow. It would take something from me, and I think it might..."

Sebastian's eyes widen with worry. "Might what?"

"No bonds have died yet," I say. "They will. They age, more slowly, but they do. But no one's died."

"Right, so we don't know—"

"I'll die," I interrupt him.

The words are heavy things that hang between us. They take up all the space in the car, weighing on us both with a future we know can't be controlled. It's confirmation that no matter what we might have said to each other about the three of us, Emry and I can't be apart. We won't survive, and Sebastian won't either without her. I've sealed our future, one that he may not want, with two simple words.

"When she goes, I'll go with her. It's a fact, a force of nature." My eyes lose focus, staring past Sebastian, afraid to face him.

The bond is life and death, a physical manifestation of love, and impossible to break. Somewhere deep inside, we all knew this, but saying it out loud changes everything.

Sebastian releases his grip on my arm, his eyes lowering to his lap. He rests his hands on his thighs face up, and stares at his palms. Hands that have killed men and tortured people, and all for Emry.

"Okay, so she's alive." His voice is barely over a whisper.

"I'm sorry." I wish my words sounded more sincere and could somehow make this better.

"What for?" he asks. There's something hollow in his words, almost defeated. "Don't be sorry for something you didn't do."

What he wants to say is, *don't feel sorry for me — don't pity me.*

Something in his face softens, moving on from the blow I've dealt. "You're sure? You're sure she's alive."

"Yes," I say. "She's cut off from me, but she's alive."

"And you're sure you can't live if her heart stops beating."

"Yes," I choke out. "I can't explain how. This isn't a ploy to keep you from killing me."

His hands close into fists, and I hold my breath. He turns to me and cocks an eyebrow. "Then I have two lives to protect. Don't do anything reckless. No skydiving."

We don't deserve Sebastian. No one is worthy of the kind of dedication this man offers with his entire soul. That's the spirit that should be tied to Emry for eternity, not mine.

My head thumps on the back of the seat, and I let myself breathe. "Wouldn't dream of it," I sigh.

Sebastian adjusts himself in his chair, looking back out to the door Deidre will walk through. "Did something happen before you were cut off? Did she say anything — see anything out of the ordinary?"

I close my eyes, trying to focus. "She was talking to me, and in the middle of her thought, just gone. And then I felt sick. I still do. Something inside me can't handle this. It's like I'm rejecting the loss of her."

Acid crawls up my throat, and I rub my stomach, fighting back the bile.

Sebastian's wide palm rests over my shoulder. "We just have to get to her," he says. "Whatever the reason for the sever between you two, it won't stop us."

I nod, reminding myself that this is only a setback. She'll come back to us.

"Should one of us try to tag Caleb?" I ask. "We could get a decoy from NeXus. Won't be as good as our Moira."

Moira hasn't moved, waiting patiently for the signal. She's another beautiful soul in this world I feel undeserving of knowing.

"Overkill," Sebastian says. "Deidre is a micromanager, and she'll check in on her investment. She used Caleb for transport, but that's where his participation ended. She's the one to follow."

"Okay," I tell him. "I trust you. Deidre's the target then."

We wait, seconds feeling like minutes that creep by with nothing to do but think of the worst possible outcome.

The tattoo on his wrist catches my attention, and I can't look away, taking note of every letter. Sebastian notices, lifting his wrist and staring at it himself.

"You know how the name is created?" he asks.

"Yeah," I say.

I want to smart off and tell him everyone knows that, but this is a delicate topic, and I'm embarrassed he saw me gawking. It's taught in school, drilled into us with billboards, and the few tattoo parlors in every city are built like castles, a shrine to the old ways.

"I meant how *our* name was created," he corrects. "Did she tell you that?"

I shake my head, eager to hear more about their history. A distraction is part of it, but listening to their love story does something to me. It's calming, almost like taking a long sip of scotch.

"Crawford and Owens," he remarks. "It was easy enough and you know the whole Crowe thing, it seemed to fit with the bird and all."

"Really?" I ask, trying to understand what he means, but the puzzle doesn't click together.

"There are dozens of different crows?" Sebastian tells me. "Maybe hundreds."

"People or birds?"

"Birds," Sebastian laughs. "Everywhere you go, you see crows, and in every location, they give it a different name. Same bird on the other side of the country, but they rename it, call it their own. New home, new bird."

"I didn't know that," I say, rubbing the back of my neck. I try to reach Emry again. It's habitual, calling out to her every other minute, but there's nothing but endlessness between us, something hiding her away.

"They can speak to other species of birds, too," he trails off. "Not just their own. They adapt."

I turn to him, curious where he's going with this, if anywhere. It could be the ramblings of someone about to snap, and I wouldn't blame him. The guy has been through enough.

"Crows don't just stay in one place," he adds. "They can be a different kind of bird in a new home, and they don't have to stay with only other crows."

Sebastian starts laughing, a chuckle at first, and then he's doubled over. "It's odd how perfect that is, don't you think?" he sputters.

I nod, even though it's possible Sebastian has officially snapped. Different species of fowl never struck me as funny, but perhaps I'm too tired to get the joke.

"You see it?" Sebastian lifts his wrist up, pointing it toward me.

I shrug my shoulders, offering a confused look. "I don't think I get it."

He runs his finger along the name, Crowe, and then points to each letter individually. "Don't you see it?" he asks again.

"See wh—" I stop mid-sentence, the point driving home.

My name fits in theirs.

Letters that could all combine together if we tried, making a new meaning for the name, and speaking a new language between us.

A new vow.

A new home.

"I see it," I say and rub a thumb over my bare wrist.

"We'll do it after we get her," Sebastian promises.

Without him speaking the words, I know what he means. There doesn't have to be telepathy between us because the understanding is there. We'll get Emry, bring our girl home, and I'll tear myself away long enough to put the ink on this wrist.

We're a new species of Crowe.

CHAPTER 9

Sebastian leans back in his seat, pleased with himself and the decision we've made. I'm just as happy, trying not to smile because there is still the problem of my bonded being kidnapped and we have yet to find her.

We will find her.

Moira checks her phone again, and I slip back into the mission, my eyes darting to the door Deidre should soon exit. A crowd of people step outside, and I worry she'll get lost in the busy street.

"There," Sebastian says, pointing to a woman in grey slacks and a tight blonde bun. She's identical to the woman I saw at the cafe, right down to the condescending look on her smug face.

"She's not dressed for a day off work," I say.

"Nope. Because she's going to check up on her investment," Sebastian growls.

I text Moira, Sebastian watching my thumbs fly over the keyboard.

THEO

Grey slacks, large red handbag, blonde bun

Walking past coffee in 30 seconds

Moira gets up, her cash already sitting on the table and her handbag flung over her shoulder. She steps outside, seemingly staring at her phone while looking for the woman out of the corner of her eye.

Sebastian shakes his head and starts the engine. "We should just grab the bitch."

My hand flies to his forearm, and I feel how he trembles. "We'll grab her if we have to, but this way leads us to Genome's front door without anyone knowing."

He nods, agreeing and tapping his thumbs nervously on the steering wheel. I release my grip and watch Moira get to work.

Deidre passes the front of the coffee shop with Moira at her heels. Her large red bag sways with every step, the back of it peeking out from behind her elbow. Moira doesn't drop the tracker, and I can only guess the bag must be zipped shut. She keeps on her without Deidre noticing, a determined look on her face, and then falls forward, her entire body weight trip-ping into the bitch.

Coffees fly up, splattering down on the two women. Deidre cries out, rolling on the ground and emptying the contents of the cup.

"Oh, I'm so sorry," Moira cries. "Are you okay? Oh, hell."

Deidre sits up, startled by the moment and in shock. Bystanders pause, reaching over to touch them both, but only one or two stop to ask if they're okay. Most just move on when there isn't a bond.

Deidre rises from the ground, wiping steams of coffee off of her shirt. The brown stains seep into the white cotton, and I imagine her front splayed with blood instead, knowing it will soon be the case.

Moira stands, looking as if she's testing her ability to walk. There's more small talk between them, and Deidre unzips her bag, handing Moira a napkin from inside and then grabbing one for herself.

It happens without anyone noticing, especially Deidre, and I can't say for certain myself until Moira hobbles back in our direction with a knowing smirk.

She's a miracle worker.

I don't know Jack's feelings about settling, but he needs to make her his wife before someone else notices her worth.

Deidre disappears around the corner, and Sebastian brings up the tracker on his phone, a blinking dot walking away from us. He pulls up to Moira and rolls down the window.

"We need you here, close to NeXus," he says.

She nods in agreement. "I heard what happened yesterday with the teeth, so maybe that's best." She frowns, but it doesn't phase Sebastian, and I offer her an apology for our harsh way of doing things, although I don't really mean it.

Moira points to Sebastian's phone. "NeXus will follow that."

"We'll be a step ahead," Sebastian says. "They know the plan, but if you hear of anything..."

"I'll let you know," Moira says. "I'll convince Jack to keep them at bay until you say go."

We drive off, not speeding this time, since the subject we're following is walking. Sebastian has to circle a few blocks before she gets into her car, but in no time we're out on the open road.

"This isn't the direction of her office," I tell Sebastian.

I'm sure he knows, but it feels good to say it out loud. We know she's going to Genome the more distance we put between ourselves and NeXus. There's nothing out this way except dead towns and buried secrets.

"Text Jack and let him know," Sebastian says. "Remind him to keep backup a step behind us. These people are crazy enough to burn the place down if they sniff us out."

The thought sends shivers down my spine, and I reach out to Emry again, reminding her we're coming even if she can't hear us.

There was a time when I thought being bonded would be uncomfortable, someone always in your head and knowing your thoughts.

After years of being alone, I'm already addicted to Emry invading the most private parts of myself. I think about what Sebastian offered earlier, and what that means, and I can't help but wonder about the physical aspect of an arrangement between the three of us.

Would he allow me to touch her and hold her? I won't be able to resist the pull to her, and how far would that take us?

He has to know.

He's not a fool.

I'd be sleeping with his wife, making love to her every chance I got. There wouldn't be a moment where I wouldn't have my mouth on her, put my cock inside her, and make her come until she passes out.

If he knows, where does he... fit in all of that?

"What's on your mind?" Sebastian asks. We've been driving for twenty minutes and I haven't said a word. The thought of Emry has me hard, and I grunt, hoping my erection will go away on its own.

"You've had this look for the drive," he adds. "Are you trying to talk to her?"

"I am," I say. "Nothing back."

Sebastian adjusts himself in his seat, weaving through a few cars so Deidre is in sight, but we aren't directly behind her. He shoots me a few looks, knowing I'm holding something back.

"You know, when Emry and I went to NeXus, we had an arrangement of no secrets," he says. "Even if it hurts the person to tell them something."

Damn. This guy's intuition might be better than mine.

"I'm, uh, thinking about..." I cough a few times, uncomfortable this close to Sebastian when I'm about to bring up how I'm rock hard because I'm picturing myself pumping into his wife. "How the uh, physical stuff would work with us. All of us. Because you know, Emry and me, then you."

I leave it at that, pushing my luck enough with the hulking man next to me.

He chuckles, rapping his hands on the steering wheel. "Well, I don't know. I think we need to do the thing women beg us to do all the time. Communicate. Talk about it."

"Right," I say, forcing myself to hold back the laugh in the back of my throat. "Well, that's what I'm trying to do."

Sebastian nods but doesn't say anything. We ride in the car, following Deidre for another ten minutes without another word. The idea of Sebastian punching me in the face makes my erection soften enough to make it bearable.

"Maybe we talk about it after we get Emry," I suggest.

"Good idea," Sebastian agrees, and we both let out a sigh of relief.

I'm glad I was honest with him, but this isn't the time. We don't know what we're doing, and the only thing that is certain is how much we both need Emry.

Another thirty minutes pass before either of us speaks again, my erection thankfully gone due to my intrusive thoughts. I don't know what's going through Sebastian's mind, but he looks over at me every so often, and then moves his eyes back to the road.

"I meant what I said at breakfast back at NeXus." Sebastian takes a deep breath before he continues, staring out the window so he doesn't have to face me. "I always knew I'd need to share my wife, in every way. I knew that when she bonded. If that's what you're worried about."

"I'm worried about..." I trail off, thinking about how to end my thought, not wanting to sound pathetic. I shake my head and say it anyway. "I'm worried I'll lose everything I've gained in this short amount of time. My friendships with Emry and with you. I can't go back to being so alone. I don't... want to."

"You won't," he promises, swallowing hard and nodding with a slow exhale. "It's the three of us from now on."

There's a gravity to his voice that kills my fear. I understand why Emry feels safe with him and why he's so trusted on the job. There's so much to figure out, but my faith is with Sebastian and Emry.

They're my family.

CHAPTER 10

EMRY

Someone checks over me, rough hands prodding and poking before tapping away at their tablet. "How long are you going to keep this helmet on?" I ask. There's no response, not even a pause. He's one of Gilbert's followers, taught to avoid looking me in the eye, let alone answer any of my questions.

I thought Gilbert was in jail, and now I wish I had made sure of it. My testimony named him, but that time of my life was a race to survive, sprinting through my fear to the finish line. When the punishments were dealt and I was handed a check and an apology, I never looked back.

The only people I spoke to were Jack and Sebastian, refusing to live in the real world and hiding inside my apartment. I never sought out Gilbert's fate.

I couldn't even get out of bed.

After months of support from Sebastian and Jack, I found the courage to go to school and start my life. The Genome Theory monsters were behind me, part of someone else's story.

I wasn't that girl anymore, and I chose to move on. My willful blindness brought me back here, but I'm stronger today.

I won't run away this time.

I ask again, louder, knowing damn well he heard me. "What is this helmet? Why are you doing this?"

No response.

"Gilbert won't find the key to the bond. He's a fool and a liar."

Those words give the man pause, but he collects himself, clearing his throat and shaking his head before he continues typing.

A glass wall separates me from onlookers. They watch a woman bound by her wrists and strapped to a cold medical bed. I'm more than what they see. The bond isn't something to be captured, and they won't find anything by keeping me here.

How long until they tire of failing and make a cut that won't heal? I'm sure someone back there wants to take an up close look at my brain.

The pen along my back is still there, but I can't reach it to plunge the sharp plastic into this man's jugular.

That would be a waste of effort. I'll save that for Gilbert if I have the chance.

"I have to pee," I announce.

"We'll bring someone in to catheter you," he answers.

"That's not necessary," I say. "I can take myself to the bathroom if you'll just let me."

"I'm told if you're being difficult, it will need to be brought to Gilbert's attention," the man says. "He'll get Alison to help you comply. Do I need to do that?"

I shake my head, my eyes welling with tears, and choke out a "no." He heads for the door, and I call out to him that I don't have to go, and that I'll be fine a while longer. I'm disgusted with how compliant I'm being with these assholes, but I'll do it for Alison. I'll keep her safe long enough for Sebastian and Theo to find us.

Over the next few hours, different people filter in and out, not worried about hiding their faces from me. The helmet works, and I can't reach Theo, but there's another reason they don't conceal themselves anymore.

They're never going to let me go.

Ever.

I'm the perfect specimen, and with so few bonded, they'll never get another chance to run their tests with someone like me.

By the time Gilbert enters the room, I'm mentally exhausted from the day and trying to reach Theo through this damn helmet. It's no use, but I can't help but try. It's the only thing I can do.

"Good afternoon, Emry," he says. "I'm sure it will please you to know that your friend Alison is not being nearly as agreeable as you."

I smile at this information, hoping she got in several dick kicks every time they came near her.

"We had to sedate her, so if you need proof of life, it's not available at the moment."

Knowing how Gilbert spews lies, the knot in my stomach tightens.

"Can I see her?" I ask. "Can you bring her to me?"

"No," he answers, without further detail. I'm in no position to beg, so I force myself to relax, waiting for what happens next. The restraints around my wrists cut into my skin, but I heal quickly. I tug at it a little, hoping they will loosen and I can claw Gilbert's eyes out.

Horrible memories surface every time I see him, things I never wanted to think about again. I put those thoughts behind me, but I can't deny them when he's so close, looming over me with his beady eyes and sweaty forehead.

I'm fourteen again, deprived of food for a week, but beaten when I don't give enough urine samples. The open wound across my back they never stitched doesn't heal as it should, leaving a jagged whelp that I still carry to this day.

Or do I?

I haven't looked, but my bond with Theo may have erased the scar.

Gilbert looks me over, and his hot breath on my skin almost forces me to wretch. I close my eyes, only to find more memories haunting me there.

I'm fifteen and dragged down a hallway where I pass out because I'm too weak to walk. I wake up, strapped to a gurney, needles in both arms and burning liquid coursing through my veins. I try to scream, but I don't have the strength, so I silently suffer and wish to be dead.

I prayed my suffering would end every day until Sebastian arrived.

This time is different. As long as Alison is safe, I can get through this.

"And you're coming, Theo. You and Sebastian are close."

They don't hear me, but I don't stop trying.

Gilbert opens the gown they've given me, exposing my breasts and not hiding that he enjoys looking. He attaches electrodes to my skin, probably the hundredth time this has happened this week, and I fight back my growl of frustration.

Weeks ago, my biggest worry was dealing with students who wanted to drop my class after the deadline.

Days ago, my biggest worry was what my mother would tell the press.

Today, I'm scared for my life and the lives of those I love.

This bond is bullshit.

"There will be some electrical impulses, and they may sting a bit," Gilbert says.

I remember these, how it felt to be electrocuted, zapped from the inside out. My hands grip the side of the gurney, readying myself for the pain.

"What's the goal?" I ask. "With this test?"

Gilbert lets out a huff. "NeXus spoiled you. You can't understand the specificities of the science we're creating here. I don't have time to explain every procedure to you."

"I'm a professor of—"

"You're nothing," he cuts me off. Leaning closer, he hisses in my face, his spit spraying onto my cheeks. "Nothing."

I shake my head but don't speak, keeping my rebuttal to myself.

I'm something special to Theo and Sebastian.

I'm a friend to Alison.

And I'm going to kill this asshole.

He puts on the last sticker, slapping it in place so hard my skin turns red. It's sadism, and nothing more.

"Wouldn't it help with the testing if I knew?" I argue. "When bodybuilders concentrate on the muscles they use, they grow stronger. That's science. If I knew what you were looking for, and I focused on it, the results may be different."

"You know what we're looking for," he seethes. "You've always known, you selfish girl. This is for our future. People are dying out there and they don't have to. I'm saving humanity."

"By electrocuting me?!" I bite back.

The slap across my face stings, catching me off guard, but it does something else.

"Theo. Can you hear me?"

The block is down for an instant. The helmet knocked to its side with the strap around my neck choking me as it hangs.

"Love, I'm here. We're almost there. We're coming."

Gilbert's reaching for my helmet, and I do my best to fight him away while I'm restrained.

"This helmet blocks me from you, and they have Alison. Gilbert took her."

It's over, the helmet securely back in place, cutting the tie between me and Theo. I want to cry from relief and frustration, but they're close and that message got through. This will all be over soon.

"They tell me you went to NeXus to break the bond," Gilbert sneers. "You know that's impossible, you stupid little girl."

I don't respond, staring at the small man who won't live through this. He won't get a chance to hurt someone else. I'll be sure of that.

My eyes dart to his fancy watch, the rings on his stubby fingers, and I can't help but notice the designer shirt under his lab coat. Gilbert has sponsors and lots of them. The wealthy are funding this charade, hiding behind this monster, and hoping for a key to the bond. The others here are desperate to find the elixir of life, blinded by hope, or they're just fools.

I see him.

I see all of them.

They may hurt me physically, but they won't break me again.

Theo and Sebastian are coming.

My family is coming.

"You're too small-minded to know what's possible," I say. "You're so very small." The smile creeps across my lips until I'm laughing, and I see his face flicker with self-doubt.

He's the one that's nothing.

His hand twitches to hit me again, but he closes his fist instead. I keep laughing louder and louder, hoping he swings and breaks this helmet.

Gilbert growls, backing away with closed fists. "Ready," he says, storming from the room.

I lose count of the hours that tick by as the spikes of pain pierce through my body and shake my bones. Slipping in and out of consciousness, I never lose hope, knowing when I open my eyes, I might see them there.

My bond calls out to Theo, just in case it can break through.

"Tell Sebastian it's okay to kill sometimes."

He doesn't need my permission. I know what happens soon, with or without my blessing.

Once they break me free of this place, I'll kill Gilbert myself.

CHAPTER 11

There aren't many cars on the road anymore, and we have to pull back, worried that Deidre will notice us. We can still see the faint dot that blinks and tells us she's close.

Sebastian's edgy, wanting to speed on the road and make this journey faster, but we force patience. Emry is within reach, and we're going to find her.

Moira messages that she's with Jack, and NeXus is not far behind. They're giving us a wide berth, not knowing what may happen if we all barge into the facility.

The last time NeXus stormed The Genome Theory, they spilled too much blood. Sebastian's done this before, and he knows what to expect, but there's so much to lose if we mess up. After a short argument about me going with him at all, I promised to follow his lead.

He was nervous I could get hurt or killed, but after explaining my bond wouldn't allow me to stay behind, he relented.

"Theo. Can you hear me?"

I jolt up in my seat. "I can hear her," I say.

Sebastian jerks forward, his hand clamping on my shoulder.

"Love, I'm here. We're almost there. We're coming."

Sebastian's biting his fist, knowing if he speaks I might miss a single word, and we can't risk that.

"This helmet blocks me from you, and they have Alison. Gilbert took her."

I'm holding my breath, my hand against my heart, so happy to hear her voice but terrified about what she tells me.

"We're coming for both of you, then. We'll get you both. Can you tell us anything about where you are? The room. The building."

Silence.

"Emry, love. Are you there? Emry."

"Emry, we love you."

It's nothing, and I know she's blocked from me. The dark haze I feel myself sift through comes back, taking away the link to my bonded.

"She's gone," I tell Sebastian. "They have Alison. Someone named Gilbert. And they're blocking our connections somehow. She broke through for a second, but it's over."

Sebastian's hand tightens against my shoulder, gripping so hard he's pushing me down. I place my palm on top of his, trying to pry him off.

"Seb, it's okay," I tell him. "We're on our way and she's okay. We'll get her."

He releases, both hands now clenched into fists, and I watch him turn and punch the window of the car, attempting to let out his aggression. It cracks, making a spiderweb in the center of the glass, but doesn't shatter.

I lean over him, grabbing his wrist and clasping my palm over his fist, stopping him from another punch. When his breathing evens, I let my other hand reach for the back of his neck.

"No," I say, my voice calm. "You can't hurt yourself. Save it for them."

The growl that escapes his chest would terrify anyone, but I know not to be afraid. He's angry, and that's what we need. That's what will save Emry and kill every bastard we come across to get to her.

His fists relax, and he pushes his back against the seat, watching the dot on the tracker move forward.

"Jesus, Alison," he shakes his head. "She's gotten mixed in with all of this."

We knew it was likely that Genome took her, but we weren't sure where. It makes sense they would keep her as a puppet in front of Emry, pulling at the strings, forcing her to cooperate.

"If it wasn't at a reception, they would have grabbed her somewhere else. You know that," I say.

"No, I know," Sebastian agrees. "It's not her fault at all."

"Who's Gilbert?" I ask. The vein in Sebastian's neck protrudes, and his jaw clenches. He knows this asshole.

"Gilbert was part of Genome when Emry was there. I thought he tricked Blaire, her mom, to put her in the program. He was the one who talked them into it. Now we know her mom is just a piece of shit."

"Why isn't he in jail?"

"He was sentenced to ten years. I'm not sure what he served," Sebastian says. "He was a low-level man back then. Nothing special. They couldn't prove he ever entered the facility. Everyone's testimony only had him doing the intake of minors for the Genome program. You remember when they had those huge blood drives, telling parents to start banking their kid's DNA for bond matching?"

"Yeah," I say. "My dad dragged me to one of those."

"They were hunting for candidates," Sebastian hisses. "Gilbert was a hunter. Seems he's gotten promoted."

I lean back in my seat, releasing Sebastian and stewing in my own fury.

"He's a fucking parasite," I say.

Sebastian nods in agreement.

"She's slowing down," he says, pointing to the screen.

The blinking dot isn't flying down the road, passing landmarks anymore. There's nowhere to turn, so she must be there, but I can't see any buildings. It's an open flat road covered in dust and dead earth. The sun's about to set, and I can't decide if that helps us or not.

"Slow the car," I order. "She'll see us."

"What if they block her signal like Emry's link to you?" Sebastian argues. "Where is she going? She's just ahead and I don't…"

I grab at the wheel. "We can't let her see us."

Sebastian brushes me off and pulls the car off to the side, but doesn't stop driving forward.

"What are you doing?" I ask.

"She'll be looking at the road. Cameras will be on the road," he says. We bump along the terrain, dust flying around the car, almost blocking the windshield until the dot is close enough for Sebastian's liking and he stops.

We both get out of the car, and I look around at the dead earth. We're in a barren field of dirt, with nothing around us but dust and sky. I raise my hands in question at Sebastian.

"She's over that lip of ground," he says. "Further down on the other side."

He moves toward a hill of raised earth, tall enough to conceal our bodies when we stand against it, and I jog after him. He walks along with me on his heels, his eyes never leaving Deidre's signal.

Our car is out of sight when we find her, the blinking dot stopping as we draw closer and close in. The hill is lower here, and we crouch down, almost crawling by the time we spot her vehicle. The sun hangs low, hiding everything with its shadows.

She's parked in front of a farmer's market, standing beside her car with her phone to her ear. There are a few other cars there, and the outside looks full of flowers and food, but the field behind the market is empty. Nothing grows out here in the middle of nowhere. I hold back my cough as the wind sprays dust into my lungs.

"Get down," Sebastian orders. "On your stomach."

He army crawls closer to the road, and I worry we'll be spotted but I slide next to him, the hot earth burning every inch of my exposed skin.

Sebastian covers my back with dust and dirt, blending me into the surrounding land, and I do the same for him. Both of us never looking away from Deidre.

One worker stands out front but doesn't speak to her. His stance is wide, keeping his hands behind his back and looking outward. He must be a guard that's keeping watch.

"It's a front," I say to Sebastian.

"Damn good one," he says. His eyebrows draw together as he surveys the space. "An expensive one."

He takes a few pictures and sends them to someone on his phone. I'm assuming it's NeXus, and I wait, holding back all the questions I want to ask. This is his mission, and I need to follow along.

Deidre goes inside the shop, and we wait. Ten minutes tick by and then twenty.

"Hey, Seb," I say.

"They're keeping her inside — underground," he responds, ready to answer the question I haven't asked yet. He points to the other cars. "You see. They're visiting the facility or they work there. It's been too long to buy apples based on the dust on the vehicles. See how it's licked up on the sides?"

"Right, so what's the plan?" I ask.

He lets out a sharp exhale, checking his phone. "We have to wait for one of them to come out."

"That could be hours," I argue.

He nods and adjusts himself in the dirt. "We can't rush this," he says. "They have surveillance, ways to ensure you don't get past the front door. They might have an exit we can't see from here."

I want to scream and argue the point, but he's right. The lone worker out front doesn't move, just looks outward at the road, making sure anyone who comes by is given some excuse to keep driving.

Maybe the market's systems are down, or they lost electricity. He'll find a reason to send them away. It's his only job. A radio sits on his hip, ready to alert anyone inside of our presence. He would recognize us. Anyone would after the media shitshow that's been going around.

Another twenty minutes goes by and no other cars speed past. It's desolate out here. A great place to hide prisoners and no place to sell fruit.

"How could no one see this?" I ask. "It's obvious they're hiding something."

"People only see what they want," he answers. "And all anyone wants is the bond."

My heart sinks with his truth. We don't look outside ourselves unless it suits us, and I'm guilty of that. All I wanted was money, my ticket to a glorious sendoff. I wouldn't have noticed this or questioned its existence.

Another twenty minutes and I call out to Emry again and again, hoping one time she'll answer, but there's nothing. Sebastian leans to the side and takes a piss in the dirt. He moves back to his stomach, his eyes never leaving the stand.

Two hours pass, my back aching, and my head throbbing, before we see someone step out and go to their car. We watch as it comes to life, the lights blaring through the dirt caked on the rear lights.

"Stay put," Sebastian says. "Get your phone."

I pull it from my pocket, holding it in my hand, my eyes remaining on the vehicle. Sebastian comes up on his knees, ready to sprint.

"I'm going to our car to run him down," he says. "Tell me east or west."

He's off, and I focus on the shop.

The worker talks to the man backing out of the parking slot, waving him off and not noticing Sebastian, who ran out of sight. The car backs to the left, the rear lights flicking off when he heads east.

THEO

East

There's no response to my text, and I wait, still lying in the dirt. A part of me knows Sebastian's finding a way, getting to this person without setting off any alarms.

Ten minutes pass before I see the text.

SEBASTIAN

Come back to the car. Don't let them see you.

I crawl for a few minutes, letting the dirt on my back remain. It slides off in small clumps until I meet the part of the land that gives us a barrier. The worker doesn't flinch, his focus on the road ahead. He can no longer see me, and I run until Sebastian comes into view.

He's standing over an unconscious man lying down next to our car. When I get closer, I smirk at the damage Sebastian's caused in ten minutes. A trickle of blood slides down the man's forehead into the dirt, his eyes swollen from whatever punishment Sebastian inflicted.

I don't ask if he's alive, just what we need to do next.

"Help me search him, tie him up, and get him in the car," Sebastian says. We pull everything from his pockets, and he whimpers in pain when we shove him into the back.

"He's alive," I remark.

"For now," Sebastian shrugs.

We look over him in the backseat, both worried about the same thing. We don't need to kill him, but if someone sees him or he gets out of the car, we're in trouble.

"The trunk," I offer.

"Good idea," Sebastian agrees.

Sebastian yanks him out by his ankle and the man moans as he throws him over his shoulder. I pop the trunk and we shut him inside, not too worried if he dies in there.

He's hurt Emry and will hurt others. We may not be judge and jury, but today this person stops whatever harm they're inflicting.

"How did you get him to stop driving?" I ask. "Any chance he's tipped someone off?"

"Nah. I bumped him. Acted apologetic until he got close enough."

We get back into our car and drive it further away and out of sight, then walk back to his. We find a keycard and identification and pocket anything else we think will help us get inside.

Sebastian tosses the man's laptop and anything not needed into our abandoned car, telling NeXus to pick it up and get what they can. We're going inside without them.

The worker at the farmers' market tilts his head when the car pulls up. We're both in the back seat letting it auto-drive. It's a familiar vehicle, so he doesn't reach for a phone to alert someone.

I hear my heartbeat in my ears, the rush of adrenaline making it hard to stay still. Every breath I take is a struggle, and I look over at Sebastian, wondering how he's doing.

The look on his face is pure hatred, focused on the employee he's about to murder because he stands between us and Emry. His focus helps me calm myself, my resolve thickening in my gut.

The car parks to the employee's right, and we both crawl out of the left back door, staying low and out of sight.

This isn't practiced or well rehearsed, but we both move in sync, inching toward the man. I stand, greeting him. Sebastian moves around the back of the car while the guard's attention is on me

"I'm a little lost," I say. "Do you—"

Before I finish my sentence, Sebastian strikes him on the back of the head, and he falls to the ground in a pile of limbs, his radio untouched.

I raise my hands to my hips and smirk at Sebastian.

"Trunk?" I suggest.

CHAPTER 12

EMRY

"They're coming," I murmur to myself. No one is in the room, but they're still around, watching me, torturing me. I remind myself they're on the way, and this won't last forever. They don't need to hear the threat because it will be here soon enough.

Amazed by how fast I can heal from electric shock, Gilbert wants to test my other regenerative abilities.

He pushed the limit.

Using a scalpel, he sliced into my legs, arms, stomach, and across my face. The last cut was so deep, that the blade goes through my cheek and slashes my tongue. The taste of copper and the spike of pain make me cough blood all over his over-sized lab coat. He sneers at me in disgust and returns later with a fresh white jacket and another scalpel.

In round two, I heal faster, the cuts closing as he slices.

"She's progressing," a woman suggests. "Her body is learning how to repair the damage."

She's wrong.

They're blinded by their desire to understand the bond. I'm healing faster because Theo is close, and I smile to myself, knowing this secret. This device they strapped to me may keep our thoughts apart, but the essence of Theo gets stronger with every passing minute.

Accelerated healing doesn't stop the pain, every slice searing hot fire into my skin. I close my eyes and drift away to somewhere else, a memory I want to keep close.

I'm sixteen.

They keep my room dark and cold. It's a cell and I'm their prisoner, taken aback when a stranger enters. He's broad and tall, different from anyone else I've seen at Genome Theory these past few years. It scares me, and I curl into myself, afraid of what's to come.

My swollen and bruised body aches from their procedures the day before, and panic sets in, wondering why someone is back so soon. The man steps forward as chaos ensues in the hallway. Unfamiliar voices say words I can't understand when this ward is always silent.

The man comes forward, apologizing for scaring me, his dark eyes searching mine.

No one apologizes in this place, and no one looks me in the eye. They don't see me here.

I wonder if I'm dreaming, or maybe I'm dead. His hand reaches out for me, touching my cheek, and I sink into the embrace. He smells like the outside - trees, and woods, a place I haven't seen in years.

"I'm Sebastian," he says.

I smile at the memory, letting it fill me and send the pain away.

I don't open my eyes, letting myself sink back in time, knowing he'll come back again. Sebastian will find me, and with Theo's help, I know it will be soon.

I remember the way his touch felt after years of being treated like an object, something inhuman. How he swallowed hard, the smell of the earth strengthening as he leaned closer before speaking again.

"I've got you," he promised me.

He's always good to his word.

"We need to record this. Get back here," Gilbert barks at someone.

There's a reprieve from the pain, and I don't let Gilbert's voice ruin the moment. I'm blissful, lost inside my memories.

The metal bed I rest upon shakes. "Ouch!" Gilbert shrieks. "That burns." The gurney slides, slamming into the wall before it comes to a shaking stop.

My eyes open, but it's nothing but whiteness, a never-ending mist with no one in sight. I pull at the cuffs around my wrists, and they're still there, shackling me to the bed.

My head pounds, the helmet tight against my skull. Gilbert's screeching in the corner, cursing about a burning. The healing cloud is back, and it's coming from me. I'm strong enough now with Theo close.

I'm healing myself, and I'm in overdrive.

I laugh, and it makes my head hurt, but I can't stop. A door slams in the room, Gilbert fleeing, but I'm still strapped to the gurney and blocked by this helmet. There's nothing I can do but wait in a sea of bright mist.

The beacon for them to find me.

THEO

Two men shoved inside car trunks in one afternoon isn't how I thought my day would look a few weeks ago, but that life is over. I'm not afraid as we descend into the depths of this underground bunker. Emry is close, and I'll walk into fire to get to her.

Sebastian grows robotic and silent, using hand motions to guide me along. We don't speak, but both of us know what each other is thinking.

He'll look in one corridor and I in another. When he leans left, I go right, and together with the credentials of our new friends in the trunks, we make it deep inside Genome's hidden lab.

It's mostly empty, and when we turn a final corner, we see our first sign of people. They're clustered together at the end of a hallway dressed up like scientists instead of sadists.

They're fooling themselves.

We stay out of sight, our backs flush to the cold cement, silent except for our steady breaths.

"I can sense her," I whisper to Sebastian. "She's that way." She's still lost, but there's a shadow of something urging me toward the crowd. It must be her.

Sebastian nods, leaning back against the wall and taking a moment to think. It's only seconds, but something inside me stirs, almost yanking me down the hallway.

I focus on keeping my feet planted on the ground, but one heel raises to step forward. It's a fight I'm losing, my palm leaving the wall and reaching out, despite the better part of me wanting to stay still.

"Sebastian, we have a problem," I admit.

My body thrums with need for her, the closeness taking away my control. I knew I couldn't stay out of Genome, waiting for Sebastian while this bond forced me to seek her out, but I've lost all restraint.

"I know. There are six men and two of us, but they don't look like they have any defenses. And we have the element of surprise," he says.

"No, it's not that," I admit. My hands shake, my heart pounding in my chest, and I'm holding myself back from sprinting into the crowd of men. "She's too close. I–I can't control it, man. I don't know. She's never been this close and awake and in danger. Fuck."

I hear my voice shake, every word a struggle, and Sebastian's hand reaches out and grabs my elbow. I'm already moving toward the group, walking away from him without realizing I'm moving. He yanks me back, and I come to my senses long enough to stop, but I can't hold back for long.

"We can move fast," he promises. "Just give me a second. I need some kind of weapon, something."

I'm pulling away from Sebastian seconds later, his hold on me slipping. My strength surprises me, and I'm about to swing at him to get to Emry.

"I'm losing it," I say. "We need to do something."

A mist of white slides in between us both, almost unnoticeable if it weren't creating a fog in front of our eyes. It seeps into Sebastian's skin, creeping into a small cut above his eyebrow. I hold my hand up, watching it pour from my fingertips.

"She's hurt," Sebastian says. "Okay, just bowl through. They're scientists, not boxers. Lead the way."

He doesn't have to tell me twice. I'm sprinting toward the group, and I roll by so fast they don't notice who we are at first, shocked that any intruders made it this far.

"Hey, it's—" Sebastian's punch to a man's jaw makes him spin in place before hitting the ground. Another man jumps on him while a few run away.

"Go!" Sebastian orders. There's another spray of blood from a punch before I'm turned around, and I know Sebastian is right on my heels. They're no match for his brute strength and seething anger.

The white mist grows as I run. I follow it, my feet flying under me, moving faster than ever before.

A few men stand in front of a large steel door, arguing amongst themselves. One sees me and calls out.

"Who are you?" His confusion turns to panic when he screams, "Gilbert, get over here?"

Gilbert.

The name sends me into a fury, and I see the culprit, small and cowardly, attempting to hide behind the others. His face is red and covered in blisters, but I don't stop to ask why.

Sebastian leaps with me, both of us descending upon him, fists flying and blood spraying.

Others try to pull us off, but as Gilbert goes limp, gurgling blood from his lips, they all slink away. I hear someone making a call through a radio, and maybe there are more we'll have to fight, but I'm certain between Sebastian and me, we'll handle anything.

"Here," I say and slam myself against the locked door. A cloud of white pours around its edges, and I claw at the metal, screaming to get inside.

Sebastian pulls at a keycard on Gilbert's belt, snapping it free. He's probably dead or dying, but we don't care.

All I see and all I think about is Emry. The mist between us touches, mixing together and sending spikes of energy through my veins. I feel our connection — her smell and taste, the joy she's feeling knowing we're here.

"Emry!" I scream out.

"Baby, we're coming," Sebastian yells.

The door opens, and I find her strapped to a table, half-naked, with a helmet on her head. The cloud isn't blinding, but a fog cocoons us all, immediately easing the ache I've been feeling.

Our bond knows we're together.

Sebastian and I leap to either side of her and rip off the restraints and the helmet, carefully removing the straps around her neck.

She sits up, the door in her mind opening to me, letting me hear every thought.

"I knew you'd come. Both of you."

Feeling her is euphoric, every puzzle piece clicking together. The three of us embrace, Sebastian and me wrapping our arms around Emry and holding her between us.

"We've got you," Sebastian says.

Those words flash a picture in my mind, and I realize it's a memory, something Emry either can't hold back or wants me to see.

It's Sebastian walking toward her. He's younger and appears a little nervous about approaching. The sense of hope that fills Emry's heart in that moment creeps into mine, and it's clear how scared she must have been then and now.

"We're here," I say, my voice cracking.

The memory of Sebastian's hand touching Emry for the

first time sends goosebumps across my skin. When the vision fades, it leaves a piece of what makes Emry tick behind.

"We have you. Always," I promise her.

"Look out!" she screams. We jerk away, and there's a flash of shock in Sebastian's eyes as she leaps from the table.

We go to catch her, but our hands can't hold her back. She tears herself from our grasp, plunging herself into a threat partially hidden by the mist.

The blood pouring from a woman's neck spurts out, hitting my cheek. Emry's fist pounds into her flesh again, slamming a weapon into her jugular and leaving it there.

Emry lets go and stumbles back into me, and I recognize Deidre, who claws at the object. She yanks out a sliver of plastic, sending more sprays of blood through the white cloud that encases us.

Emry doesn't react, her face blank as she watches Deidre slump to the floor. The scalpel Deidre intended to stab me with slides from her hand and clinks on the cement.

Sebastian turns Emry to face him, and he looks her over, checking her for wounds.

"She's okay," I tell him. The cloud fades around us with nothing left to heal.

He smiles, his lips meeting hers and I feel the joy from their kiss. His hands plunge into her hair, and he kisses her as if her mouth gives him life. She's his source of oxygen, his reason for living.

I'm gripping the gurney, the metal bending under my hands, trying with everything I have not to steal her from him and scoop her into my arms.

It doesn't bother me that she's kissing Sebastian, but I need to touch my bonded and feel her skin on mine. I need to hold her, to wrap myself around her. My body tingles with fire, limbs twitching, eyes unable to look away, heart beating only for her.

The metal groans, and Sebastian breaks their kiss, a smirk on his face when he sees the warped metal.

She looks at me, Sebastian's hands still tangled in her hair, and without pause, he moves her mouth toward mine.

CHAPTER 13

EMRY

Sebastian's hand nudges me toward Theo, encouraging me to kiss him. My heart races and instinct takes over with that slight push. His permission releases what resistance I'm able to hold on to. I wrap my arms around Theo's neck, my body sinking into his.

Theo wraps his arms around me, our lips barely touching, breaths mingling together in each other's mouths. I can taste him before our lips meet, the sweetness of his soul sending flutters into my stomach.

When our mouths collide, the kiss sends fireworks throughout my body. Any pain or worry fades away, and all I think or feel is Theo. It's electricity, sparking all of my senses, and I'm ravenous, dipping my tongue inside his mouth, letting our lips move in a perfect rhythm, making a heaviness sink into my core. He moans, his hold on me tightening and taking the breath from my body.

I'm so close to coming just from this kiss, my whimpers

growing, hands clawing at his neck and back. It's the first kiss, but the familiarity shocks me. We fit together just as Sebastian and I have, and something about that feels wonderful and terrible all at once.

"Sebastian."

The thought hits us both, but Theo doesn't have a worry in his head. All he thinks of is me. Kissing me, holding me, making love to me.

"Wait, Sebastian."

Our lips separate with my thought, Theo pulling back and staring at me with confused eyes. My heart pounds so hard I feel it beat against his chest.

I let out a breath, long and shaky, and a mist of white pours out between our lips. It seeps away, and I follow it with my eyes, noticing how it curls into Sebastian's bloody knuckles. He's pacing the room, looking for someone or something, and I'm relieved I don't have to look into his eyes and see the disappointment I'm sure to find there.

Theo brings his mouth to my neck, and I'm lifted from the floor, my legs wrapping around his middle. He lets out a moan, and my eyes flutter closed, unable to stop myself from this embrace. His lips find mine again, the euphoria taking over for a moment before I let myself think about what we're doing.

"Stop it. We're hurting Sebastian."

I yank my head back, breaking the kiss once more, a flare of white shooting out from our mouths. My hands curl into his chest, and I tell myself to push him away, to break from our embrace, but I can't.

"We're not, love. Sebastian wants this."

His thoughts make little sense, but Sebastian offered Theo to me, and he's not ripping us apart. The words spoken about all of us together were true, and of course they were. Sebastian doesn't lie.

This bond pulls Theo and me together like magnets, and my devotion to Sebastian does the same. If Sebastian wants to try a life with the three of us together, why would I fight that? Maybe I need him to say it in person and hear the words from my husband's lips.

Sebastian is turned away, rummaging in a closet, yanking a lab coat out from inside, and holding a metal rod in one hand. The last wisp of white still circles him, finding the parts that need healing and burrowing its way inside his skin.

All the while, Theo still reaches for me, unable to keep his lips and hands off of me. He's clinging to my body, his lips once again on my neck, and finding the sensitive spot that makes me wilt in his arms.

The bond between us wants him and begs me to rip off his clothes. I'm a second away from fucking him on the metal table I was just strapped to, but I fight it. The knowledge that we're still trapped underground by Genome stops me and gives me enough pause to hold back the frenzy inside.

Sebastian kicks the closet door closed and turns to us. There's a small part of me that worries I'll see regret in his eyes, or some sadness he'll feel at the sight of his wife in the arms of another man.

His wife, who he saved once again, with someone else's lips on her skin. He might have given me to him, but this is all new.

Except, when Sebastian faces us, my legs still wrapped around Theo who's trailing kisses along my collarbone, there's a wide smile on his face.

"Clothes," he holds up one hand, holding a lab coat and some other items. "Weapon." He shakes the metal rod in the other.

"Theo, that's enough," I say begrudgingly, patting him on

the back. He separates our bodies with a grunt, and Sebastian shakes his head, still smiling.

My bare feet hit the cold ground, and I realize I'm almost nude in front of both of them. Sebastian hands me some clothes, and I shove one leg through the scrub pants, eager to get dressed.

"What's the plan?"

"I'm following Sebastian's lead here, love," Theo answers my internal thought aloud.

"You gotta speak out loud when I'm around," Sebastian says. "Or everything will take twice as long."

I shove the top over my head, ripping the tangle of cloth they kept me in and throwing it to the floor. "Okay, what's the plan?" I ask.

"We get the fuck out of here," Sebastian answers. "I've already alerted NeXus, and it won't take them long to get inside. Are there others down here?"

A wave of dread hits me, and Theo brings his hand to his throat, feeling it as I do.

"Alison's here," I say. "I haven't seen anyone else, but there has to be."

"We know about Alison," Sebastian says. "We'll find her."

I nod, finding it difficult to speak. She could be hurt or dead and it's all my fault.

"It's not your fault," Theo reassures, pulling me against his chest. He gives me a quick kiss on the lips and turns me to Sebastian, who does the same.

"Are you ready?" Sebastian asks.

I nod, eager to get the hell out of this place and never return, and follow between them as we head for the door.

Once we step out into the hall, I see him.

Gilbert lies in a pool of blood. He's motionless, eyes half

open and unblinking, his oversized lab coat covering him like a blanket.

"Gilbert's dead."

"Good," Theo says.

"He can't hurt anyone anymore."

He reaches his hand out for mine, and I smile at his thought. Taking it, I'm yanked forward with them at a steady jog.

"Out loud," Sebastian repeats. "I can't help if I can't hear." He taps one ear with his finger and takes a left down a hallway streaked with blood.

I hope he knows where he's going. I've never left the room without being drugged and blindfolded, so I don't know the way out.

"I know where I'm going," Sebastian says, almost as if he's reading my thoughts as Theo does. "Don't worry."

He turns again, and we see dozens of men coming toward us. They're silent even when opening doors and signaling commands. Part of me wants to run before I realize they're NeXus employees. People dressed in the same uniforms Sebastian wore all those years ago storm another Genome Theory building, rescuing the stolen people from inside.

"We'll have you out in five minutes," Theo says. "Just over here."

I twist my arm, pulling away. "Wait, we can't."

"It's safe," Theo protests. "It's NeXus. They're here to help."

"No!" I scream, ripping myself free of Theo's grip and rubbing my wrist. A few NeXus employees look up, one of them waving at Sebastian.

"We have to find Alison!" I beg.

Sebastian turns around, catching me as I squirrel away from Theo. He's strong, but this bond gives me just as much muscle when I want, and right now, I could lift this building if I thought Alison was under it.

"We'll get her," Sebastian says. "I promise."

"I'll get her," I demand.

I storm up to a NeXus employee. "Have you found her, Alison? She's my height and age. Hair about to here." I hold my hand up. "They said they knocked her out but kept her alive."

They give me a blank stare and look at someone else for help.

A woman in uniform comes over. "Our intel shows there are several people held here against their will. We'll look for the one you're describing."

Someone pulls a long black body bag into the hallway, dragging someone's lifeless body along the floor. I race for it and yank back the plastic, my eyes flooding with tears.

It's a stranger, a man in a lab coat with broken glasses and what looks to be a broken neck. Someone Sebastian might have killed on his way to me.

I stand up, my body trembling with fear and adrenaline. "Alison!" I scream throughout the hall, making my way back from where we came.

I'm a terrible friend, always arguing with her about how stupid the bond is, and then getting bonded myself. She couldn't get to work without being harassed by reporters, and no doubt had her picture taken against her will. They didn't need much to find her and steal her.

Theo and Sebastian are at my heels, pleading with me to let NeXus look for her, but I refuse to listen. It's my responsibility to find her because I'm the reason she's here.

"Alison!" I call into an empty room.

Sebastian rests a hand on the small of my back. "You said they drugged her," he says. "She won't hear you. Please, let NeXus do their job."

"You all want to be together? The three of us?" I scream at them. Theo and Sebastian freeze, my outburst startling them speechless. "Well, then help me. This isn't going to be two against one for the rest of my fucking life. I'm not leaving here without her."

My body shakes, tears welling in my eyes. Alison's my only friend, the only one who stayed by my side even when the world thought I was insane. She didn't deserve this, and I can't let her down.

They look at each other, shoulders relaxing in some sort of agreement between them both.

"We'll look together," Theo says, coming to my side while Sebastian wraps an arm around my shoulders.

Satisfied with their answer, I collect myself and think. Alison's in this place somewhere. They wouldn't risk taking her above ground where she could be seen.

Sebastian juts his chin in one direction, and Theo nods, unspeaking. Sebastian nods back seconds later, not a word said between them. They stare at each other expressionless, and I huff out an exasperated sigh just before Sebastian takes my hand and drags me along with him.

"What was that?" I ask. We're going down a different hallway. I'm grateful I won't see Gilbert again, even though he can't hurt me anymore.

Sebastian looks at me and squints his eyes. "What was what?"

He looks inside a window before opening the door to another room. "Stay here," he orders.

"What was that thing between you and Theo?" I ask, ignoring his command and following him inside. The room is empty except for some storage of spare gurneys and medical equipment. "What's the plan to find Alison? You and Theo just had a whole conversation without words. Kind of like..."

"I don't know what you're talking about, baby," he says. "Nothing here. Let's go."

I grab him by the elbow before he's out the door, my grip stronger than I realize, stopping him in his tracks.

He looks back, meeting my eyes. "I want to get you out of here. So, we're getting Alison, so you will leave."

His mind is elsewhere, unsure of what I'm asking or why. I don't know either, but I can't shake this nagging feeling.

"Back there, before we split up, you didn't speak to Theo," I said.

"Yes, I did," he argues. "I said I'll take you east so you don't have to see the room where they kept you, or... anything else."

He means Gilbert, and I shudder at the thought.

"And he told me to he'll double back from where we came and check it out."

"He didn't say any of that," I argue.

"Emry, we need to move before NeXus takes over this entire operation," Sebastian says. "Come on."

I let him go, following him, and refocused on finding Alison.

I reach out to Theo.

"Anything yet?"

He answers right away.

"I'll tell you the second we find her, love."

Another few rooms of nothing except NeXus employees and dead members of Genome. We turn around when we reach a dead end, jogging back to the stairwell where Sebastian says we can check back in with some of his coworkers.

Theo checks in with me. He's partnered with another NeXus employee, and they've located the security system, scanning through video of everyone that came in and out. I feel his rage when he sees me brought inside.

"Do you see my mother?"

I don't know why I asked him. It's instinctual, needing to know if she did any of the dirty work, wanting to hate her more if that's possible.

"No. Still looking for Alison. Come to us."

I tell Sebastian where they are, and we head in that direction. Turning a corner, my heart drops, and I choke back the tears that threaten to escape.

They can't see me cry.

That's not fair and won't help anyone.

There are children, a dozen of them. They're standing in a long line, some of them worse off than others. I don't recognize any of them, and that's the worst part. There should be news articles and cover stories about these missing babies, but that's all hidden away.

Something has to change. We need to protect these kids.

A teenage girl stands in front of two smaller boys, both of them much younger and smaller than her. She's wearing a fresh gown, her hair clean and straight. The boys look malnourished, skinny, and weak, with dark circles under their eyes.

"They're doing it all again. We can't let this happen again."

"I know," Sebastian says. "This doesn't end here."

It's not until we reach Theo that I realize it.

I never spoke those words out loud, only thought them.

Something is shifting with the three of us.

Something that might let him hear us.

CHAPTER 14

THEO

"There," I point to the image, and the men from NeXus shift their attention to the right-hand screen. This room has four monitors and one dying Genome Theory employee. He's bleeding out in the corner and none of us put much energy into treating him or putting him out of his misery.

There are no files in this room, only the monitors, and we're lucky they didn't lock up before the tech noticed us. We've been combing through the video, watching children shuffled into labs, carted back and forth for testing, and we also watched the moment Emry's dragged inside.

Knowing what they do to Emry, treating her like an object they can torture with their tests, no part of me feels bad about killing Gilbert.

None.

We focus on the video of Alison. She's a fighter, kicking and flailing her body around in protest. When someone brings her into a room, removing the bag over her head, she bites them with such force, that another man has to step over to unlock her jaw. Blood sprays on the floor when he rips his arm away.

"Atta girl," I say under my breath at the video of her, and others nod in agreement.

"Where is she?" Emry says when she rushes inside. We all point to the monitor and watch, speeding through hours of Alison left alone.

"She's not in that room," I say. "Keep going. They move her at some point."

The images sprint forward at high speed, people buzzing in and out until finally, we see Deidre and another man. They stun Alison and then inject her with something, dragging her out and down the hall until...

"Oh my god," Emry shrieks, sprinting out of the room.

Sebastian and I exchange a solemn glance at each other before we follow Emry. She's in a dead sprint, and her worry mixes with mine until we're both frantic to get there. Still, I let Sebastian lead, knowing he will calm her better than me, especially with how entwined our emotions are to one another.

Where they took her had two drawer-like compartments. She was placed on a metal slab, and then pushed inside, locking the small door at the handle. It looks like a morgue, but we have to be sure.

We fly down the hallway, knowing where this room is, not realizing the cabinets on the floor reached back so far when we checked it for the first time.

Sebastian lunges at Emry to stop her from entering the room, and I tumble into them.

"Let me go first."

Both Emry and Sebastian yell back different responses to my thought. Emry screams, "No," while Sebastian says, "Yes."

Sebastian holds Emry back, struggling against her increased strength. I breeze past them, doing my best to ignore the agony that sinks into my gut. Emry's hysterical, unable to control her madness, and I'm eager to end her fear, one way or another.

Bending down, I yank at the first drawer and break the lock. It flies open with nothing inside, and my shaking hands reach for the second.

Emry screams behind me to let her see, and the sorrow she feels makes me want to vomit.

"Please, no. This is all my fault."

"It's not your fault," I tell Emry, giving the second drawer a pull. The weight of it tells me something rests inside. It jerks to a stop, Alison's bloody body lying out on the slab, still and unmoving.

My eyes meet Sebastian's, Emry screaming and desperate to slip from his hold. We both think the same thing, knowing this is the exact reason we didn't want to look for Alison. This image will haunt Emry forever.

The strike to my face catches me off guard, cracking my jaw and making Sebastian blur in my vision. Falling back, I rub my cheek, my other hand catching me from hitting the ground.

I scramble up, and even though it hurts to smile, I do. I've never been so happy to have a woman punch me in the face. She could swing again, and I'd keep on smiling.

"Oh, shit, I'm sorry, Theo," Alison apologizes. "You're Theo, right? I thought you were one of them."

I'm laughing, my cheek healing an instant later, so relieved to find Alison alive, pretending to be dead or knocked out so she could strike.

Before I can answer her, Emry squirrels away from Sebastian and throws herself onto her, breaking the sliding base of the cabinet. Both women thud to the ground happier than ever.

A NeXus employee steps inside, asking if everything's okay.

Sebastian and I step to the doorway to give them both a minute to talk. It's mostly sobbing noises between the women, but they may not need words to get across the joy they're experiencing.

"We want to get Alison and Emry out of here," Sebastian says. "We need to skip whatever debriefing NeXus has planned."

He knows this person, both of them shaking hands and talking with ease.

"Shouldn't be a problem," the guy answers, giving Sebastian a few pats on the bicep. "But I need you both to take care of something."

"What's that?" I ask.

He turns to me with a lopsided grin. "Jack and Moira are out of their skin worried about what's going on, and for us, it's classified, so—"

"I'll call them," I tell Sebastian and step outside, motioning for him to stay with Alison and Emry.

"Tell him no debriefing," Sebastian orders.

I flick him a salute, not entirely sure what a debriefing entails, but agreeing to bypass the event.

The phone rings once before Jack picks up, and he tells me Moira is with him. I give him all the necessary information, sparing the gory details. They don't need to hear about the murders and bodies we left inside trunks.

"When you get back to NeXus, we need to take a break on the testing," Jack says.

I hear Emry and Alison inside the room, Emry apologizing again and again while Alison tells her it's not her fault. Sebastian goes over to them, wrapping his arms around each one, and they rest their heads on his shoulders.

"I don't know if that's happening," I answer.

"It's too much for Emry. She's revisited years of horrible trauma," Jack argues. "She needs help."

"We'll help her," I stop him. "Listen, what I mean is I don't think we're going back to NeXus. Sebastian said he doesn't want to put Emry through debriefing, whatever that is. I think NeXus would force us into it if we go back there. Not to mention, a NeXus employee was a part of her kidnapping. Deidre orchestrated this whole thing. Before that, you tried to shock us half to death because that Bob asshole lost his mind."

Saying all of this out loud solidifies my decision that we are not stepping into that building anytime soon. They need an overhaul before we even think about going near the place.

Jack exhales into the phone, Moira in the background supporting everything I've said.

"Look, you're right. She'll need some support," I tell Jack. "You can see her at home. Help her there."

"He can't see you nodding through the phone," Moira chimes in.

I chuckle to myself, picturing the two of them.

"We should get security to her house," Jack says after some thought. "NeXus is on the line for this, so it shouldn't be a problem, but Theo..." he trails off.

"Yeah?"

Sebastian, Alison, and Emry stand up, walking over to me. Streaks of tears on Emry's face almost send me over the edge. I hold back from running to her, not wanting to upset her or Alison.

"Where will you...?" Jack asks, his question unfinished.

Moira pipes up in the background, announcing I can stay with her in her daughter's room.

"What's going on?" Sebastian asks.

"I'm talking to Jack, letting him know we won't do a

debriefing. He said he can get security over to your house," I explain. "I can stay with Moira."

"No," Sebastian says and takes the phone.

I knew he would disagree, but I wanted to offer what might be best for Emry. There's a lot of change happening, and fast.

"He'll stay with us," he tells Jack. "It will take us several hours to get home. Send our things back so it's all there when we get home."

His words send me into overdrive, thrilled with the idea of being close to my bonded.

I can't help it when I reach for Emry, pulling her into my arms and kissing her forehead and her cheek, trailing my lips down her neck. Alison's eyes grow wide, shooting back and forth between Sebastian and me, but it doesn't stop my assault on Emry's soft skin.

"Are you seeing this?" she whispers to a NeXus employee who simply shrugs in response.

Sebastian hangs up, patting me on the back to signal it's time to go and telling the man we're leaving and we need a car.

"We brought yours here," he tells Sebastian.

"I need another car," Sebastian says. "There's a guy in the trunk of mine."

"I'm sorry. What?" Alison asks.

"There's a Genome guy—"

"I heard you," Alison interrupts, raising her open palm. "You are insane, Sebastian Crowe. I'm not complaining at the moment, but damn."

A small smile reaches her eyes as she holds hands with Emry. We make it outside, someone from NeXus empties a vehicle for us, and everyone piles inside.

"Hey, Mills," Sebastian calls over to another co-worker.

He clasps hands with Sebastian when he steps over in

greeting. "You head out. We'll take care of everything here. I'll send you my notes."

"Thanks, I appreciate that, but uh, there's a guy in that trunk, too," Sebastian admits, pointing to the Genome worker's car.

"Wow," Alison says from the back.

Mills raises his eyebrows. "So, two guys in trunks? I heard about the other one."

Sebastian speeds off without responding, sending a cloud of dust in our wake.

Emry's in the backseat with Alison, her head resting on her shoulder, and Alison's worried eyes scan the horizon. Emry's growing tired, her eyes heavy with the need for sleep. It pulls at me, and I fight the urge to rest.

"I knew you'd come for me," Emry mumbles, eyes closing.

"We've got you," Sebastian says. He pats me on the thigh a few times before returning his hands to the wheel.

"I've got my family. All of us."

It's Sebastian's voice in my head, but his lips don't move. Maybe I'm imagining this, wanting to hear him say those words—wanting this to work with the three of us.

When Emry's head pops up from Alison's shoulder, a smile on her lips and her eyes wide with surprise, I realize I'm not imagining things.

She hears it too.

CHAPTER 15

Alison's stuff is all over the house, or rather, my stuff that she's been wearing and then discarding in tiny piles.

"I'll clean it up," she offers, breezing past me and gathering things in her arms as she goes. She's walking in a haze, and I tell her not to worry, but I don't know if the words leave my lips. It's getting difficult to determine what I'm speaking out loud and what's only in my head to Theo.

And maybe to Sebastian.

"You will not," Lucas, Sebastian's brother, says as he strides through the hallway. I'm more grateful than surprised to see him. He's a distraction, and it never hurts to have more muscle around. He greets Sebastian and me, and then nods to Theo, narrowing his gaze a bit at the stranger that upturned his brother's life. He's level-headed but cautious about the man.

Alison keeps shuffling around, picking up items that over-flow from her arms. Lucas pulls her toward him and takes the dirty clothes from her hands.

"After what you've been through, just sit down," Lucas tells her. "I'll take care of this and make us some coffee."

He looks us over, noticing how disheveled, dirty, and chaotic we all appear.

"Irish coffee," he decides with a nod. "Extra shot."

"I need a shower," I say and Alison lets out a sound of agreement.

"I don't want to be the bearer of bad news," Lucas says, discarding the dirty clothes into the laundry chute. "But police need to do a few things. They're pulling up, well, now."

He points to the window at the marked cars heading down our drive. "There they are. Just a few pictures of any injuries. Take a quick statement."

"I don't want this. I said no debriefing. They need to eat and sleep," Sebastian argues. "Let me make a call."

"No," I say, resting a hand on Sebastian's shoulder. "We need to talk to them soon so any case against Genome doesn't get thrown out."

I take in a deep breath and lean into his side, trying to wrap my arms around his thick torso. "Or any case against whoever is giving Genome cash. We need to do this right for all those kids."

Theo moves closer, wraps a hand around my waist, and kisses the top of my head.

Lucas's jaw drops. I'm not sure if it's my mention of children or our embrace. Maybe it's a combination of both.

"I know," Alison murmurs to him loud enough for all of us to hear.

I don't have the energy to give her a side-eye.

Sebastian raises an open palm to Lucas, urging him to relax. He shuts his mouth and crosses his arms over his chest.

"I have no idea what's going on," Alison adds. "I'm just happy I'm not dead."

Lucas lets out a huff of air, glaring at his brother. Once the dust settles, he'll be having a talk with him, but I don't know what to say at this moment. We need to talk, the three of us, but I can barely keep my eyes open.

"I'll go deal with the police," Lucas says, pointing toward the door. "At least buy you some time to sip an Irish coffee."

"Me too," Alison pipes up. She rushes after Lucas, eager to get away from the awkward moment. We must look ridiculous, this immediate throuple that no one understands, even me.

"Is that what we are?"

Theo and Sebastian both look at me, and I close the door to my mind, feeling the block back in place. It makes Theo let out a huff, knowing he's been shut out. Sebastian's reaction was different, shutting his eyes and rubbing his temples.

A police officer walks inside with Lucas. She's young and smiling, and I raise my hand like a schoolchild.

"Can I go first?" I say. "I just... really need a shower."

She nods, and when I follow after her to my kitchen, both men are reluctant to let me go. I look back, seeing their large hands clasped over my wrists, and I smile, my thoughts so loud I think they might break free for the world to hear.

I want this. I want us to be happy together.

Alison steps in when I'm finishing up with the officer. The process is quick and simple, answering questions and having photos of my body taken. After the torment of Genome, this process seems too easy.

I'm not surprised there isn't a mark on me, but it makes my accusations sound ludicrous. With Theo, no injury sticks. They electrocuted me, sliced me with scalpels, and performed unknown tests after drugging me, but my body shows nothing —no bruises or cuts.

When I explain this to the officer, she writes it all down, not questioning my honesty. I've signed a document with my full statement even if it's unbelievable. I just hope it's enough to go after everyone responsible.

Everyone knows the bond gives you youth and health, so my healing abilities must make sense, but it's different when it's happening to you. Watching my skin close and heal, not leaving a single scar behind, is nothing short of... magic.

"Are you ready, Alison?" the officer asks.

"No," she says, taking a seat next to me. "But does it matter?"

The officer's eyes are kind, and she tilts her head in understanding. "Would it help if your friend was with you?"

Alison reaches for my hand. "Is that okay?"

"Of course," I tell her, interlacing our fingers together and closing them tight.

I didn't know what happened to Alison, or how she was captured, and my throat constricts with unease. She was scared and alone, not knowing what Genome Theory was capable of, or even that they were responsible. I brace myself to hear all of this again, my heart racing under my shirt.

Theo busts through the door, and we all jump from his dramatic entry.

"What happened? Are you upsetting her?" He points to the officer.

Sebastian's at his back, pulling him away, hissing something in his ear. I can tell he's saying something to the tune of, "Let's cooperate and get these people out of our house."

Our house.

The thought hits me as Sebastian drags Theo away, and I compose myself, not wanting to upset my bonded. I mouth to him, "I'm fine," and he retreats with Sebastian, the door slamming closed behind them.

Theo's upset because I am, and that's something to remedy if I'm able. Closing my eyes, I picture something that will put him at ease. It's all of us sitting on the outside patio with the snow falling down, sipping hot coffees, and talking about shows we're watching and books we're reading.

"That's us soon."

I feel Theo relax, the stream of consciousness between us softening to a steady vibration of calmness.

Alison and I take in a deep breath, listening to the officer type away on her laptop before she begins.

"Hi, Alison," the officer starts over, pretending that the interruption didn't just happen. She reaches over to place her hand atop Alison's. "I hate to ask this, but there are three other officers here. Did they?"

"They already touched me, Sara," Alison says.

I look at her uniform and notice Sara scrawled above her badge, feeling terrible I never asked or used her name.

"No bond," Alison quips, rolling her eyes.

How could I forget the standard protocol?

My time at NeXus took me away from all the unwanted touching and strangers in my personal space.

I didn't miss it.

Bonds are so rare, and it won't be long before everyone in this town knows I'm off the market, if they don't already. That may save me from a lot of skin-to-skin in the future.

"We've received footage from the event where you were taken," Sara explains. "It's clear and we're able to identify those involved."

"Who was it?" Alison asks.

Sara taps on her tablet a few times and brings up a picture of three men. It's their intake photos, and we're both relieved to know they're already in custody. We don't recognize them, but the list of small crimes under each of their names doesn't make sense. They jumped from stealing food and breaking into receptions to kidnapping.

"Unfortunately, they all have the same story," Sara explains. "Someone approached them with an offer. Money in exchange for transporting you to a second location, away from the reception. They don't know by who, and they received untraceable transfers to blocked bank accounts for their services."

Sara pulls the tablet back, swiping through as she continues. "It's likely Genome Theory pre-screened who they would approach. They were all seekers with overdrawn bank accounts."

Alison frowns. "Well, us seekers get pretty desperate. We go to receptions we know are sketchy."

"This is not your fault," I assure her, and she gives me a small smile.

"It's not," Sara agrees. "They would have gotten you one way or another and used you to find Emry."

I frown and sink into my chair, Sara confirming what I already knew.

"Not your fault either," Alison tells me, squeezing my hand.

"What we need to get are more details about when you were put in a second vehicle," Sara says.

Alison tenses and my back shoots ramrod straight, Sara waiting for us both to breathe. It's such a simple action, but I'm having to force myself to remember, holding my breath until I'm dizzy.

There's the flash of us on the patio once more, Sebastian laughing at a joke someone has said. Theo's leaning forward, blowing into his hot coffee cup and staring at the falling snow. I can't tell who's creating this, me or Theo, but it helps.

"The three men took you to this storage room attached to the bathrooms here," Sara says, showing us an aerial picture of unfamiliar buildings.

Alison shrugs. "I don't remember where exactly, and it was dark."

"That's okay," Sara says. "We can see where you were grabbed and that they bring you inside. But here, see that black vehicle?"

"Yes, but they blindfolded me. I didn't see anyone."

"We have an image of a passenger, but it's not clear," Sara says. "It seems she came out to the shed and then went back into the car before you were put inside. We think it may have been to identify you as the target, so you may recognize this person. She's covering her face and wearing a hood, so it's a long shot, but one we should take."

"Super." Alison's sarcasm doesn't hide how her body trembles.

I lean forward, ready to see who did this to her.

Sara enlarges an image for Alison. "Do you recognize her?" She gives Alison a moment to look and then swipes to a video of the person walking, doing their best to cover every identifiable part of themselves.

Alison grabs the tablet, holding it closer to her face. She squints her eyes at the pictures and sets it back down.

"I'm sorry," she sighs. "I don't know who that is."

"I do," I croak, the words hard to manage. I let go of Alison's hand, sure that if she didn't hate me before, she will now. She won't want to be anywhere near me, least of all have me comforting her.

"I know that person's mannerisms, the way they walk. That's Blaire Crawford," I admit. "That's my mother."

CHAPTER 16

I sit out on the patio alone, dirty and trembling, doing my best to hide my sadness from Theo.

He feels it anyway.

"It's not your fault. You have to know that," he reminds me. He stepped outside without me noticing, Sebastian at his heels.

Theo sits down, reaches for my hand, and runs his thumb over the back. His comfort passes through me, but it doesn't change what I know to be true.

All of this started with me.

"No, it's mine," Sebastian says.

Theo rests a hand on Sebastian's shoulder. "It's not your fault, either. Why is everyone here so focused on being the person to blame? If anyone's the villain here…" he trails off, realizing he's about to do the same thing.

Alison's been in the shower for forty-five minutes, either avoiding me or rubbing off her top layer of skin. Both are reasonable explanations. She said she was fine, and just needed to get clean and have a good sleep, telling me over and over again that this doesn't change anything about our friendship and Genome is to blame.

We're all left feeling guilt and hatred about the things we can't control and the people who have hurt us. No matter who's to blame, we're all stewing in the anguish inflicted on those we love.

"I've always encouraged her to have a relationship with her mother," Sebastian admits. "Jack said that it would be normal for her to hate Blaire and that wouldn't be good for her, and so I kept the door open to that evil woman."

"And it wouldn't have been good for me," I tell Sebastian. "Having all that hate inside would have destroyed me. That's not what I should have focused on. I needed to forgive her, even if she didn't deserve it."

He lets that sink in, but I know he despises himself for keeping her in our lives. No one could have predicted this, and we need to move past the hurt, together.

Sebastian runs his hand down his face and leans back in his seat. "I still can't believe she would do this."

"Because your parents would never," I sigh. "I miss them."

"Are they?" Theo stops short of finishing his question.

Sebastian turns to Theo and takes a deep breath. We've talked about his family so many times, but all of this is new to Theo. We haven't had the time to get to know each other.

"They're fine. We haven't seen them in a while is all. My parents should have just said they were settlers, but they never took the plunge," Sebastian explains with a smile. "They had me and Lucas back-to-back, lived together to co-parent but never separated."

I prop my chin into my hand and feel myself smile. Sebastian's parents are always traveling, so we don't see them often.

Every time they visit, it's a joy, and I forget they aren't settled. Legally, that is.

"When we were little, they would have dates at receptions, and then after a while, they stopped going. Now they live like nomads." Sebastian laughs to himself and strokes his chin. "They have this list of a hundred places they want to visit. I think they're on sixty or something."

"Sixty-two," I correct him.

"That's really nice," Theo says. "Settled or not, it sounds like you had a good life and they're... happy together." He swallows hard, hiding something behind his eyes. Sebastian tilts his head and there's something he sees, or maybe hears.

Theo takes the cue, and slaps his hands together once, staring out at the vast thickness of trees when he speaks. "My mom wasn't as bad as Blaire, but she didn't give a shit about me. After she found out about my heart, she left. My dad never said anything, but she wanted another kid in case I, you know."

I grab Theo's hand. "I'm so sorry."

"She wanted those checks, and if I was dead, well, there goes her payday."

He squeezes my hand, still staring at the treeline. "My dad though." He clears his throat, his voice catching when he speaks about his father. "My father was an amazing man. He raised me better than..."

Theo lets me go and runs his shaking hands through his hair. When he continues, he's fighting back the tremble in his voice.

"I wasn't living the life I should have before," he admits. "He didn't raise me to be that person. My father was the kind of man who did the right thing for people, even if it wasn't for him. Everyone truly loved him. He never cared about the bond, just people, and when he died, I was just so angry. All I could see was death in front of me, and I thought he was someone to keep on a pedestal, not someone I could aspire to be."

I bite my lip, fighting back the tears that may fall. The feelings Theo emits are impossible to ignore, and I don't want to. I want to feel all of it and help him in any way that I can. The adoration for his father and regret about his past fill me, and then there is a profound sadness. It's not something I've experienced, the loss of a parent who you love.

Sebastian rests a hand on his shoulder. "He would be proud of who you've become. You tried to break the bond, thinking that would save our marriage. You risked your life for Emry —for me."

Theo places his hand over his mouth and nods, and I sense he's done with the topic. His father is someone I want to hear more about when it's time, and even though I can only experience the ricochets of Theo's love for him, it's different from anything I've ever known. It makes me want to care for a child and give them that kind of feeling.

There's a knock at our back door, and Lucas steps outside. "Sebastian, they're ready for you."

Sebastian stands. "Hopefully, they can leave soon." He gives me a hug and a kiss on the cheek, pats Theo's shoulder, and tells him to stay out here with me.

Thunderclouds roll in the distance, promising rain, and I'm ready. I love storms and the idea of washing everything away.

"Will you sit with me?" Theo asks.

I rise and make my way into the chair with him, curling up in his arms, my eyes looking at the sky. He points and I nod, both of us eager for the storm.

"You know what I would like to do?" I say. "If it's possible."

"Anything's possible."

I smile at his thought, and Theo's grip around me tightens.

"I'd like to make a world together again," I say. "But something from your memory. Something you may not be ready to talk about, but you'd like to show me."

"I'd like that."

Theo's chest rises with a deep inhale, and I close my eyes.

We're standing together in the field again, me in dirty scrubs and him still splattered with blood.

"We really need to take a shower," I joke.

Our clothes transform before our eyes. I dress myself in a beautiful green floor-length gown. It's something in my closet I bought in case there ever was an occasion to wear it, but so far, this is the first time it's seen the light of day.

Theo does something else entirely. He changes into a young boy, maybe nine years old, wearing jeans and a shirt streaked with grass stains.

"Is this weird?" he says. His voice is Theo's, older and masculine, but I'm looking at a child with all of Theo's traits that haven't matured yet.

"Is it weird I'm wearing a ball gown?" I ask, pulling at the fabric of my skirt so it floats out around me.

He laughs, shaking his head before he turns and jogs forward. The world around us changes with every step.

Grass below our feet becomes a dirt path, and it's early morning, the sun barely lifted into the sky. Birds chirp and a faint dew catches in my mouth with every breath.

I run after him, staying far enough away so the dust from his feet doesn't fly over my dress. He stops at a river bank where a man sits on a blue cooler with a fishing pole in his hand.

The man places his hand on Theo's back, who settles into the dirt and plucks at the line that reaches out into the water.

"Anything yet?" Theo asks.

"No, but it's not about the fish, son," the man says.

"Then why are we out here at the crack of dawn? No one's awake this early," the boy complains.

This memory is rehearsed, something that he's played over and over again in his mind. He knows every word spoken, every leaf on the surrounding trees, every pull of the line on the man's fishing pole, and the feeling he had as a nine-year-old boy.

It's beautiful.

He's safe and loved, happy in a way only a child might experience. It's a time in his life when nothing terrible could happen and every hurt disappears.

At nine years old, Theo is thinking about how this is the best day of his young life, and that feeling is so pure that it breaks my heart and puts it back together.

The man turns, his profile unmistakable.

"This is your father," I choke out.

Theo's eyes don't look back at mine, focused on the man he misses, the man who left us all too early.

"We're out here to be together," his father says. "The earlier we get up, the more time I get with my son."

"You said fish don't bite in the afternoon," Theo wines.

"That is also true," his father admits.

He rustles Theo's hair and tickles his stomach.

Theo lets out a bellow just as the line pulls, sending the tip of the pole downward, almost touching the water.

"You've got one!" his father shouts, standing and giving the pole to Theo. "Reel it in. Great job, son. Wow, look at it."

The memory fades away and we're back in the field together alone. My eyes flood with tears and a smile stretches so wide on my face that it hurts my cheeks.

Theo's himself again, older but still wearing jeans and a dusty shirt.

I step forward and wrap my arms around him. He clutches

to me so tight, I can hardly breathe, but I let him hold me, giving him a moment after showing me something so special.

"Do you know I love you, Theo?" I tell him. "And not just because we're bonded. I love... *you*."

His chest shudders against mine, and he loosens his grip, pulling back to cup my face in his hands.

"I do. Something inside me knows without you saying it, but I'm glad that you did," he admits. "I love you, too. Very much."

I bite my lip, feeling the bond inside me thrum with excitement. Theo is so easy to love.

"I'm so glad I got to meet your father," I say. "Thank you."

"Me too, Emry," Theo chokes out. "Would you like to see something else?"

CHAPTER 17

Somewhere in the night, Theo and I fall asleep outside, the rain never coming down on us. When my eyes crack open, the sun is high in the sky.

Sebastian sleeps beside us in another chair, a blanket wrapped over him.

I sit up, my mind spinning with all the memories Theo shared with me. I've experienced years of his life, felt his joy and disappointments, and I gave the same to him. Every hurt and happy memory we could manage passed between one another until exhaustion took over.

I only have one regret about the experience.

"Sebastian needs to see all of that to know you as I do now." Theo's voice whispers in my head.

"We'll find a way to share it with him."

"You're awake?" I say as Theo stirs, adjusting me in his arms. Sebastian wakes as well, sitting forward, stretching his arms to the sky with a yawn.

Sara opens the back door, and my eyes widen, realizing that they're still here. She must notice my reaction as she steps forward, clasping her hands at her front. "We wanted security in place before we left," she says.

"Thank you," I say.

"I'll catch you up before we leave. Blaire Crawford." The name makes us all stiffen. "They're on their way to arrest her. She shouldn't be hard to find."

"What's their plan?" Theo asks.

"They messaged her about an interview," Sara explains. "Big payout, said they got the media ban lifted. She's already on her way to meet them. She doesn't know they infiltrated Genome, so we'll need to act fast."

"Fish in a barrel," Theo says, and we all nod, Sara turning to go back inside.

"Do you feel... bad about her getting arrested, Em?" Sebastian asks.

"Hell, no," Alison chimes in from the doorway. "Come inside and get some coffee."

She doesn't have to tell me twice, and I'm sitting on the counter of my kitchen with a cup in hand before I notice I'm still covered in filth. Looking at Theo and Sebastian, I'm grateful I'm not the only one.

"I still need to shower," I tell Alison, who refills my cup. "I was so tired, I just fell asleep."

"In Theo's arms." She winks and pours herself some coffee.

She's wearing my blue pajamas covered in stars. The bruises on her cheek are growing darker, and there are gray circles under her eyes.

Lucas trails into the kitchen, holding her luggage in both hands.

My back straightens, another apology at the ready when she shakes her head and lifts her hand to stop me. "I'm not leaving because I'm upset with you or with... whatever this is," she says, pointing to the three of us. "I promise. None of this disaster is your fault, and I'm team bonded. Have fun with all of this."

She waves her finger at Sebastian and Theo.

Lucas rolls his eyes in the distance, and I do my best not to laugh at his reaction.

She moves her hand to her chest, touching her heart and patting it a few times. "I went to an underground reception. They are dangerous and that was fucking stupid. Your mom is a grade-A bitch. And the bond picks who it picks."

She takes a sip of coffee and plants a smile on her face. "I had a lot of time to think while you were playing campground outside with your men."

"I'm going to take these to the car," Lucas says. He's not amused by her on-the-nose remarks.

"Let me arrange something more comfortable than your apartment," Sebastian says. "NeXus will pay for it. You can't stay there."

Alison smacks her lips and turns back to Lucas, who's waiting to head out the door. "About that..." she trails off, setting her cup down on the table. Lucas sets down the bags by the front door, shoving his hands in his pockets and rocking on his heels.

"You're staying with Lucas," I blurt out.

"I think it's best," she says, trying and failing to keep the smile off of her face. "I'd be scared to be alone, but my apartment is full of annoying people. Lucas lives alone in a beautiful house with two bedrooms."

"Isn't one an office and gym?" Sebastian asks.

"Okay, we're going," Alison announces, her voice an octave too high.

Lucas turns and opens the door without answering Sebastian's question.

"You know I'm not prying about this mess," Alison whispers to him while pointing to the three of us. "So you stay out of mine, okay?"

She winks and plants her hands back on her hips.

Sebastian raises his hands in defeat and chuckles. "Just making sure you didn't need more comfortable accommodations."

"I'll be plenty comfortable," she quips and comes over to hug me.

I plop down from the counter, her arms wrapping around my back, and we hold each other tight.

"Seriously, we are talking about this situation," she says. She turns her head, so she can speak directly into my ear. "For the record, I approve. Should be really hot, but dear lord, take a shower first."

My face turns crimson, and the image that comes through sends my libido into overdrive. I'm unsure if it's from my imagination, or someone else's.

Theo's hand moves to his crotch, and he grunts, adjusting himself. I can't bear to look at Sebastian, curious if he's really seeing and feeling anything we are.

"How would that even be possible?"

"I don't know," Theo says without words.

I close the wall in my mind, not wanting to embarrass myself, at least until our guests leave. I step over to the door to walk Alison out.

"I'd say be careful, but what else could happen?" I joke.

"I'm not going to be careful," she says. "I'm throwing all caution to the wind."

She smiles and heads out, Lucas holding a car door open for her. He's grinning, but trying to hide it, and even though

I'm not happy she's leaving, she'll be comforted and kept safe with Lucas.

Sara asks for Sebastian, telling him that they're packing up, but they have officers scattered around the property. I can't decide if that's necessary, but if Sebastian agrees, then so do I. They have our information and will contact us if they need anything.

He thanks everyone and then calls Jack just to check in and let him know we need a few days to recover. It's a not-so-subtle way of telling him to leave us alone, but Jack won't mind. Hopefully, it gives him some time with Moira.

Even after a night's rest in Theo's arms, the shower I felt so desperate for now might take too much energy. I'm afraid I'll fall asleep and wake up when the water runs cold.

The clock on the wall says it's late in the afternoon. I lost sense of time in Genome, but it will be bedtime again before long. I let out a sigh of relief, and wonder if eating will help me regain some energy.

"Are you two talking to each other?" Sebastian asks.

"No," we both say in unison.

"She, uh," Theo pauses, slapping his hands on his thighs with a devilish grin, "won't let me in right now."

Sebastian cocks an eyebrow. "So, you can control that?"

"Yeah," I admit. "I don't really know how, but I can. I just didn't want to, um, I had this thought, and it was kind of embarrassing, but now that everyone's gone..."

I let my mind open, hoping that by some miracle, it's to both of them.

Sebastian nods, and I take a seat on the couch with my coffee, knowing I'll need to wash the cushions later. They join me, sitting down with sighs, grateful we have the house to ourselves.

"You two seem to be getting along," I say. "What all happened in your time together?"

They look at each other, both of them silently deciding who will go first.

"We never didn't get along," Sebastian corrects me. "I never hated Theo, just the situation."

"You know what I mean," I say. "You two have one breakfast before all hell breaks loose, and before that, you're each other's worst nightmare, no matter how civil you can pretend to be. And now... now you're just..." I trail off, not sure of the point I'm trying to make.

Is the idea of the three of us together too good to be true? Nothing in my life has been easy or worked out the way it was supposed to, and I don't expect this situation to be different.

"We went after you together, and that put a lot of things in perspective. What mattered to us... what matters to us, is you," Theo explains. "That time helped us to get to know each other. To understand each other, you know."

"So is that when you..." I trail off, afraid of the question I need to ask. I'm too tired to small talk about little things, but this conversation is like climbing a mountain. "Did you come to some sort of agreement when I was gone? About us?"

"You make your own choices," Sebastian says. "But I'll speak for myself and what I think would be best for our family."

Family.

The word makes my heart beat faster, happy to hear him refer to us as something so sturdy. It's a title I like and one I want to keep. I sit up straighter, ready to hear what he has to say.

"I never thought you would be able to break the bond. Never," he admits.

My mouth drops and I shake my head to argue. "But you

said we went to NeXus together for that, and we agreed not to keep things from each other."

"I know and I'm sorry," he says. "There may have been some moments of hope, you know. I clung to that. Thinking maybe, just maybe, Jack could create a miracle. Maybe there was something in that lab that they kept secret that would change things, but inside I knew. I know. The bond is unbreakable."

"My love for you is unbreakable," I say, my voice shaking.

"He knows," Theo says. "So is his love for you."

I cover my mouth with my hand, trying to hide how my jaw shakes when I speak.

Theo and Sebastian lock eyes, and I see both of them take in a deep breath. "Let him speak his piece," Theo says.

I nod and sit back on the couch, bringing my knees to my chest and wrapping my arms around my legs. Holding myself, I urge him to continue and promise to stay quiet.

"I've loved you since I was a teenager, and I'm the luckiest man alive because you chose me."

There's a sinking feeling that Sebastian may feel trapped by us and that he's accepting this three-way relationship as a consolation prize. Biting my lip to force myself to stay silent, I listen, allowing him to get everything out in the open between the three of us.

"If there's a chance I can still have you, then I'm happy to share you," he admits. "The bond you and Theo have makes you both happy and healthy. It's saved Theo's life. How can something that does that be so terrible? I won't fight that. I want to be a part of that."

"You don't have to fight it," Theo says.

"That's the decision, I guess," Sebastian says. "Theo and I haven't figured it all out, and maybe we never will, but he's a part of this. He's a part of us."

I let his words hang in the air until they seep into my mind, clicking into place.

"What about what you wanted?" I ask. "For your life."

"I want to be someone who changes as I get older," Sebastian answers. "For the better."

The question from NeXus is at the tip of my tongue and I can't shake it. What if Sebastian was able to stop loving me? He could be free. I never asked him, and he doesn't know. It's not fair to keep that possibility from him after all he's done.

I'm on my feet, my arms wrapped tightly around my middle. I could lose him forever, but telling him is the right thing to do. Everything should be out in the open, even if that means I don't have them both.

He deserves to have all the information before he makes this choice.

"Emry, this is what I want. I want the three of us to stay together," Sebastian repeats.

"That's what I want, too," Theo says.

"We don't have to figure it all out now," Sebastian says. "But no one's going anywhere. We're going to be... a family."

"We already are," Theo chimes in. "Right?"

I'm shaking my head, biting my lip so hard I taste blood. Theo's looking at me with such happiness and hope, and the wave of joy washes over me, pulling me under.

He desperately misses his father - his family, and he wants that more than a bond.

I want to give that to him, but not at the expense of someone else's happiness.

"This is too much for her," Sebastian tells Theo in a whisper.

"It's not," I protest, my voice cracking with the words. "It's just... I know something that I need to tell you, and I'm scared when I do..."

"What?" Sebastian questions. "Scared of what?"

"That we will lose you," I say.

Theo stands. "What's wrong? Why are you so upset and worried?"

I let Theo see the interview from NeXus, giving him the chance to understand what we need to tell Sebastian. All the while, I'm worried Sebastian will hear, but his face doesn't change, so I'll need to tell him in person.

Theo's face contorts, his eyes filling with understanding and the smallest bit of sorrow. I sense his disappointment. He doesn't want to lose Sebastian either, and that breaks my heart.

We both love him, but it's enough to let him go.

"What's going on?" Sebastian asks.

Theo takes in a shuddered breath and looks at his friend.

"Give him the choice, Em," he says. "And for what it's worth, my vote is no."

CHAPTER 18

"Let's go in the bedroom to talk," I tell Sebastian.

He gives us both a wary look, uncertain about what's coming.

"Why not with Theo?" he asks. "I just said I want us to be a family. We should talk together."

"This one last thing, Sebastian," Theo tells him. He places a heavy hand on his shoulder, and they both go in for a hug, sensing something tragic may be around the corner.

He holds the back of his head and speaks into his ear. "Just this one last thing between husband and wife, and then... we'll see."

"We'll see?" Sebastian questions, his voice slipping into anger. I go into our bedroom, and I hear him follow, his steps dragging and slow.

Everything in the room looks the same, but nothing is as it was.

We're different, so this space and the people standing inside of it, feel different.

When we left for NeXus, I felt sure of what I would come back to. They would break the bond and we would slip back into the same life.

It sounds foolish now, especially after Sebastian admitted he never thought we could change nature, especially a science no one understands.

I sit down on our bed, and it doesn't feel right. Our world is off-kilter, slanted on one side without Theo to balance it out. I tap the space next to me for Sebastian to sit, and he takes my hand when he does.

"What's going on?" he asks, his eyes pleading for an answer.

"You may not know what you want because you don't have all the facts," I tell him. "Or, the possibilities."

"I think we've discovered anything is possible," he jokes, trying to make me smile.

My heart sits heavy in my chest, aching at the thought of Sebastian leaving me—leaving us. There's a split second where I want to back out and tell him nevermind.

Theo would go along, but the idea quickly fades. My entire existence has been nothing but unfair to this perfect man. If it weren't for me, he could have the calm life he desires with some other woman, one he doesn't have to share.

He deserves to know.

"I kept something from you at NeXus," I say.

Sebastian's eyes cast down and his jaw tightens, ready for the worst.

"And when I tell you, I want you to think about it," I continue. "You're going to say no right away because of the man you are, but I need you to promise me you'll think about it."

"Okay," he says, his voice barely over a whisper. "Out with it."

"The day they did the questionnaire, and they had a thousand things they asked us, there was something they asked that I couldn't answer," I tell him. "They asked me something along the lines of, if either of us would agree to a round of treatment that would kill off your love for me. It's hormone therapy to subdue your chemical reaction and your feelings of love. It seemed to be solid. Something that would make you indifferent to Theo and I being bonded and you being... alone."

"And you couldn't answer?" Sebastian asks.

I let out a long breath of air, feeling him tighten his fingers that intertwine with mine. My hand throbs in his grasp.

"I would never do that without your consent," I explain. "And I couldn't answer if that might be something you wanted, not knowing if we could break the bond or not. Being free of feelings for someone can save a lot of heartache."

"But I said—"

I cover his mouth with my free hand. "I told you to think about it," I argue. "And that's what you should do. This means you could let go of this marriage and me, start over, find someone else. You wouldn't love me anymore, wouldn't feel anything. It's possible."

He scrunches his eyebrows, but I don't remove my hand. With little effort, he could shake me free, and I'm glad he's taking a moment to think about this.

"I want you to consider a life where you don't love me. You don't hate me. You feel nothing," I say. "Really think about that, and then we can talk."

I remove my hand, and Sebastian opens his mouth. My hand jerks back up, but he leans back and blocks me.

"Do you still want me in this relationship?" Sebastian asks. "With you and Theo?"

"Yes!" I almost scream. "I don't want to lose you. And neither does Theo. If you saw what he showed me about his past, how lonely he's been. I don't think he wanted to admit it to himself until now, but the last thing either of us wants is to lose you. I just want you to have all the options before we go forward."

"What did you see?" he asks.

"After he lost his father, and he knew he would die soon, he cut everyone off. He knew when people were genuinely trying to get to know him or be kind, but he stayed away. He felt so afraid that he would hurt someone when he died, the way..." I choke on my words, struggling to get them out. "The way he hurt when his father died. He stayed alone, so no one else felt that pain."

Sebastian's eyes look down at our entwined hands, and I see them move over the tattoos on our wrists.

"That must have been very hard for him," he admits. "Even before you, I had Lucas and my parents. I've never felt alone like that."

I nod in understanding. My family may have been non-existent, but after my first round in Genome's clutches, I knew Jack and Sebastian would be there for me.

"How long?" he asks. "How long do I need to think this over?"

My eyes close and I wonder if I can open them again, the exhaustion making me sway where I sit. I turn and climb into the bed, chastising myself for all the laundry I'm creating by spreading my filthy body all over everything.

"I'll have a quick nap, and you think," I offer. "An hour."

Sebastian climbs over next to me, sinking beneath the covers and pulling me against him. "Would you still love me?"

"Always," I admit. "I'll never stop loving you."

My answer may not be fair, but it's honest. There isn't a

future where I don't love Sebastian Crowe. The bond expanded my love, stretching it over these two men, but it never lessened my feelings for Sebastian.

He breathes deep, his chest expanding against my back, and before long I drift off to sleep.

There was no chance of an hour's nap. Once my head sunk into the pillow, the covers yanked up to my neck, I was done. Much-needed rest came quickly, and I fell deep into a dreamless sleep.

The sounds of the outside woke me the next morning. Soft winds make the tree branches slap against our window, and I lay in perfect bliss on the soft mattress, refusing to open my eyes.

Rolling over, I feel Sebastian pull me closer, and I remember the conversation from the night before. He has a decision to make, and it pains me. I'm pulled tighter against him when he whispers in my ear, "Don't worry, love. It will work out."

My eyes fly open, and I'm staring at Sebastian. He's lying on his back, one hand flung above his head and another draped over his stomach.

It's Theo that pulls me against him, and it's his sleepy words that tickle my earlobe.

I freeze, my brain still catching up to the fact that I'm in bed with two men.

"How long have you been in here?" I whisper.

"What?" Theo mumbles, already half asleep again.

"How long..." I stop speaking when Sebastian rolls on his side toward me.

"All night," Sebastian says with a smile, his eyes still closed. "Did you sleep well?"

I sit up on my elbow, Theo's arm slipping off of my body.

The bond inside me screams a rebuttal, wanting me back safely in my bonded's hold.

"I slept well. So well I didn't notice this one come into the bed," I joke.

Sebastian smiles and sits up to kiss me. All the while, Theo's hand is running up my back, sending pinpricks of delight across my skin.

Sebastian's not bothered, content with another man resting under the sheets. I can't hold back the question any longer, desperate to know what his thoughts are about our talk.

"Did you decide?" I spit out.

"He did," Theo mumbles into the mattress. "He's sticking around."

I smack Theo's arm, trying to will him awake. He's half alert, drifting in and out of awareness.

"Don't answer for him," I protest. "I need to hear it from you, Seb. What did you decide?"

"Em, I could never be apart from you. There isn't anything powerful enough to tear me away," he promises. "I'm still here after you bonded with another man. You think there's some prescription out there that's going to break us up?"

Theo laughs, his fingertips tickling my skin, and I smack him one more time.

"Seb, if you want to try, we support it," I tell him.

"We do not," Theo interjects.

I glare at him, but I can't help but smile when I see his tousled hair against my pillow.

"The decision's made, Em." Sebastian swings his legs over the side of the bed. "I feel so much better. We really needed sleep."

We.

We are in this bed together.

We decided we were going to be in a relationship.

We aren't wearing pants.

"Where are you going?" I ask.

"To shower and make coffee," Sebastian says, standing up and stretching his arms to the ceiling.

"I'm coming with you," I say and crawl out of Theo's grasp. He looks at me bewildered, curious as to why I would ever leave the comfortable bed. I'm in panties and a fresh tank top, meaning someone changed my clothes in the night.

Sebastian kisses me on the head and I grimace, knowing I haven't washed my hair or body in over a week.

"I'm showering first," I announce. "And... who changed my clothes?"

Theo and Sebastian share a look and both make the same smirk before turning back at me.

"Love, nothing happened," Theo says. "It's just... you only have one bed, and we were all exhausted. Sebastian came out and told me to get some sleep after he changed your clothes. You never woke up is all."

"I know you wouldn't do anything while I was asleep," I say. "It's not that. I'm just... taking everything in. And to do that, I need soap and coffee. Food would also be good."

I turn to leave, and Theo reaches out and grabs my hand.

"We're okay," he says. "The three of us. We're good. We're doing this."

Sebastian wraps his arms around me, and it fills my heart with joy. The thought of us three on the patio finds its way into my mind, and I share it with Theo, hoping someday Sebastian will see it as well.

It's snowing and Theo is sleeping, wrapped in a big grey blanket while I'm talking with Sebastian. Theo feels it, letting his eyes close slowly from the hit of dopamine.

"She'll be good after coffee," Sebastian jokes. "Lesson one of being a Crowe."

Theo jumps from the bed, looking perfect in nothing but boxer briefs. I'm salivating when his eyes linger over my body and he says, "Well, I better get up and see how she likes it."

CHAPTER 19

THEO

I love the pictures she shows me of what our future might look like. She's not psychic, but we can make the visions true. It's such a small dream, sitting on a patio with people you love, but it's all I want in this world.

She and Sebastian just gave me everything I could ever want.

A life.

It's not only the added years, it's something to fill them with besides an endless accumulation of money I was planning on spending on some going-out party. A celebration I would have had by myself before I died.

I'll live longer than most and with a healthy heart and as a part of their family. It feels surreal. What did Jack say before?

Magical.

Sebastian and I brew the coffee and take it to the patio. Emry steps outside a few minutes later, the aroma calling to her.

"Hey, Em," Sebastian says. He kisses her forehead, and she smiles from his embrace.

Her hair is wet, and she smells like soap.

"That was quick," Sebastian says.

Emry's eyes grow wide. "The pilot light is out again. That water was ice, so let me tell you, I'm awake now."

"Oh, shit," Sebastian says. "I'm sorry. I'll go take care of it."

"It's okay," she calls after him. "We can somehow blame Lucas for this, right?"

"Right," he yells back before he's out of sight.

She strides over to me, and I run my fingers through her wet strands. "I'm glad you braved it out to clean up," I joke with her. She gives me a smack in the stomach with a giggle. She's beautiful no matter what, but I know she feels better washing Genome off of her.

"I'll need another shower. I'm clean enough, but I want to scrub and wash my hair again." She shivers, picking up her coffee and sitting down.

Her heart slows while she sips, sitting outside in her favorite chair. A juxtaposition of sorts that makes me smile.

"I'm genuinely relieved that Sebastian isn't leaving us," I admit to her.

She tilts her head to the side and curls her legs underneath her. "I know you are."

"I know, but I wanted to say it again, and really make sure you know that this is what I want," I say. "More than anything."

"I know, but you don't have to repeat yourself because I just know."

"You can feel it, right?" I ask her.

She nods. "Yes. Not that I've ever sensed you lying, but when you feel emotions during a conversation, it kind of..."

"Hits you. Like a wave," I say.

She takes another sip of coffee, keeping her eyes on me.

"I could feel your admiration for Sebastian while I was at Genome - how much you liked him, dare I say, loved him."

She's right that my feelings for Sebastian have grown strong in a short amount of time. He's impossible not to love.

"And in a way, that makes me feel this deep love for you, because the bond..." she trails off, rubbing the side of her temple, trying to find the right words. "You almost have to love me because of the bond. We both feel that connection like we're soul mates."

I nod in agreement, the tie between us tightening, pulling us toward one another. It's so much easier to fall into the feeling now that we're not fighting it anymore.

"But you don't have to love Sebastian. You just do because he's a wonderful person. I love that about you."

"Thank you, love," I tell her. "I can't imagine our life without him, and honestly, if he wanted to leave, I don't know if I could have let him."

"Oh, yeah?" Sebastian says, stepping out to the patio with some sandwiches. "I'm a little stronger than you if you haven't noticed."

"Well, I have the power of the cloud," I say before I take a bite of food.

Sebastian and Emry look at each other in confusion before they laugh.

"I don't think your special healing mist could help you hold a man back," Sebastian jokes.

"It could if it heals our broken hearts," Emry adds with a grin on her face.

"Oh, so corny," I joke, even though I don't disagree. Losing Sebastian would devastate us.

We finish our cups outside in pleasant silence, everyone squinting to see if we can spot any security. They're around,

Sebastian made sure of that, but I'm grateful they aren't so close as to spy in on our situation.

I'm sure the news outlets are nonstop about everything that's occurred, the three of us, and whatever relationship status we keep will be the top headline.

Who cares about abducted children when they can gossip about our bedroom?

I set my cup down and stretch my arms over my head, letting my back pop as I yawn.

"This is my favorite spot," Emry says.

"Your favorite spot in the house is outside of it?" I mock. She does look peaceful, curled up in her chair, holding the porcelain cup against her chin.

She chuckles to herself. "I think it's my favorite spot in the world." Taking another sip, she leans back and stares at the tips of the trees. They reach for the blue sky, so tall they must be hundreds of years old. I notice how their house sits at an angle, and part of it juts out to avoid disturbing an especially large trunk.

"You built around the trees," I say, noticing the careful floor plan and how it weaves around the woods. "It's beautiful."

"And private," Sebastian adds. "Do you feel out of place? You're used to cities, right?"

"I'm sick of cities," I tell him. "I traveled for work, going from place to place. Hotels and takeout and sterile offices. People touching the new guy everywhere I went. I won't miss that."

Everyone gives a sound of agreement, none of us enjoying the constant and unwanted rubs and pokes from strangers.

"I love it here," I say. "It's amazing."

Emry smiles into her cup, pleased to know I'm as enamored with this place as they are. They've built something special, a secret world they invited me into, and I'm honored to live here.

Sebastian clears his throat. "What do you think about a shower?"

His chest rumbles with a laugh at the unsaid joke we don't dare say out loud.

I shake my head and chuckle as well, unable to make an argument.

Sebastian and I stink terribly.

Emry nods. "I'm sorry. I know I need a second one. And you have Gilbert's blood on you." She points to Sebastian's neck, a streak of red that splatters across his skin. I haven't dared to look in a mirror since last night. Even though I put on fresh clothes, the evidence of our mission is still caked onto my skin.

"Are you all going to make me suffer through another one of your showers?" I ask. As soon as it's out, I regret the joke, but I can't take it back.

Emry looks at me with wide eyes, while Sebastian tilts his head, confused, not understanding my meaning.

"Theo," she hisses, but there's no malice behind the words. "This is why I shut you out sometimes. In fact, I'm going to do it right now."

With that, Sebastian pieces together what must have happened, and a wide smile appears on his face.

"Oh, man! I bet you hated that." He slaps his knee and takes another sip of coffee. "So, could you just hear her, or did you see something?"

"Oh, my," Emry says, getting up. "How long until that water heater revs up again?"

Both of us take her in, her hair uncombed, wrinkled clothes, and her cheeks a rosy pink from the topic. No matter how dirty she might be, she's gorgeous.

I'm hard in an instant, thinking about all the possibilities.

"Fuck, she's gorgeous."

"Isn't she?" Sebastian says.

"Isn't she, what?" Emry asks.

Sebastian leans back in his chair, wrapping both hands around his cup, and looks at me, jutting his chin in my direction.

"You said..." he trails off, thinking about what he's about to admit. "Didn't you just say she's gorgeous?"

"I did in here," I tell him, tapping a finger on the side of my head.

"Can you hear me?"

Emry doesn't respond, but Sebastian nods, and I'm on my feet, excitement running through my veins.

"Emry, keep your wall up," I tell her. She shrugs and nods in agreement.

"Sebastian, if you can hear me, take your wife to the shower and tell her to lower the wall when the time is right."

He lets out a hoot and shakes his head.

"What's going on?" Emry asks. "What did you say?"

She lowers her wall, reaching out to me to hear something, her heart thrumming with excitement.

All of this is new, and I expect it's going to take some practice to figure out, but there's something happening with our telepathy. It's reaching Sebastian, at least some of the time.

Sebastian stands up, takes her by the hand, and they head toward the house, Emry objecting with every step. Her voice raises with questions as her eyes become frantic, looking back and forth between us, curious about all the possibilities that we're both thinking.

This changes things.

I cackle a laugh and bring my hands to my hair, pulling at the roots in shock.

"I asked him to take you to the shower and keep the wall

down," I call out after them. She turns back, standing in the open doorway, and I wiggle my eyebrows at her. She opens her mouth to object but snaps it back shut.

"You heard him?" she asks Sebastian. "Really? Truly?"

He nods, and she kisses him, bobbing on her toes with excitement. She releases his mouth with a pop, beaming a smile in my direction.

"Now really, gentlemen? Getting me naked is all you can think about at a time like this? Don't you think we should explore this more?" she objects. "Call Jack and talk to him about it."

"Jack's leaving us alone for a few days," Sebastian reminds her as he tries to pull her inside. She shakes him off and steps back out to the patio. Sebastian rolls his eyes, trailing behind her in defeat.

We were only partially joking, but the idea of Emry in a shower with one or... maybe both of us is one I'd never turn down.

"Do you think I can shut you both out?" Sebastian questions. "Like Emry does. How do you do it, Em?"

"I–I don't know," she admits. "I just decide and then it's done."

"Honestly, Seb, I don't think you even know how to open it. I'm not getting every thought, so this is sporadic, or maybe." I bring my hand to my chin and think for a moment. "Maybe it's like a muscle you have to work and get stronger. We could all try. We've got nothing but time."

"I have a job," Sebastian says.

With his words, I remember I have to check emails from Robin, and I groan. Sebastian nods, knowing what I'm internally complaining about. Robin isn't bad, and she's been a huge help to us, but I don't want to do this kind of work anymore.

It's so empty and requires me to move around. I'm not leaving Emry and Sebastian, so I may not have a choice, even if I wanted to keep up with the business.

"Well, if we aren't going to call Jack, then I need to take a real shower," Emry repeats, grabbing her empty cup from the table. "So very badly."

She sniffs her shoulder and makes a face of disgust before turning away and heading inside.

"You going after her?" I ask Sebastian.

He doesn't answer but turns on his heel to leave. I'm jealous, but I decide to refocus on work and maybe check in with Moira. Sebastian said that Jack was giving us a break, but he never mentioned her.

I let them disappear inside the house before I go in myself. The thought of Emry naked, Sebastian washing her, and anything they might do could send me over the edge. I'm eager to occupy my mind with something else, something safe.

Our things have arrived from NeXus in large unmarked boxes, and it doesn't take me long to find my laptop. It powers on while I grab another cup of coffee, mentally hyping myself up to face reality.

There are over three-hundred emails but they've all been funneled into separate folders, meaning Moira got to work.

Bless that woman.

I call her immediately and smile when I hear her voice on the other line.

"Hi, stranger," she says. "I thought you were taking a break from the outside world. That's what Jack said."

"You two spending a lot of time together?" I ask. "Is that pillow talk?"

She shushes me through the phone. "Don't be naughty."

"Okay, but you should be," I joke.

She laughs, and I know if she were standing in front of me,

she would chastise me more for the comments. I'm guessing Jack is within earshot.

"Thanks for organizing my email," I say.

"Are you back to work already?" Moira asks. "I think you need to take time off. Figure things out."

"I am," I tell her. "I mean, we are."

"We?" Her voice hints at the question.

I'm nodding, but I know she's waiting for an answer. "Yes, we," I confirm, still surprised this is my new life, afraid it could all slip away from me in an instant.

I'm smiling, and I know Moira hears it on the other end of the phone. She's like that, someone who listens well enough to hear people's emotions.

"I'm going to work out an end date with Robin. She won't need me much longer. I can still spot consult if something needs a sign-off for another month, but you'll be off the hook soon."

"I can't say that I'm disappointed," Moira sighs. "Not that I don't like Robin."

I snort a laugh. "She doesn't care if she's not liked," I say. "She cares about money. It's okay to feel relief."

"Okay, well, I kind of don't like her. Just a little. And I'm ready to get back to my store," Moira admits. "Oh, that reminds me. I'm delivering some food to you all. Just a drop and run. Don't say no."

"Oh, I won't," I tell her, my mouth salivating at the thought of her cooking. "Thank you."

"So, will you stop working when the month's over?" she asks. I hear her moving around the kitchen, drawers opening and shutting, and a pan clanging around. "You could, right? With the government money. I hope you don't mind me saying it doesn't sound like you, though."

She's right. I don't want to do consulting anymore, but I'll need to do something. Sebastian made it clear he was going back to work.

I scroll through my inbox and read the offer from NeXus once more, curious if it's still available. They presented an opportunity in the acquisitions department but left an entire section available for counter offers in other areas of expertise.

They want their investments close, knowing the bonded have the first choice about what labs they visit. They want us as a research opportunity, and because of that, I hold the upper hand.

A thought comes to mind, one that I can't let go of, and it scares me. It's terrifying because I've never thought of work giving me purpose, only money. There is something I could do with NeXus that would bring me joy and change things for the better.

My dad would approve.

He would love this idea.

When your work is also your passion, it shapes everything. Emry and Sebastian wouldn't object, and in fact, I want Sebastian to be a part of this.

"Theo, are you still there?" Moira asks. I hear something sizzling through the phone and wonder how long I've been mute during our conversation.

"Yeah, sorry," I apologize. "I–I need to go. Listen, when you send food, bring Jack and have a visit with us."

"But Sebastian said—"

"I know what he said," I cut her off. "Please. I'll talk to him. Come over for dinner. I'll make sides and we'll have some drinks. I have something I need to run by Jack."

I hope Sebastian isn't furious when he finds out about this invite, but this idea isn't something I can propose without an insider's help.

"Okay, if you say so," she says.

"Thanks, Moira."

I hang up the phone and start typing, my mind bursting with ideas. My fingers fly across the keyboard, writing out the draft for a business plan.

I'll have this ready by tonight, or so I think.

A force I can't explain or control interrupts my thoughts, taking over my mind.

It's my bond. It pulls at me, almost painfully, bringing me to my feet. I can't stop myself as I'm forced forward, making me sprint toward the bathroom door.

I'm about to ruin everything.

CHAPTER 20

"I had suspected this," I say. Sebastian motions for me to lift my arms, and even though I can undress myself, I adore his attention.

"Suspected what?" he asks, pulling the shirt over my head. He moves his hands to my waistband, untying the knot there.

That you could hear us.

He looks up, one side of his lips upturning in a smile.

"Since when?" he asks.

"Earlier, in Genome. I tried to talk to you about it, but we were looking for Alison."

My voice cracks, and I swallow hard to cover up how much the mere mention of that place affects me. "You and Theo had a conversation with no words," I explain. "You didn't even notice. It was second nature."

"I don't remember that," Sebastian admits.

"Why aren't you more surprised?" I ask him.

He's taking everything with such calmness, and it's making me a bit manic. We've always balanced each other well, and Sebastian's never been one to react strongly, but every man has a breaking point. I would think he would have hit his by now.

"Have you been reading everyone's thoughts this whole time?" I mock.

My pants hit the floor, and Sebastian pulls his shirt over his head before he flips on the water. He turns back, looking into my eyes for a moment before his gaze drifts down my body. He takes his time, looking over every inch of me before he steps closer and takes my face in his hands.

I should feel some embarrassment knowing I'm still in need of a full body scrub, the cold rinse from earlier doing nothing, but the way he looks at me takes away any shame. He adores everything about me, even if the package isn't always perfect.

"I haven't," he says. "And I don't know why I'm not more surprised. Maybe I've maxed my quota of being shocked by things."

"I don't know how this is possible," I say.

"How is the bond possible?" he asks.

I shrug, accepting his point, and step into the shower, but Sebastian doesn't follow.

"You aren't coming in?"

He shakes his head, no, and takes a seat on the bench that faces the shower wall of etched glass. I'll be on full display if he stays out there, which I don't mind, but I want him inside the warmth with me.

The water hits my skin, so hot it stings, but I like it that way. It can burn away every molecule of Genome Theory. I'll remove every fingerprint that those bastards placed on my skin.

"So, what do you think you're doing?" I ask him.

He offers a wicked smile in response and remains seated.

"I'm testing the boundaries of this bond," Sebastian says, one hand moving inside his pants. "Why don't you see what Theo is in tune with during this shower?"

"I don't know if that's a good idea," I say.

"Pity," he sighs. He leans back, hooded eyes drifting over my form that he can't quite make out. He's memorized my body, and I wonder how much Theo has seen without ever using his own eyes.

"Why don't you just come in here," I beg.

It would be nice to relax in Sebastian's arms underneath the steams. The patio might be my favorite place, but my shower is in the top three. Number one if Sebastian is with me.

He pauses to think over my offer, adjusting himself in the seat. "It's... too soon," he objects.

He's right, and I know that as much as I want my husband to hold me, to make love to me, it's somehow not right. Theo's sitting only a few steps away, and even though he's heard us before and he practically asked Sebastian to give him a mental show, I think we're walking a thin line. We don't want to hurt Theo.

I nod, taking a bar of soap from the shelf and rubbing it over my body, starting with my shoulders and working my way down. There's still evidence of dirt and grime from my skin running down the shower drain, and I grimace at the sight.

Closing my eyes, I keep the door to my mind open. Sebastian isn't in here with me, and I don't like staying closed off to Theo for long. He's a part of us, and I like to know what he's doing and feeling.

Nothing specific comes through from Theo, but he's still wafting through me, and maybe through us both.

The soap slides between my legs, and I hear Sebastian grunt. Keeping my eyes closed, I lift my leg to the lip of the tub and continue to wash myself, letting my head fall to the shower wall. Sebastian can't see me, not all of me, but he can picture it in his mind, let everything we've done in here replay to his heart's content.

I like how comforting that is, knowing he's sitting so close, thinking of me and waiting for the right time. That's what Theo suffers through, and maybe Sebastian thinks he's being a brother in arms of some sort, both of them holding back together.

My mind drifts to the possibilities.

How would it look with all of us?

Would Sebastian watch for the first time? Every time?

I think I would like that.

Would they both—

Bang. Bang. Bang.

My eyes fly open at Theo's knocking on the door, so hard it shakes, threatening to come loose at the hinges.

I startle, dropping the bar of soap and letting out a squeak.

"Sebastian, I need your help, man," Theo orders. His strained voice begs him, and he bangs on the door again. "Emry, keep your head closed because I can't–fuck, I can't."

"Oh, no. Theo, are you okay?"

He doesn't respond, and I sense the open line of his thoughts attempting to close, like a door that's too heavy to shut. Theo wants to block me out, but he can't.

"Hey, I'm coming out," Sebastian says. "Can you stand away from the door?"

"No, I can't," Theo admits. "I can't move. I'm afraid I might break it down. This is too much. Don't look at her. Don't think about fucking her. And fuck Emry, what are you doing to me? You know what you're doing, what you're thinking about."

His voice is pleading and desperate, and my stomach sinks. I shut off the water and step out of the shower, grabbing a towel and tying it around my body. Water drips off of me in thick puddles on the floor and I move toward the door, only for Sebastian to hold me back.

"Close yourself off, Emry!" Theo yells.

His strained voice comes out somewhere between and scream and a cry. Sebastian's looking at me in question, not sure of what we should do.

Theo's thoughts are scattered and manic. He's fighting the urge to break down the door and take me, fuck me on the bathroom floor the second I'm within reach.

There's another part of him, one that I sense is gaining control, that knows this is the bond's need bubbling over. He knows it's forcing its way through after holding back for so long, and he's fighting his body's response, knowing we should wait.

"I won't cut myself off from you. Not when you need me."

His thoughts are a mess, both sides of him fighting for control, and it pains me to hear how he chastises himself for what's happening.

"Let me go to him," I tell Sebastian.

His eyes widen. "I'm not hearing everything, Em, but he's not himself right now. If you open the door, he might..."

"That won't happen," I say. "Trust me."

Sebastian frowns but steps to the side, and I place my palms and forehead on the door, talking to Theo in silence.

"Theo, you're okay. I'm here. Your bonded is with you."

His heart beats so fast, I feel its rhythm in my bones.

"Can you take a step back so I can open the door? You can do this. Put your back against the wall, and I'll come out."

Theo pauses before he responds. *"I don't want to hurt you."*

"You won't."

I feel when his presence shifts back, and I turn the handle of the door, water sliding down my arm and onto the floor. It's silent except for the steady *drip, drip, drip.*

Sebastian takes in a sharp breath, and I reassure him it's okay before stepping into the hallway.

I feel drawn to Theo, but it's not as desperate. There's a need there, but it's shared with Sebastian. I don't know if that's why I'm not as animalistic. Theo only has me to think about, his side of the bond forcing him to act.

I let out a breath of air I didn't know I was holding and step toward Theo, who is practically shaking against the wall, his eyes shut and hands clasped into fists.

"You're okay."

I move my hands to his shoulders and then run them up to cup his cheeks.

My body leans against his, and I think of us cooking in the kitchen together, Theo popping a bottle of wine while I sit on a countertop, watching Sebastian cook over the stove. I imagine us starting a firepit outside, roasting marshmallows, and projecting a scary movie in the fall. My mind drifts to the picture of his father on the riverbank, me as a girl sitting next to Theo, watching the line catch in the water. His father smiles down at both of us, and with that final image, Theo's body relaxes.

He wraps his arms around me, and I feel Sebastian on my back, embracing us both in a hug.

"I don't know how much longer I can fight the bond's... physical needs."

Theo's worry passes through us all, something inside Sebastian letting me know he hears him. He exhales at my back, squeezing us both tight.

The piece of me that thought I needed to have all the answers fades away, and my only focus is Theo no longer suffering like this. Now isn't the time, but very soon, I will end this fight.

I want him just as much.

CHAPTER 21

EMRY

We stand in the hallway for a half hour, and I'm almost dry when we all separate, relaxed enough for me to go back into the shower.

"Do you want me to block you out?" I ask Theo.

He tells me to, just in case, and he and Sebastian head into the living room while I finish up. We got through that together, no one regretting their actions, and it proves that we're growing stronger as a family.

As difficult as it was, I'm glad it happened.

Another hour passes until I step back out into the living room, clean with dry hair and moisturized from head to toe. They both stop talking and turn to me with gentle smiles, and I open the door to my mind, knowing the coast is clear. Both of them look cleaner, and I surmise they washed themselves up a little while I spent forever in the bathroom.

"We're not as good as you," Theo says.

I cross my arms in front of my chest and step forward, tilting my head in question.

"Theo can't close himself off," Sebastian explains.

"But we're working on it," Theo adds.

"Ah," I say. "How are you feeling, Theo?"

He leans back and nods. "I'm good," he says. "I just got overwhelmed."

"I texted Jack to let him know about this... development," Sebastian says. "He's coming over for dinner."

"Which development?" I ask. "The telepathy between three of us or the..."

"Loss of control over my dick," Theo interjects.

Theo isn't the only one struggling, but I'm better at keeping myself in check.

My bond with Theo has my panties slick with want, and I keep looking at Sebastian, imagining him inside me. The known and unknown pleasures that sit on my couch may be too much to resist, and I know I could have just as easily lost control like Theo, unable to control my bond's urges.

I sigh heavily and sit down between them, resting my head on Theo's shoulder.

"It's okay."

Theo rubs my thigh and nods.

"I know."

"I don't want to go back to NeXus," I say to both of them. "Do they know? That we're not... breaking the bond."

"We were never going to break that damn bond, baby," Sebastian reminds me, and Theo nods.

My thoughts from just a few weeks ago sound silly, idealizing this company as being stronger than a force of nature.

That's grief for you.

I grieved the loss of the life I thought I once had and went straight to bargaining. We're sitting in the acceptance phase, and that's just fine. Things change and life moves on. We're turning this corner together.

"Is Moira coming?" I ask, sitting up and positioning myself to sit cross-legged.

"Yes, she's coming," Theo says. He turns to Sebastian. "We should invite Alison and Lucas, too."

Sebastian raises an eyebrow. "One big happy family."

"Something like that," Theo agrees.

"Are you sure you want to mix business with pleasure?" Sebastian asks. "Didn't you want to talk to him about the job?"

Theo nods, slapping his hands on his thighs. "I think making it a big family-style dinner would help with that—makes it less formal."

"What job?" I ask.

"I'll let you take this one," Sebastian offers, rising from his seat. He takes my chin in his hands and kisses my lips.

"I need to shower and clean up whatever Alison did to this damn house," Sebastian says, looking around.

I mouth a thank you to him and he strides away, Theo letting out an exhale with his eyes closed.

"Are you alright?" I ask. "Really. It's okay not to be."

He takes another breath, opens his eyes, and scoots closer to me, wrapping his arm around my shoulders. It's a simple action, but one he's never tried before. It feels comfortable and normal, something a boyfriend does when you sit to watch a movie or walk down a street.

His calmness flows through us and puts me at ease. The manic episode that occurred before has left him, and he's back in control.

I thought it might be impossible to have any contact with him without ripping our clothes off, but something has stilled between us just enough to bear it. We're in each other's proximity, our orbits circling one another, and the bond isn't lashing out, forcing us to do more.

That is, as long as I don't imagine Theo's cock inside me.

"I'm feeling better," he answers. "Can you tell?"

"Yes." I touch my stomach and lean into his embrace. "Something here. It flickers, lets me know when you feel, I don't know, at peace."

"I'm happy," Theo says. "And I'm sorry about earlier."

"Let's move on from it," I say, turning to see Sebastian stepping into the bathroom. "We got past it together, and that's what counts."

Theo and I are alone, and although Sebastian's given his blessing about this bond, I know we need to tread lightly. I've decided anything physical with Theo will be with Sebastian... in some way. He needs to be a part of this, of us.

"Good idea," Theo agrees.

"Job?" I question, looking back at him with wide eyes.

Theo nods, biting his lip and I sense the excitement there. He's thrilled about the opportunity for something new.

"You know we would get monthly stipends, and large ones if we..." I trail off, thinking about our future. "So you don't have to work."

Sebastian could stop working too if he wanted, but he wouldn't do that. He finds pride in what he does, protecting people, and I know he won't let that go.

Theo shakes his head. "I need to work," he says. "I want to if this works out. I really want to, shit. It's almost meant to be."

I tilt my chin up, waiting for him to continue and he draws his eyebrows together, a worry crossing his mind that wafts into me. A sliver of apprehension slides between us.

"I don't want it to upset you," he explains. "We need to make this decision together."

"Out with it," I order. "My curiosity is piqued."

He smiles and sets his palm on my thigh, squeezing it gently. "I received an offer from NeXus, and I'm countering with a proposal. The offer was perfunctory. They want me to do anything, just keep me on the payroll, really. Jack let me know they would try. Keep assets close, and it's easier to have me pop in for a blood draw if I have an office there."

He lets out a nervous laugh, and I nod, not wanting to interrupt him. If he's comfortable going back to NeXus in some capacity, I trust he has a good reason.

"NeXus agreed to... help break the bond because they wanted, in a way, the same thing Genome did."

"Yes, yes," I muse. "Everyone wants the key to the bond."

"They wanted you," he corrects me. I stiffen, taking in the information.

"NeXus had all of the data from Genome when you were young. When they rescued you, it wasn't because they had your best interests at heart. All that information, it's worth something to them," Theo explains. "Now you're back and bonded. NeXus wants the key to the bond. Yes, you're right about that. I think I can convince them to find others like you, or others that may be like you."

My head spins, not understanding anything about this fantasy job Theo has dreamed up.

"I don't know if I want to go back to NeXus," I say. "If that's what this is."

I shake my head and feel myself pull away from Theo. He holds me close, urging me to stay at his side.

"No, no, no," he assures me. "Love, this would be only me. You don't ever have to go back into that building again if you don't want to."

I relax and nod, letting him continue.

Theo takes in a deep breath and looks at his hand that rests on my leg. I cover it with mine, sensing he's about to unleash something difficult. "I think there are over a hundred missing people. That's a rough estimate going through some archived articles."

"What? How did you?" My words are jumbled, confused about what he means.

"I consulted at a company that would... control media. I wrote some of the software, so I can see what's been altered or removed," Theo explains. "You were in the shower for another, I don't know, hour or so. I told Sebastian what I wanted to do and we might have... snuck in."

"Snuck into a previous company's private data?" I ask.

"I had a good reason," he whispers.

"Just confirming details," I say with a smile. "Continue."

"I found a story detailing missing kids and adults for the last ten years. Then I found another and another. The data is close for all of them. Looked to be close to a hundred," he sighs. "Maybe more."

"Shit," I say. It's the only word that comes to mind while my stomach lurches with the thought. All those people, lost and alone, going through torture.

"What do you want to do?" I ask him, my voice cracking with the despair of this news.

Theo meets my eyes, his excitement and hope rushing through my veins.

"I want to find them."

CHAPTER 22

"Find them," she says out loud. Her mind spins with the possibilities. A second ago, I felt her sick to her stomach over those missing, but she's thrilled with the idea of saving them all.

"Yes, love," I say. "NeXus has an interest in these people. Genome has done—no wait—is doing terrible things. But the data is out there. Imagine comparative data between you and another person. Bonded versus unbonded, and what if one of them bonds? NeXus can't buy that kind of information, but they can get it and front the whole thing as a savior mission, and their stock prices rise."

Emry frowns, and even though I can't read her thoughts, I know she's thinking about her time at Genome. I hate that I've brought these memories back to the surface, but I need her support.

"They're all still out there?" she asks, her voice small. "In other places?"

I nod, sure of what I'm telling her. It didn't take long for Sebastian to find out that Gilbert flew in from a thousand miles away. He got word of his former project, Emry, and ran to her. There was somewhere else where he tortured others. I'm sure of it.

It's not my intention to keep that from her, but I don't want to bring up that bastard's name. There will be a trial with all the gory details, and she'll face it, but not today.

"The funding for Genome is huge, and it's coming from a large corporation or several," I explain. "They wouldn't put all those eggs in one basket."

She takes in a shuddered breath, nodding in understanding.

"I can't say we'll find out who's behind that, but maybe we can shift their focus," I say. "We have to try."

"Who is a part of that we?" she asks.

"Sebastian will help me," I tell her. "If you're comfortable with that. I can't say it would always be the safest employment, but considering he's somehow in this bond, and I can speak with him without talking, it would make us unstoppable."

I move my hand to her cheek, turning her to face me.

"We want to do this. We need to help them." I'm pleading with her because I won't approach NeXus without her blessing. Her bonded and her husband could both be gone at once if things went wrong on a mission. That's a huge risk, and maybe it's too much to ask of her, but something inside me, the part that feels her desires, knows she wants this.

She hates Genome more than the rest of us, and she knows the terror they cause.

She smiles, her eyes watering. "I think it's amazing. You're both so amazing."

My heart explodes with relief, and I jump up.

"Jack and Moira are coming over for dinner," I tell her. "We're going to talk with him. He'll know the best way to approach this, how to get them to say yes."

"And Alison, too," she reminds me.

"Oh, yes, could you call her?" I ask. "I don't want to upset her, but if she advocated for this as a citizen... People will want to believe her story, and she could be good marketing."

"She'll agree, and if we have to..." Emry looks away, swallowing hard before she continues. "If we have to, we'll all go to the dreaded media. Maybe I could even... make some arrangements with NeXus to test me. I just need some time."

I'm in awe of my bonded. She's strong and kind, and giving me everything I could dream about and more.

Without thinking, I bend down and bring her lips to mine. It's not our first kiss, but the same fireworks explode, making my body tremble with anticipation. I'll never let her go, and everything I do from here on out will be to please her.

Our lips move in rhythm as the endless minutes tick by, and we only stop when Sebastian clears his throat, standing over us.

"I–I'm sorry," Emry says. Her hair is tousled, and several of my shirt buttons are undone. I want her hands on me again, exploring my skin and feeling my warmth. It takes all my strength to back away, almost tripping over a piece of furniture behind me.

"No need to be sorry," Sebastian brushes her off. "Just letting you know the shower's free."

He turns to me and I look down at myself. "Oh, hell," I say, laughing a little when I realize I'm disgusting. "Emry, how could you kiss me like this?"

Sebastian heads to the kitchen laughing. "No clue, man," he calls out. "When you're done, I need some help. We're feeding seven tonight."

The shower is still steaming, and I push any thoughts from earlier away. Hot water sears my skin, and I scrub endlessly, washing my hair twice, and scouring myself with soap. I have to stop when I'm halfway clean, wash the tub and walls, then clean myself again.

I step into the kitchen a new man, ready to help Sebastian, leaving Emry on the couch curled into herself and reading a book.

"She wants us to do it. To take down Genome," I tell Sebastian.

He grabs a few pots from the bottom cabinet, cursing Alison for whatever disorganization she caused under his breath, and spreads them on the counter. There's a plan here, and I'm thinking of confessing to Sebastian I've only had takeout for the last ten years. Hopefully, his need for my help doesn't extend past washing dishes and stirring things.

"I knew she would be," Sebastian says. "Once we get NeXus on board, I'll build a team. I already have a few guys in mind. This will be good."

"It feels almost..." I trail off, unsure of how to finish my thought.

"Meant to be," Sebastian says, slapping me on the shoulder.

I nod, bouncing on my toes. There isn't a time in my life I've felt this kind of excitement, not even as a child. The last several years, especially, have been a ticking clock until my inevitable end, and there wasn't a lot to be grateful for along the way.

He looks me over, noticing my nervous energy. "How are you doing?"

"I'm great," I tell him and realize he's shifted from talking about the job.

I shove my hands in my pockets and lean against the

counter. "I'm calmer now. I can control it as long as, you know..."

"As long as no one thinks about sex," Sebastian says. "That's not going to last."

"Well, I don't think you'll be in a shower with Emry again today, right?" I point out. "Let's just take this day by day."

Sebastian ushers me to step outside with him, and we go over to an outdoor grill. He opens up some cabinets around it, digging out the cleaning supplies. We get to work before he continues our conversation. It always helps to have your hands busy when discussing fucking someone else's wife.

"And what about tonight?" he asks.

"We should wash those sheets," I joke.

Sebastian stops scrubbing and turns to look at me. "What about tonight?" he repeats.

I know what he's asking. The last thing I want to do is lose control again, and what if I hurt Emry in the process or scare her? It's a terrible start to this relationship and not something either of us wants.

"I think Emry should take the lead," I tell him.

"Okay, you and Emry take it one step at a time tonight," he says. "I trust you'll let her call the shots. You've shown that kind of restraint, and she knows the risks."

"What do you mean me and Emry?" I huff. "Where are you going to be?"

I raise my hands to my hips and rock back on my heels, waiting for him to offer the suggestion he's holding back. It's times like these I wish his thoughts weren't so sporadic. I can't hear what he's thinking right now, and it's frustrating.

"You want me in the room or not?" he asks.

"In the room," I say without a second thought.

Sebastian jerks his head to look at me, shocked by my answer.

"You sure?" he asks again. "I can be on the couch. I get it."

I shake my head, sure of what I'm wanting, what I'm needing.

"At the beginning of all this, I don't want to do things without all of us," I explain. "We need to be solid before any solo adventures."

"You're bonded," Sebastian says, resuming his scrubbing. "You can't get any more solid than that."

"You and me," I tell Sebastian, grabbing him on the shoulder. "I want *us* to be solid."

His arm stops the assault on the grill, but he doesn't look up, frozen by my words.

"I want our... relationship to be just as strong as me and Emry. It's important to me." I squeeze his shoulder, forcing the words to leave my lips. "You're... important to me."

He nods but doesn't say anything, and I wonder if he can't. I'm coming on strong, but this family is too important to hold anything back.

"So, we'll share the room," I say. "You'll be there."

Sebastian tosses the scrub brush to the side and wipes his hands off on a towel, and smiles. "Wouldn't miss it for the world."

CHAPTER 23

I'm failing at desserts, yet again, while everyone sits in the living room, snacking on something delicious Sebastian whipped up with little effort. I should accept defeat, but I want to be useful.

Theo is apparently also a subpar cook, and Sebastian's been messing with him all day about how the only spices he knew about were salt and pepper. That helps my confidence, but only slightly.

"I wanted to talk to you alone," Jack says. I jump, not hearing him come into the kitchen. He closes the divider that acts as a door to the hallway, giving us privacy if we don't speak too loudly.

"Sounds serious," I joke, flinging another scoop of icing at a deplorable cake. It leans to one side, and I wonder how high I can stack up the sugary goodness to even it out.

"It is," he deadpans.

I appreciate his direct nature, but I don't know if I have the energy for what he's bringing into the kitchen.

"It helps if you freeze or refrigerate the cake," he says, pointing to my mess.

"Well, that wasn't as bad as I thought," I say. I frown, smearing the icing full of cake crumbles across the top. "I think it's too late to cool this enough to save it."

"Agreed," Jack sighs. "But that's not what I want to talk to you about."

I slap more icing onto it anyway, because no one in history complained about too much sugar. "I figured," I shrug.

Jack hands me a leather zipper pouch, and I take it, surprised at how cold it feels in my hands. It's unzipped, and I let it fall open, finding a row of needles inside.

Worry settles inside my stomach, and a flash of fear about what I'm looking at makes my hand shake. The divider slides open, and Theo steps inside.

"Oh," he says, seeing the needles I'm holding.

"Theo, I let you all know I needed a moment with Emry," Jack objects.

"Did Sebastian— Did he change his mind?" I whisper, my voice so low Jack cranes his neck to hear, and Theo steps over, lowering his face to mine.

I swallow hard, trying the question again. "Did Sebastian change his mind? Is this the hormone therapy?"

"Oh, no, no, no," Theo says, ripping the container from my hand and pulling me into a hug.

"Not at all," Jack assures me.

A weight lifts from my chest, the roller coaster of emotions making me dizzy.

"This is for Theo."

Jack turns to him, giving him a knowing look.

Theo pulls away, releasing me and excusing himself. "I'll be right outside if you need me," he says, shutting the divider once more.

Jack grabs the pouch again, opening it for me to see.

"Is it his heart?" I ask. "I thought you said he was better."

"He is better, but he's also in a bit of trouble," Jack says.

"Could you please just tell me what's wrong?" I beg. "You wasted five minutes judging my cake, and we could've gotten to the point by now. My lectures are quicker."

"Theo and Sebastian informed me about the incident from earlier. The one in the bathroom," Jack explains.

I bite my lip and look down at the syringes.

"He needs a way to control the neurotransmitters that are overstimulated. I didn't dare bring in a blood draw kit at the demand of your husband. He's insistent we don't have any debriefing, but I'm sure Theo's testosterone levels are through the roof. This will help."

There's a needle missing, and I know Theo's already taken a dose. I can't blame him, and considering how he struggled before, it's the right decision.

"It won't hurt him in any way," Jack explains. "And it won't stop his drive. We don't know much about mating when it comes to the bond."

"Jack, honestly," I lament with the use of the word mating.

"You are a professor, Emry," Jack chastises me. "I know doctors make the worst patients, and an evolutionary biogenetics professor doesn't want me to use scientific terms in regards to her sex life, but this is a genetic response. You need to turn on your medical mind and help Theo."

I feel foolish for not thinking of this earlier, and worse for not taking Theo's struggle seriously. If we're going to be a family, we need to make sure we take care of each other's health.

"You're right," I tell Jack.

He smiles and hands me the pouch.

"I'm not a great patient, but I want to help Theo."

"One shot, fatty buttock, once a day," Jack explains. "Until your sex life is routine and normalized."

It takes all of my energy not to groan at his medical transcript about my bedroom, but I bite the inside of my cheeks and nod.

"You know this would have been helpful in NeXus?" I point out. "When he was wandering to my room in the middle of the night."

"It would have muddled results," Jack says. "We also needed more of a workup on him for proper dosage. I wasn't trying to keep something from you."

I nod, not wanting to continue the discussion and go back to frosting my cake while Jack continues staring, not moving from my side. Setting down the spatula, I raise my hands to my hips and turn to him.

"There's something else, isn't there?" I ask.

Jack nods, mirroring my stance, hands on his hips and leaning on the counter. My guard goes up knowing what he's doing. Years in therapy with this man and I've learned all of his tells.

"If you don't want to talk with me, I understand," he says.

"Oh, here we go," I grumble.

"But you need to talk with someone, and soon," Jack insists.

"Didn't I graduate from therapy?" I say. "I know there was a time when I struggled, and you helped me. You saved me, Jack, but that was a long time ago."

Jack takes my hands, setting them in prayer in between us, his clasped over mine. My shoulders relax, and I let out the breath I'm holding.

"In my medical opinion, what you are deciding to embark

upon with Sebastian and Theo is the healthiest option," he says, his voice even. "Even so, you've revisited a lot of trauma, Emry."

I almost faint, shocked to have his blessing, sure a lecture about polyamory was coming my way. At least he would have some detailed report about making rash decisions after psychological stress, but instead, he's telling me to jump in bed with two men.

"It will keep you grounded in your relationship with Sebastian as well as soothe the bond that, again, in my medical opinion, would take decades to break, if that's even possible," he admits.

"You know you neglected that fact before?" I smirk.

"Would you have listened?" he asks.

I shake my head, knowing he's right and I was grasping at any straw to keep Sebastian.

Jack's hands squeeze mine, and I feel my pulse under the skin.

"But those decisions don't wipe away what you went through," he adds. "You were kidnapped by someone who tortured you as a child. A biological parent sold you and discarded you. Sebastian and Theo may mask the pain, but it's there. If you don't want to see me about it, please see somebody."

I nod, agreeing without thinking.

"For what it's worth, Emry, I would love to be a part of your healing," Jack says. "I'm not saying I have favorites, but if I did..."

"I'll talk to someone," I promise. "I'll... I'll talk to you."

Jack's right.

Even the bond can't fix the damage that's been done, and it's my responsibility to be the best version of myself for the best men I've ever met.

"You look good," Alison tells me. She's holding a large glass of wine, sipping the contents with a grin.

"I look showered," I say.

"Just accept the compliment," she argues. "You look… peaceful."

I think about her words, letting them sink in, and I smile. "You know, it's been a wild month, but I think I am at peace. As much as I can be."

"That's so nice to hear," Moira adds. She sits down next to Alison, filling both their glasses with the rest of the bottle.

Jack is outside with the guys, talking over their business plan. I look over to find everyone's expression is calm with lots of nodding. Moira turns to see what's caught my attention.

"What's so important they aren't in here with their women?" Moira asks.

"Their women?" I raise my voice with the question. "Moira, are you and Jack, you know?"

She brushes me off. "I'm too old to play games or pretend I'm not interested in him. We're together I suppose. Oh, my, I guess I'm a settler now. What name shall we use? This should be fun."

Alison lets out a cackle and shakes her head, swallowing another sip of wine.

"What is Lucas doing out there?" I ask her. "He doesn't have to suffer through their business plan."

Alison leans forward, a wicked look in her eye. "I sent him away so you would talk to me about screwing two guys at once."

I spit out my wine all over Alison's shirt. It's technically mine. Our clothes co-mingle while we still live out of suitcases, so I don't feel so bad.

"Alison, that's not, we haven't," I sputter.

"But you will?" she asks.

I look over to Moira, and she gives me no help. She offers to go get Alison another shirt, her face crimson but grinning.

Alison taps on the table, refocusing my attention. "You really haven't. That would have been the first thing I'd do. The first person, people, how are you saying this? Are you a throuple?"

"Please, stop," I beg Alison. "It's been one night, and we have our whole life to figure it out."

"Sebastian doesn't," Alison says.

I groan at her. "What do you mean?"

"He's not going to live forever like you and your bonded hottie," she remarks.

The wine glass wavers in my hands when I try to set it down, Alison's statement hitting me like a truck. Theo and I will live for hundreds of years, but Sebastian will age like the rest of the population.

Her face falls when she notices my reaction.

"Sorry," Alison murmurs. "I didn't mean to upset you. I thought you all had talked about—"

Theo bursts through the door, out of breath with Sebastian on his heels.

"What's wrong?" he asks. He has to stop doing this, but our situation is new, and he's yanked toward me every time I'm sad or scared.

Sebastian moves next to Theo, both of them shoulder to shoulder, and I look at them, really look. Today, even with the differences between the two, they could be brothers.

Sebastian's thicker, his shoulders wide, and his build so broad I can't wrap my arms around him when his hands are by his sides.

Theo is lean, with long lines of muscle that cut around his

body, but he matches Sebastian's height. He looks at me the same way Sebastian does, meeting my eyes before he lets them drift over my body.

Both have hard lines on their jaw and brow with a five o'clock shadow that's morphing into a beard.

"You have to trust I'll call for you when I need you," I tell them both. "You can't burst in every time I'm upset."

"He's done this before?" Alison asks. "He gets some kind of my-woman-is-emotional signal? Damn, that's lucky."

I nod and roll my eyes.

"Are you okay?" Sebastian asks.

"I'm in our kitchen," I remind them, keeping my tone sympathetic. "And I have emotions when talking with my friends. That's normal, okay?"

"You're right," Theo says.

"Damn, did he just say you were right? Two perfect dicks *and* they admit when they're wrong," she mumbles into her glass.

"Oh, my," Moira says, walking into the kitchen with a fresh shirt.

It's the wrong time to talk about my worries, so I send the men outside with Jack and Lucas. My heart sinks when they turn, deflating with the first crack in our perfect reality.

"I'm sorry," Alison says. "I didn't realize you hadn't thought about that yet."

"I haven't had time to think about anything," I admit.

Alison fills Moira in on her comment and she gives me a look of pity, the first I've seen since bonding. Everyone thinks I'm the luckiest woman in the world, but the way Moira sighs, her shoulders hanging low, I know our family won't be free of heartache.

Sebastian will age, and he will die, and Theo and I will watch it happen.

"You don't have to figure it all out today," Moira tells me. "This all just happened and things are changing all the time. Just get through today, enjoy your new little family in the here and now."

"And please call me as soon as things get spicy," Alison says.

Moira covers her ears and shakes her head. "Do not call me. Theo is like a son, and, ew, oh, for the love of biscuits."

I break the news to Alison. "I'm not calling anyone."

She frowns and shrugs. "Oh, well. I had sex with Lucas like five times so far, and if his dick is anything like Sebastian's—"

"I'm done," Moira announces. "You girls are lovely, and I'm so happy to be invited to dinner, but I'm joining the men."

She excuses herself and goes outside, and I shoot Alison a look.

"Could you behave?" I ask, but I don't really mean the words. I miss our banter and the smile on my friend's face. It's familiar in my new strange world, and I find comfort in that.

"I'm happy things are working out, Emry," Alison sighs. "I was worried there for a while."

"Around the time you got kidnapped?" I joke.

"I've always worried about you," she admits. "I thought you were ignoring reality for a long time."

"Sebastian said that, too," I say, taking another sip of wine. "He says he knew we could never break the bond."

Alison shakes her head. "Not about that. I thought that every settler was just…" She pauses and shrugs, making an admission that she realized herself not too long ago. "Wrong. I thought searching was the only way."

She looks out the window over to our friends, her eyes lingering on Lucas.

"And now?" I ask her.

"Now, I think I think we choose our own fate," she says.

"You picked Sebastian, and when the bond came to you, you decided on a life with both men."

She glances at my tattoo. "Snow has a nice ring to it. Or Newson."

"Wow, how quickly the mighty have fallen," I mock.

Alison cocks an eyebrow. "I got knocked over by Lucas's dick."

Once more, my wine spews out of my mouth. Another shirt ruined.

CHAPTER 24

Emry's being overly quiet as we get ready for bed. She's dressed in a soft gray pajama set, the cotton thinned out from years of wear and showing the shape of her curves through the shadows of the fabric. Her perfect breasts bounce while she brushes her teeth, her nipples peaking and begging for my mouth.

I grunt and re-adjust myself, Sebastian holding back his laugh while we all finish up our lengthy nighttime routine. Emry's stretching out the time, avoiding the fact that we're all getting in bed together. She spent fifteen minutes applying moisturizer.

I've never had a long-term relationship, nor have I ever spent enough time with a woman to memorize her routine, but this has to be too much.

She's avoiding us.

"Emry, are you alright?" Sebastian asks.

She nods, brushing her teeth for the second time, maybe the third.

"Really? Because we've been in this bathroom for thirty minutes, and before tonight, I didn't know we owned two types of floss. I've never seen you floss, let alone twice," he points out.

"Everyone flosses," she bites back, slamming down her toothbrush.

One side of Sebastian's mouth lifts in a smile. He shifts his eyes to me, and I shrug, and then he looks back at her. "You never floss," he says with a chuckle.

"We don't have to share a bed," I say. "This is all moving really fast, and we don't have to rush it."

My bond aches inside, arguing what I've offered, but I ignore the pain. The drugs Jack gave me fight off the urges enough to give me control, but that doesn't mean it isn't uncomfortable.

"Especially for you, Sebastian," I continue. "I know you say you're alright with all this, but you could change your mind."

"I mean what I say. If I get... upset or something, I'll say so, but Theo's right." Sebastian places a hand on the small of Emry's back and kisses the top of her head. "It's just a bed and nothing more. We don't have to rush anything. There's nowhere you have to be. Nothing we have to do."

Her face falls, and she grips the side of the sink, avoiding our stares.

"But we do have to rush it," she whispers, tears welling in her eyes. "We're going to run out of time. It's all going to go by too fast."

Sebastian and I both rush over to her, encasing her in our hold. She places her head on my chest, and Sebastian strokes her hair, both of us confused about the shift in her demeanor.

"It's been a month, babe," Sebastian says. "I'm not trying

to downplay your feelings, but what the hell are you talking about?"

She turns her gaze to him, and I feel her fear and sadness. Sebastian must hear it, the thoughts in her head, the worry.

It's an image of him.

He's an old man in a hospital bed situated in our living room. Soft light from the window exposes the deep wrinkles that cover his face and hands. Emry reaches to hold one, a stark difference from hers, his fingers turning inward with age while hers looks as smooth as today.

She pictures me sitting on the other side of the bed in a large chair, reading something. My hair is a bit longer, but nothing else changes about my appearance.

We aren't a day older while Sebastian is near his end.

"Oh," Sebastian says.

His hold on Emry loosens as he steps back in shock, his eyes losing their focus. I can see what he's imagining a moment later, and I know Emry sees it too. Emry and I are holding hands at a gravesite, fresh flowers covering the dirt.

He swallows hard, and we both feel silly assuming what bothered Emry was sex when it was something much deeper. Silent tears stream down her face, and I feel the lump form in my throat, my eyes welling like hers.

"I thought all of us being together would fix everything," she says. "But it doesn't. There's still going to be so much pain. I can't imagine losing you. Watching you grow old while you're forced to watch us stay the same. I think you should consider NeXus's offer about hormone therapy."

"No," Sebastian and I say in unison.

Emry jolts, her spine straightening, and she meets our eyes in the mirror.

"I can't bear to put you through more pain, Sebastian. If you would just consider this," she begs.

Sebastian closes his eyes in frustration, holding back the argument he wants to start. I've seen his thoughts, his fears that flash through when he can't help it. He won't live without Emry, and with every passing moment, our friendship grows stronger. I'd like to think he needs me, too.

It's visceral, something inside us all changing. We are a part of something together, and he's not letting that go.

Neither am I.

I tilt her chin toward me. "Did you think this would be easy?" I ask her, not meaning the harshness in my voice, but it's there. "Damn, you're the strongest person I've ever met. Everything you've been through, but the slightest hint of someone else in pain, and you're a damn mess."

"That's about right," Sebastian sighs.

She jerks away from me, backing up and sitting on the side of the tub with her arms crossed tight around her middle.

"I didn't think that far into the future," she hisses. "Did either of you?"

"I'm lucky I remembered to brush my teeth. I was so distracted looking at you in that shirt," I admit.

Sebastian elbows me on my side. "Did you notice the variety of floss we have to offer as well?"

"Why can't we have a serious conversation about this?" she asks. "Sebastian, you are going to get older every day, and we aren't. That... complicates things."

Sebastian shrugs, widening his stance and his smile.

"You know, a few weeks ago, I thought our time together was over. I never thought we'd all be here together. My wife and a new telepathic best friend." He whips his head at me. "We should join the rugby team. We'd kill 'em."

"Isn't that cheating?" I ask.

"Who cares?" Sebastian counters.

"Are you fucking kidding me right now?" Emry shouts.

Her voice takes me by surprise, and Sebastian's eyes grow wide. She's not the type of person to lose her temper like this with Sebastian, and she's shaking with anger.

"I'm terrified of our future together, and you're talking about getting a leg up at a stupid ball game?" she hisses. "You saw what I did, Sebastian. That's your future with me. With us."

Sebastian takes a hesitant step forward, gets down on his knees, and places his hands on top of hers. She doesn't pull away, which surprises me. I feel the calm wash over her. He's so good at knowing what she needs, and how to approach her, and when he leans forward and kisses her lips, the last of her defenses drop.

"My lifetime, however short it may be, with you, is more than I could ever have dreamed of," he says. "And when I'm gone, I'll know there's someone who loves you as much as I did, who's looking out for you when I can't. What husband could ask for more?"

"Damn, Sebastian."

The thought slips freely from my mind, Sebastian's smirk giving away that he heard me.

Emry lets out a shuddered breath, and leans forward, softly pressing her lips to his once more.

"I'll love you forever, even when you're old and wrinkly," she promises. She holds up her wrist, and he does the same. It's the first time since we've been here I feel a twinge of being left out.

Sebastian and Emry must sense my moment of self-doubt, both of them lowering their wrists, faces falling.

"Did you... want to get a tattoo?" Emry asks. She turns to Sebastian. "Could he?"

"That was my plan," Sebastian says. "I'll make some calls."

"It's not a rush," I say, but inside I'm desperate to share the same name. I want to see it on my skin, mirroring theirs. It's futile to lie when others read your thoughts and Sebastian scoffs at me, promising it's at the top of his priority list.

Sebastian rises and offers his hand to Emry, and her nervousness peaks now that we've talked about what is bothering her. The idea of sex may have been why she was flossing for twenty minutes, after all.

I tuck a strand of hair behind her ear, running my thumb along her cheek. Every part of me wants her, and knowing that we'll be in a bed together only amplifies my anticipation.

That won't change the agreement that Sebastian and I made and what we told her earlier. She leads in all things.

"No matter what you think, Emry, none of this needs to be rushed," I promise. "Let's take it one step at a time."

"Step one, babe," Sebastian says, leading us all out of the bathroom. "Let's go to bed."

CHAPTER 25

EMRY

I'm split in two.

One woman longed for Sebastian since she was a teenage girl. No one else touched her, and she never dreamed of another man in her bed.

Sebastian knows that woman. His touch is familiar and always right. There's nothing dangerous with him, but yet, there are still the flares of excitement. Moments of uncontrolled lust when I'm with my husband.

The other woman is desperate for Theo. Desperate for him to take off her clothes and ravage her, show her new needs and desires. That woman doesn't want to wait for another second, ready to satisfy urges hidden deep inside, buried where only the bond could find them and bring them to the surface.

Both women stand at the edge of the bed in old gray pajamas, wishing I'd thought through this more, or at least enough to wear something more desirable.

I haven't made promises to anyone, but we're sharing a

bed, and I want this. It's not just easing the stress of Theo's bond, it's pleasing mine as well. There's also something symbolic about being physical with both of them. We can talk all day about this relationship, but until it crosses that threshold, we're friends and roommates.

There's only one complication.

How does this work?

I chastise myself for not being more adventurous or taking an interest in those that are. This was never on my horizon, yet here I am, standing in thin pajamas.

Clearly, I don't know what I'm doing, but I don't want to wait anymore. It's been a month of fighting this bond, something that felt so natural and impossible to ignore. With Sebastian's blessing, I'm free to explore a physical connection with Theo, and I can't imagine waiting one more moment.

Jack didn't give me any syringes to calm down my libido. They're in the kitchen, and if I gave him a call, I bet he would tell me the dosage.

Do I need that?

I'm the one leading, the one deciding. They're ready to try the intimate side of this, and all I need to do is grant them permission.

"Emry." Sebastian draws out my name. "You've been standing there for five minutes."

Shit.

They both share a look, and Theo hops up and makes his way around the bed. It's larger than a king, necessary for Sebastian's height, and we've only ever taken up half of the space. Even with the three of us, we would never need to touch in a night's sleep, but that won't happen.

My bond won't permit that to happen.

He tilts my chin up, and the touch sends sparks over my

skin. "I'll take the couch. When everyone's asleep, if my back can't take it, I'll slip in," he offers.

No.

He leans down to kiss me. It's light and gentle, a goodnight kiss. Except I cling to his wrists, something deep inside me begging him not to leave. Our lips linger together until his body is flush with mine, his hands dipping into my hair.

I reach for his waist, feeling every muscle. My fingers find the hem of his shirt and slip underneath it. His skin burns with heat when I slide my palms up, finding every cut and curve until I moan into his mouth.

Forcing myself to pull away, I look over at Sebastian, his face unreadable. There isn't anger or jealousy, but maybe a hint of curiosity.

"I don't want to go too far," I say, the bond arguing, but since this started, I'm better at controlling myself. The proximity helps too, knowing that Theo isn't going anywhere. "I know I said we don't have all the time in the world, but I don't think I can..."

I drift off, unsure of what I'm asking.

"You lead," Theo says. "We don't have to have sex."

I nod, unsure if that's possible.

Theo places his hands over my shoulders and down my arms, giving me a kiss on the neck. He runs one palm along the small of my back and directs me to the spot next to Sebastian. Going to my other side, he slips into the bed and curls his body around mine, his erection throbbing against my backside.

I reach for Sebastian, my hand resting on his bare stomach, and he turns off the light before he rests his hands behind his head.

"You let me know if you..." Theo trails off.

I don't know what to say and neither does he. Are we

taking turns, and they flipped a coin earlier? There's a part of this that requires some discussion or someone to take the lead.

Shit, that's me.

Theo's arms wrap around my body, holding me tight, his heart beating against my back.

"Theo, if you want to, um..." My eyes adjust to the dark room, seeing the outline of my husband. I'm struggling with the words, so I do the most logical thing.

I dare to let the thoughts buried deep in my mind slip out, and with the sight of my secret desires, theirs flow forward. What's in their heads makes me gasp. Theo envisions taking me in every way possible, my body naked and misted with sweat, with his cock buried deep inside me.

Sebastian is, in some way, sharing that same vision. He's watching us, and he's liking what he sees.

Need creeps inside my core, my center growing slick, begging for attention.

"I know you said not too far," Theo whispers into my ear. "It's just difficult to know what the line is. You need to tell us because those thoughts you just shared? Fuck, love. I'll give you that and more."

I nod, wishing I could make out the expression on Sebastian's face. My hand shifts, moving downward, fingertips creeping underneath the band of his sweatpants.

His stomach shifts, taking in a long pull of air, and he runs his touch along the length of my arm, urging me to keep going.

My nipples harden, the vision of myself with both men circling in my mind. The desire for them takes over, and I need to feel Sebastian's hard cock in my grip, and I want to be touched by Theo just as much.

There are so many things we can try together. It doesn't have to be sex to find relief.

And I need relief.

I'm dripping between my legs, arching my back, and pushing myself against Theo's cock. He grunts, burying his face into the pillow while I slide my hand down to Sebastian's cock.

The hot skin under my fingertips feels smooth, veins throbbing when I wrap my fingers around his length and pump. Sebastian lets out a groan of satisfaction, pulling at the sides of the pillow but keeping his hands to himself.

We've always touched each other, found satisfaction together like this, but he's holding back.

When Theo's hand shifts, dipping lower, I know why. He's letting Theo touch me, and Theo brings his lips to my ear, asking, "Is this okay?" before moving further.

"Y-yes," I stutter, my heart beating faster with every tiny movement of Theo's fingertips. I want to grab his wrist and shove his hand into my panties, pressing his fingers inside my wet opening. I'm rocking my hips against him, begging for him to keep going, all the while milking Sebastian's cock. "Please, Theo."

He doesn't hesitate, reaching for my leg and lifting it so it rests on top of his. I'm open, the thin shorts doing nothing once his hand dives beneath my waistband.

My breath is shallow and my body is on fire. He doesn't make me wait before he's stroking against my clit and sliding a finger deep inside.

"Oh, fuck," I gasp. The explosion of pleasure is unlike anything before. I don't just feel *my* exhilaration rocketing through my body, but his as well. His satisfaction amplifies mine. He's getting off on making me come, and we won't be able to hold off our orgasms for long.

Theo's wet mouth is against the back of my neck, heavy breaths and groans escaping while he rocks his hard cock across the small of my back. His fingers slide out of my center, and I whimper at the loss. When he sheathes my clit between two fingers, rubbing them back and forth, I explode.

The sensation is too much, sparks of electricity firing between us both and the feel of Sebastian's throbbing cock in my hand sends me over the edge. There's a flash of something, a colorful light, but I can't focus on anything besides the climax.

It's an orgasm felt across all of us, Theo's touch in the same rhythm as mine while I cry out, my body shaking in response. I keep pumping Sebastian, but my grip weakens with every wave of pleasure that crashes over me.

Sebastian's hand covers mine, helping me continue, the slick of his pre-cum warming my palm.

"Are you?" I ask. I'm not really sure what I'm asking or who. This is the first time my focus has been split between two men. "Did you?" I rush out.

Sebastian lets out a growl, his cock thickening before it spills over my fist and his. Theo dips his hand lower, sliding two fingers deep inside me, and I gasp before my back arches with another orgasm.

"Is that good, love?" Theo hisses into my ear. "Is this how you like it? Show me."

I remove my hand from Sebastian's spent cock and join it with Theo's, pressing the heel of his palm against my clit. It's animalistic - rabid, and I'm vibrating with the sensations.

Sebastian's mouth finds mine, his tongue slipping inside while I moan against his lips. Theo's movements grow stiff, his harsh breath coming out in short bursts against my neck before I feel his warmth spread against my back.

Knowing he's come, his fingers deep inside me, the rhythmic pressure against my clit, I cry out with another crushing orgasm. "Oh, y-yes!"

My body trembles uncontrollably, and Sebastian's face is

now an inch from mine, his soft words making my climax only intensify. "That's it, baby," he urges. "You come for us. Tell us how good it feels."

The wave doesn't stop, crashing again into me and flooding into them both. He growls and Sebastian moans as another spurt of warmth sprays against my back from Theo and another on my stomach from Sebastian.

"Say it," Sebastian demands. "Say how good it feels."

"It…" I gasp in a breath of air. "Feels too good." After another few breaths, sweat trickles down my chest, my hips still rocking against Theo while his fingers massage my inner walls. "So good, oh, fuck."

Sebastian's mouth finds mine as his fingers slide into my hair. His kiss is ravenous until he yanks his head back, his grip on my hair tightening while another wave of pleasure has me trembling in their arms. I see Sebastian's reaction to this even in the dark, the way his eyes roll back and his face slackens.

His free hand moves into his sweatpants while his chest vibrates against mine.

He's still coming.

Another flash of color brightens the room for an instant, but it doesn't shift their focus. Sex with Sebastian never left me unsatisfied, but there's something more happening in this room. It's the bond and us, creating a visual of the pleasure we're all experiencing.

Theo's movements have slowed as the height of my climax slips away, the trickles of ecstasy still swirling through all three of us.

Our orgasms are fast and hard, a testament to how long we've waited for this moment, and although I'm sad it's ending, I know this is just the beginning. I'll never tire of this and what we can do together.

"Fuck," Theo says before he rolls onto his back, removing

his fingers from me and placing his cock in his hands. He empties himself before he sits up, his chest heaving as he looks down on us in the dark. Sebastian is spent, his limbs falling to his sides as he lets out a sigh.

"That was good," Theo says. The statement is so blunt and honest that I have no response.

"Yeah," Sebastian agrees, sitting up and swinging his legs over the side of the bed. He rises, adjusting himself as he walks to the bathroom.

He's leaving?

"Where are you going?" I ask, shooting up in bed, terrified we've just done something that crossed the line.

It's one thing to say you're okay with a lifestyle, but once that boundary is crossed, you can't undo it. We can't take back what just happened, and now he's leaving Theo and me alone.

"I'm going to clean up, babe," he says, flicking on the bathroom light.

"I think I'll jump in the shower if it doesn't bother anyone," Theo says.

"Nah, that's fine," Sebastian tells Theo, who pauses on the side of the bed before he heads to the shower.

"Are you okay, love?" Theo asks. I'm sitting up in bed, my pajamas twisted and covered in... everyone. I can't imagine what I look like, but I know the look on my face is of a stunned woman in a haze.

"Uh, yeah," I say.

Theo's swirling around in my head, and without thinking, I shut off my thoughts. He tilts his head, narrowing his gaze.

"Habit," I explain, offering him a coy smile. "You know, private thoughts are good sometimes."

The sound of the shower starts when Sebastian flicks it on for Theo.

"No, I'm just fine," I repeat with a small laugh. "I think I'll use the hall bathroom for a minute."

Sebastian steps over, running a towel over the back of his neck, his chest muscles pumped and strewn with a mist of sweat.

"Hey, are you okay?" Sebastian asks again. "Really? Do we need to talk about what just happened?"

"We can do that," Theo offers.

It's the most awkward offer from both of them who are obviously fine with what we just did. They're ready to clean up and go to sleep satisfied. I pull myself together enough to put a genuine smile on my face even though my shock is overriding the pleasure. In time, I'll get used to the normalcy of this.

"I'm really good. That felt... amazing." It's true. I came so hard my abdominal muscles will be sore in the morning. "But, yeah, I'm going to use the spare bathroom so we can all get to sleep sooner. I'm still exhausted."

"So, no talking?" Theo asks, heading for the shower.

"No," I answer, grabbing my cell phone before heading out the door. Sebastian and Theo don't stop or follow me, and I let out a breath of relief before I hide in the bathroom and call Alison.

She picks up after I call for the third time.

"Are you okay?" she rushes out.

"No," I mutter, turning on the water so no one hears our conversation.

"Okay, I'm coming over. Did you alert the security people on your property?" she asks.

What if someone walking around our house just heard us all messing around?

"No, no, no," I say. "I'm okay. It's not like that. It's just..." I don't know how to finish my sentence, and I regret calling Alison, knowing I'll have to tell her why I'm calling.

I hear the rustle of bedsheets and Lucas's voice in the background, asking what's going on. Alison tells him she'll be right back, and a door closes before she hesitantly asks her first question, which gets right to the point.

"Did you have sex with Theo?"

"Not, technically, but we did some things," I admit. "I don't know why I called. I'm in the spare bathroom, and they're in the bedroom acting like this is normal."

"Okay," Alison muses, thinking about what to say next. I know her and she's holding back from asking for details. "Did something cross the line to make you uncomfortable?"

"No, not at all. They made sure I made the call of what and when," I say. "I just don't know how to act right now."

"Did you enjoy yourself?" she asks.

"Yes, definitely." My heart flutters with the flash of memory that comes when I answer.

Alison clucks her tongue. "And Seb and Theo are good. They aren't acting weird?"

"That's the thing," I admit. "It's weird how normal they are acting. We all, um, enjoyed... touching each other."

"I want details later, but you don't have to get into that now," Alison sighs.

"Okay, well after, they just popped up to wipe off and get to sleep," I rush out. "They're probably washing each other's hair right now. What the hell?"

"Did you want them to hold you or give you comfort?" Alison asks. I'm astonished at how poignant her questions are, grateful I chose such a thoughtful best friend.

I shake my head even though she can't see me. "No, we needed to clean up first."

Alison sputters a laugh. "That good?"

"Yeah," I admit. "Really good. Like fireworks good." I think about the light, curious how I would pose that question to Jack without feeling awkward. Hopefully, he won't use the term "mating" again.

"Okay, then." Alison lets out a long sigh before she continues. "I thought this first encounter would make you spiral a little, and that's normal. But if everyone consented, the guys seem fine, and you enjoyed yourself, then it's the best outcome. Did you get there? Did you come?"

"A few times," I tell her.

"Damn, well, okay," Alison says. "Have a shower, calm yourself down, and give yourself some time to adjust to this. Everything's fine. They seem to want to share you, and that's what's happening."

"Yeah, but..." I trail off, not sure why I'm trying to argue. She's right, but I can't accept the fact that something inside me is scared of everything that could go wrong.

"It doesn't always have to fall apart," Alison says. "All your struggles led you here, and if you're happy, weren't they worth it?"

I nod but don't answer, staring at my disheveled self in the mirror.

"If you're nodding I can't see you," Alison says. "Are you happy?"

"Yes," I say, shocking myself with the admission.

"You've even got me thinking about settling with Lucas, woman," Alison jokes. "You should be damn near ecstatic."

"Really?" I ask, my mind shifting focus.

Alison laughs but doesn't answer my question. "Rinse off and go to bed with your two hunks. Everything is fine. You're okay."

"Right. I'm okay," I say to myself as well as Alison.

We offer each other a goodnight and I strip off my clothes, reminding myself I need to find some pajamas purchased in the last decade. A shower would feel good, but a small part of me doesn't want to wash away the scent of them both on my skin. Alison could be right. Not everything is a lead-up to disaster. Haven't we all been through enough?

The handle turns, and there's a soft knock before the door slowly opens. Both men step inside. Steam creeps out through the open door, reminding me of the mist. I wonder if the lights are like that, something that's created in moments of passion.

Theo's standing with a towel around his waist, and Sebastian has changed into shorts.

"I'm fine, really," I tell them. "Are you two okay?"

Sebastian leans against the counter and looks at Theo, both of them having a conversation inside their heads.

"We are great," Sebastian says as Theo nods. "But if that went too far for you, we can, um, talk about it."

I shake my head. "I enjoyed myself," I admit. "I... I want to keep going."

Both men stand straighter, and I correct my wording. "Another night. I want to keep going, continue, you know, another night. Not tonight."

Theo laughs and sees himself out. "I'm beat and heading to bed."

We both give him a goodnight, and Sebastian checks in with me one more time. I promise him I'm fine, which is true.

When I make it back to bed, I find both men passed out on fresh sheets, a space between them meant for me. I crawl in and slip underneath the covers, looking them both over before I lean back into my pillow.

"Goodnight," I whisper, but the only response is the soft breaths of Theo and Sebastian on either side of me.

Weeks of worrying about this bond kept me awake, but I sleep peacefully tonight, not knowing what tomorrow will bring.

CHAPTER 26

THEO

My phone buzzes again.

It's done so more than once, maybe half a dozen times. I'm used to sleeping in different places all the time, but that doesn't mean I do it well. Never feeling comfortable in my surroundings, I developed a habit of being a light sleeper.

This night, I drifted off into a deep sleep before Emry came back to bed, but that phone continues to vibrate over on Sebastian's nightstand where I left it, keeping me awake.

I sit up and squint my eyes at the dull light the screen makes facing downward on the table.

Sebastian's sleeping on his back, one hand reaching over to Emry. She's on her side, facing me, her face at peace.

His eyes open, and he flings the phone in my direction. It's not forceful, but there's a hint of irritation there, probably because it's still dark outside and no one should call this early in the morning.

My eyes can't adjust to the bright screen to see what's

setting my phone off, so I lock the screen, toss it on my night-stand, and hope it stops.

I'm at the precipice of being able to fall back asleep, not fully awake where the damage is done, and I'm forced to start my day when the fucking phone buzzes again.

"Who the fuck keeps calling?"

The thought screams inside my own head so loud that Sebastian jerks, and I know it's my fault. Sebastian's retort comes right back at me.

"I don't know. Maybe answer your phone."

The bed shifts as he rolls to his side, trying to fall back asleep.

The buzzing continues, and I shove the blankets off, sitting up to reach for it.

Emry stirs, moving her soft body towards me, disturbed by the loss of warmth. She lets out a small grunt but doesn't awaken.

I was dreaming about sex with Emry, thinking about how wet she felt and the way she whimpered when she came. This piece of garbage phone keeps pulling me away from that, and it's leaving this room. I don't give a fuck who's calling.

"Good plan," Sebastian agrees.

My fingers fumble to turn it off, and when I can't figure it out half-asleep, I stagger from the bed, ready to throw it out of the room. That or bust it with a hammer. Whatever makes it stop.

The name on the screen saves it from destruction.

Cutthroat Robin.

It doesn't make sense. There's nothing I owe her, and even though I don't think that vampire sleeps, there's nothing she could need at this early hour.

Sebastian rubs his eyes, still trying to wake up. "Who is it?" he asks. The phone buzzes again.

"I've got to get this," I say. The sound of Sebastian's feet hit the floor before I can tell him to stay in bed.

I look over at Emry and frown. She's curled into the covers and fast asleep. I jut my chin to the door, and Sebastian nods, following me into the kitchen.

The clock on the phone reads a little after five in the morning, and I wonder if the smell of coffee will awaken Emry.

"I'll make the coffee."

I nod at Sebastian, head to the living room, and answer Robin's thirteenth call of the morning.

"Robin, why do you keep calling?" I hiss through the phone. "It's five in the morning."

"I'm calling because I have information you'll want to know immediately," she answers with no inflection in her voice. "I set it to auto-dial until you woke up. They say geniuses rise before the sun."

"I guess I'm not a genius."

"No," she agrees. "You are not."

"Okay, out with it so I can get back to sleep," I say.

"I don't have time to detail it for you, but I received alerts of several articles releasing in succession this morning. They named you."

I can hear her typing away at a keyboard, and my phone buzzes a few times in my hand.

"I've sent them to you," she says and then promptly hangs up.

I stare at the screen of my phone, my eyes shifting through the titles of news blasts released less than ten minutes ago.

Blaire Crawford, mother of Emry Crawford (Crowe), WANTED AT LARGE.

Crawford's last known address was found abandoned. Click *here* for any known whereabouts or sightings.

Crawford escaped, creating a late-night search. We advise everyone to remain off of roadways.

Police have Crawford in a stand-off. She's inside a home with two unknown males.

I head into the kitchen with Sebastian. He runs his hand down his face and pulls out a chair from the table, stretching his neck from side to side as he sits down.

"They left here with a warrant for her," I say. "I–I didn't follow up. There's been a lot going on."

Sebastian yawns, his eyes still heavy. "What are you talking about?"

Sliding the phone across the table, Sebastian catches it in his hands. He scrolls through the articles Robin sent, becoming more alert with each one.

The coffee maker rumbles to life, and I ask Sebastian if he wants some.

"Shit," he says, reaching his hand out for a cup. "I mean, yes, I want some coffee."

There's a creak from somewhere in the house, and we both freeze, fearful Emry woke up. A minute passes by, and there's nothing, so I hand Sebastian his coffee and join him at the table.

"Emry doesn't need this," he says, a pained expression on his face.

"How does Blaire think this is going to end?" My question is rhetorical, but a part of me is curious. She's trapped and surrounded, not to mention, guilty.

"She's delusional," Sebastian explains. "She probably

thinks she was being a good mother in her warped head. Or she'll lie and say Genome tricked her again."

"Look at this," Sebastian says, holding my phone up for me to see. It's a stream of news articles identifying Emry's mother as responsible for collusion with the Genome Theory.

"She must be desperate with this out," Sebastian muses.

He clicks on one, and we read through it together, skimming the article with tired and bleary eyes. Coffee helps, but it isn't the magic Emry acts like it is.

"She can't think she's getting out of this," I say. "Fuck, this is all over the news. Emry will find out as soon as she wakes up."

Sebastian groans, gulping down a large swig of coffee. "That woman won't stop disrupting our lives," he grumbles.

"Glad someone else has the title for a minute," I joke.

Sebastian nudges me in the arm. "Don't. I get it's funny to a point, but that's not what you did. Things change. That's life."

I nod, taking in his words and reminding myself I'm a part of this family. I'm here, not as a disruption, but as someone who loves Emry as my bonded and Sebastian as my brother.

We're interrupted by a soft knock on the window behind us, and I jump to my feet so fast that I knock over my chair.

Sebastian walks over and opens the door, letting someone wearing a NeXus uniform inside, a man I've seen walking the grounds.

"Shit, if my heart wasn't better I would have died just then," I say, picking up the chair and putting it back on its legs.

The man tilts his head to the side, confused by my statement. Maybe he hasn't caught up on all the online gossip about how Emry quite literally healed my broken heart.

"Theo, this is Milo," Sebastian says. "We work together."

"Nice to meet you. You can't be here by accident. Any developments?"

Milo stands with his thumbs in his belt loops and leans against the counter. "I saw the light was on, so I radioed that I'd let you in on the news. We were letting you sleep."

There's the hint of a grin there telling me someone on the property heard something last night, but that's the least of our worries.

Sebastian hands him the phone with an article open. "This news?"

Milo nods. "Seems she's barricaded herself inside with some male friends. They're identified, but nobody is of note. There's concern she'll hurt someone, maybe herself. She's asking for you and Emry."

"Where's Emry's phone?" I ask, worried that she'll be getting this news by herself.

"She turns it off at night," Sebastian says.

I think how that would have been good advice for me earlier, but then we wouldn't have this information first with a chance to break it to Emry gently.

"We've been notified some officers are at the gate," Milo says. "To talk to Emry, see if she can de-escalate the situation."

"Absolutely not," Sebastian argues.

"Shouldn't that be up to me?" Emry asks from the hallway.

She steps out of the shadows, her phone in hand. "I can sleep through a lot, Theo, except for breaking the furniture."

I wiggle in the chair with a lopsided grin. "Chair's fine," I tell her and she smiles.

Sebastian introduces Milo to Emry, and he catches us up on everything. Blaire was tipped off about the search and fled, but they were already in pursuit.

There's a knock at the door. Milo gave permission for the officers to come through the gate, and we join them in our living room. Strangers in uniforms and us in pajamas, and all I can think to do is offer them some coffee.

"I don't want to see her," Emry says. "I won't be of help even if I do."

"And that's alright," Sara says. She's the officer who took Emry and Alison's statement, and I'm glad it's her that's here. Something about her is trustworthy, and I sense Emry is at ease when they talk. "We wanted you to know what's going on, and give you the opportunity. Our concern is bystanders, and we've evacuated the nearby houses, but we can't make the perimeter much wider."

"People love the drama," Emry scoffs.

Sara offers a close-lipped smile in response.

"I know that she's my mother," Emry continues. "But I'm done with her."

Her voice chokes on her words, and I feel the pain rise up through the bond. My hand flies to my heart where sorrow seeps inside, the agony of a child torn apart by their parent.

My mother rejected me, and that hurt, even though my father loved me enough for both of them. But she never set out to harm me. That's a different kind of evil, and the hurt is worse when it's someone who is meant to protect you.

Sebastian's brow creases, seeing us both in pain. "I'm going," he offers.

"What, no!" Emry says.

"I'm ending this," he argues.

Emry turns to Sebastian, her eyes wide.

"Does Blaire know we saw her picture? Does she even know why there's a warrant?"

"To our knowledge, no," Sara says. "She's aware of her own wrongdoings. Her dealings with Genome Theory. But how that was discovered, and if you all are aware, that's not something she's said. She thinks you and Emry will help her, is what I'm hearing."

"Okay, then let's go," Sebastian says. "I'll need twenty... maybe thirty minutes."

"I'm going with you," I say, stepping toward Sebastian.

He places a hand on my chest, stopping me in my place. "You stay with Emry. I'd feel better knowing you are with her."

I think about it, knowing I won't be much help to him, but hating that he's going alone. "Okay," I agree, knowing I'd feel the same way.

"Did anyone hear me say no?" Emry asks, her voice shaking.

Sebastian leans down, taking her face in his hands. The sorrow in her gut softens with his touch, and I feel the relief myself and let out a sigh.

"Em, baby, this is what I do," he tells her. "This is my job, and there's some personal interest in this one, but you don't need to worry. I'll get her out with everyone unharmed."

"I'm not too worried if she's harmed," Emry admits.

"She'll have information on Genome," Sebastian says. "And if I do this and get some names, it helps Jack's case to NeXus about our business. Theo and I could start doing what we've set out to do sooner. Help kids that Genome is holding hostage."

Emry can't argue with those words, and she nods, biting her lip. "Please be careful," she whispers to him before she throws her arms around Sebastian's neck, kissing him goodbye.

Sara gets up, informing the other officers of the next steps. "I'll be outside with a car," she tells Sebastian.

With that, the living room is empty again.

It's not even six in the morning, and this is setting up to be another long day.

CHAPTER 27

EMRY

The news stations are relentless. Helicopters circle the house where Blaire is hiding, and there's a constant stream of articles and chats that never end as Theo and I watch the television curled up on the couch.

I'm on my third cup of coffee, my hands shaking from the caffeine. It's been a few hours since Sebastian left, and he appears on the screen, dressed head to toe in riot gear. My mother isn't a large woman, but she's capable of anything. She'd kill him just like she tried to kill me.

"Are you okay watching this?" Theo asks me. His hand runs up and down my spine, and I rest my head on his chest, listening to the perfect rhythm of his heart. I feel his nerves, worried for Sebastian.

"I'm fine and Sebastian will be fine," I tell Theo. "He's very good at dealing with criminals."

"Oh, I've seen him in action," Theo admits, letting out a chuckle.

"Damn, this has gotten so much attention," I sigh. "But no one is talking about why she's being arrested. They need to focus on Genome Theory, not fill the television with people on the street asking if she has a bomb."

"You know they're trying to kill the feeds that don't suit the receptions," Theo reminds me. "But Sebastian and I will handle that. We've got two purposes in life. Loving you and destroying every last member of Genome Theory."

I smile, the joy emanating out of me and into Theo. He feels it, sinking lower into the couch and wrapping his arms around me.

"It feels good to hear you say that," I admit. "Not for me, but for everyone else. Maybe I could..." I drift off, a sinking feeling in my stomach. Fear creeps in with memories of cement walls and needles, hidden faces that hurt me over and over again. I want to help, but I can't even bring myself to say the words.

"It feels good to have a purpose, a family," Theo says, pulling me closer. "But you need to go your own path. Leave Genome to us. I know you're strong, but that's too much for you to handle. Especially so soon."

He's right, and I hate that. Those missing people need my help, and who better to help them than someone who's been through what Genome does to people? I need to get stronger, and I remind myself to schedule a session with Jack.

Theo changes the station to find another reporter on the other side of the house. It's a large one-story surrounded by woods. There isn't anything nefarious about the property. A corporation is renting it out to one man trapped inside, and I would guess that the company has ties to Genome. Maybe we'll dig deep enough when this is over and find out.

"What do you want to do?" Theo asks. "As far as work, I mean?"

"I want to go back to the university," I answer. There's a lot about my job I might find annoying, but I love my work and my students. "I won't have to sit at the gates on the first day anymore and get touched by everyone."

"You had to do that?" Theo asks. "I guess I get it, but still."

He shivers a little and I know he would find the process as disagreeable as I once did.

"Do you think they would take me?" I ask. "I'd be a bit of a spectacle. I don't think any bonded ever went back to work. They just do their annual testing and get paid. What do they do all day?"

"We aren't doing what other bonded are doing," Theo says. "We're making our own choices. You want to teach, then they'll be lucky to have you. They won't take you back, we'll move or start our own damn university. Between testing stipends and our income, we'll have enough damn money."

I smile and watch the news reporter point to the house, explaining how many hours, seconds, and minutes have passed since Blaire first barricaded herself inside.

Sebastian comes into the camera's focus, standing on the front grass. His name rolls along the bottom of the screen in bold letters.

Sebastian Owens (Crowe) – ex-husband of Emry Crawford,
Blaire Crawford's daughter.

"Ex-husband!" I sit up, ripping myself from Theo's hold, and scream. "What the hell are they talking about?"

Theo wraps his hands over my shoulders and pulls me back to him. "They're looking for reach, getting people to watch. They'll do some small retraction, but you know they don't care, and more importantly, Sebastian doesn't care."

Theo kisses the side of my head, the sparks of our bond sending his soothing nature through me.

"Don't let those assholes get to you."

I check my phone again and huff. No messages from Sebastian, but I understand. I can see him, but not talk to him. He moves with another man toward the door of the house, a weapon in his hand. The news reporter who I now hate steps as close as he can to the police tape, making assumptions about what Sebastian is doing or the plan to get her out.

I wrap my arms around Theo, holding him tighter. "Sebastian's very good at what he does. He'll end this soon," I say, mostly to myself.

"Yes," Theo says. We watch without blinking, feeling that something big is about to happen. I hold my breath as more men block my view of Sebastian.

"Shit," Theo mumbles.

A few minutes pass, and I think about muting the station so I don't have to hear this reporter's voice, but I don't want to miss anything.

"Do you think—" Theo stops short, sitting up suddenly, and I let out a scream. Something's happened, sending news reporters and bystanders ducking to the ground, smoke billowing out from the windows of the house.

I'm on my feet. "We need to go!" I scream.

Theo's already putting on his shoes, opening the door to scream at one of the security guards surrounding our house to get us a car.

"I'll get dressed," I say.

Whipping by him, I see Milo jogging up to our door and responding to Theo. I throw on some jeans and a fresh tank top, running into the living room before I button my pants. The screen of the television is nothing but smoke, and the dread hits me, almost sending me to the floor.

Theo holds his stomach, the pain etching into his soul as well.

"We're ready," he tells Milo, ushering me to his side. We sprint to the car, and another man in the driver's seat blares the sirens when he sees us. The engine roars, and I watch as the NeXus employee shifts it into automatic drive, sending me into a rage.

"You need to speed," I argue. "Get it off fucking auto-drive."

"Oh, honey," the man drawls. "You've never seen auto-drive like this before."

The car jerks forward, sending me rolling into Theo without my seatbelt fastened. Billows of dust hit the windows while the sirens blare louder, and we fly off of my property.

The screen in the dash lights up, a flickering light moving over the grid of streets, sending red blinking dots green, and then moving to the next.

"Are you controlling the traffic?" Theo asks, securing my seatbelt into place.

Cars flash by our window, and our vehicle screeches as it turns. My shoulder catches in the belt, pinching my skin, but I'm happy we're moving at breakneck speed.

"I'm not at liberty to speak about proprietary information," the man says. He turns back and gives us both a wink as we pick up speed before entering the highway.

They should be forty minutes away, but at the rate of speed we're driving, I'm hoping we're close after only five minutes into the drive. I check my phone, searching for anything about what happened. Every article tells a different story, and I don't think any of them are true.

The driver radios, asking for updates and we get one before pulling up to the house.

Blaire is in custody, using the explosion as an attempt to

distract everyone and killing one man inside in the process. They say nothing about Sebastian.

"Has anyone left for the hospital? Any ambulances?" Theo asks.

"An ambulance was on site, but it hasn't left," the man says. "Not to my knowledge, that is."

The car jerks with another turn, and my head whacks into the windshield. A billboard comes into view.

What you crave is with the one of your choosing.

I scoff at it, and at every other bullshit propaganda we see on the way.

Your life mate is waiting. Are you looking?

Fulfillment is companionship.

They mock me, and I vow to turn every one of them into marketing for the lost people Genome has stolen.

"We're here," the man says.

I unbuckle, shocked at how fast we arrived, but I think we were going over two hundred miles per hour for most of the drive.

Sprinting out of the car, I hear Theo behind me, calling out my name. A few people touch me, and I slap them away, pushing myself through the crowd.

"Emry, wait!" Theo yells.

He's stuck behind me, trapped by people reaching out for him, but I can't make myself stop. The same undeniable pull toward Theo that I could never break now pushes me, rushing me forward to Sebastian. He's still here. I can feel him, sense that he's close.

"It's her," someone calls from the crowd.

I ignore them, as well as all the cameras and phones that get shoved in my face when I get to the police line.

Sara is standing on the field, the smoke still hazy but mostly cleared. There are several people crowded around someone on the ground.

"Sara!" I call out. There are men lining the police tape, ready to stop me. I'm strong, but I'm not wanting to test it and hurt someone. "Get me through."

"Hey," someone says with their grip on my elbow. It's the newscaster from before, the one broadcasting that my *ex-husband* was at the scene.

"Get away from me," I brush him off. He comes back to my side, Theo screaming at him to get off of me from behind us.

He thrusts a microphone in my face. "Emry Crowe, here to lend aid to her ex-husband—"

He doesn't get another word out before I hit him in the jaw and he falls to a pile of limbs on the ground.

"Husband," I seethe at him. "Not ex, just husband, asshole. Husband!" Everyone backs up, fearful of my anger being let loose on them, but they don't stop recording or taking pictures.

I try to get past the police line, but they have an electric field that shocks me when I step forward.

"Take it down," Sara orders. Someone pulls out a keyboard to follow her command.

"Emry, are you alright?" Sara asks. "Oh, Theo. What about you? Are you both okay?"

"Us?" I question in disgust. "Where is Sebastian?"

Theo grabs my hand a moment later, and that's when I see it. The mist in front of us isn't haze from the bomb anymore.

It's us.

The white smoke is pouring off of our bodies, an obscure

fog that makes its way to someone who lies in the grass up ahead.

CHAPTER 28

THEO

"This means he's alive," Emry says, her voice shaking. She holds up her arms, smoke billowing out of her limbs. "Because why would this happen if he was dead?"

Not wanting to upset her, I don't remind her that this gift brought me back from the dead once. The electric field comes down, and Sara jogs us ahead toward Sebastian, our mist blinding everyone along the way.

We find him with his shirt open and a tube down his throat. He's not moving and several scratches line the left side of his chest.

"He was hit by debris," Sara says. "He was wearing a vest, but the impact broke some ribs, collapsed his lungs. We have a pulse, but barely. What is this? What are you two doing?"

I can't see her when she's talking, blinded by a blanket of white.

"I can't explain it, but it will help him," I say, lowering myself to the ground.

Something inside me drifts away, making me weaker by the second. I'm tired again, reminiscent of the little strength I had before Emry, my eyes closing when I hit the grass. His injuries must be bad, but he can take everything I have to give as long as he gets better.

I see the outline of Emry, her body resting on Sebastian's broken body, and I hear her sobs. This lawn, which bustled with people and voices moments ago, has grown quiet.

There's the soft movement of feet that shuffle around us, the beep of a machine, and the ambulance engine running at our side. I'm aware strangers record us, holding up their phones in hopes they can be a part of the latest story. They won't see much through this mist, but they watch in silence and awe.

I lay down next to Sebastian. *"We've let her down."* My thoughts whisper to him. *"I promised Emry that things don't always have to fall apart, and we would build our lives together. We deserve more than just a few days."*

"You have to make it, Seb," Emry cries. "We need you."

He doesn't respond to either of us, his mind blank, and I reach for his shoulder, squeezing it as best I can in my weakened state.

"Please, man," I say. "We just found each other."

My limbs grow weaker, and I'm limp at his side. I watch the mist sink into his chest, waves of it cascading through his wounds. Emry loses consciousness first, becoming lifeless, her hand rolling from his face and flopping to the ground.

I'm not far behind her, letting what life force remains in me go to Sebastian.

"Come back to us," I say aloud before it all goes black.

"Come back."

I open my eyes and shiver from the cold.

Emry, Sebastian, and I are sitting on her back porch. It's

winter, snow falling and making everything so white my eyes need a moment to adjust. Bare trees don't look as dead when it snows like this. Something crackles, an animal running through the woods that surrounds our home.

Sebastian hands me a cup of coffee, steam billowing from the cup. He's wearing his NeXus uniform, but it isn't ripped open and splattered with blood. There's not a mark on him, and I take the cup, the sides burning the palms of my hands.

"It's almost too cold to be out here," Emry says.

"Never too cold for your favorite spot," Sebastian tells her.

"You better drink that second cup quick," Emry says. "You'll be late."

Her eyes meet mine, and I'm taken aback by her beauty. She's sitting in her favorite chair, a large gray blanket wrapped around her shoulders. Her hair flows over her shoulders, longer than I remember, and her cheeks flush with a rosy hue.

I set the cup down and see the black cuffed sleeve of my shirt, noticing I'm wearing a uniform that matches Sebastian's.

"Ten minutes," Sebastian says. "I can get us there faster if I drive."

"I wish you wouldn't do that, Seb," Emry argues. "It's not safe."

He chuckles into his cup. "Nothing we do is safe, but I know the best healers in town. Makes me kind of like Superman."

I don't know what to say, staring at them both with longing.

Is this real?

I jolt upward from the dream, my body covered in wires and sweat.

"Hey, hey, hey," a voice calls out.

I leap from the bed, unsteady on my feet. In a panic, I rip off the cords attached to my body. A nurse enters the room and she must find the scene too much to handle because she turns on her heel to leave once we make eye contact.

It stings when I pull the tube out from inside my arm. Someone lays a hand on my shoulder and I shove them away.

"Hey, calm down."

I don't stop peeling at the tape stuck to my arm.

"Emry and Sebastian, where are they?" I ask.

I dig at the skin, needing to get free and find them.

"Theo, stop!" Jack yells.

"Jack?" I question, looking him up and down. Hurried footsteps enter the room and Moira comes to Jack's side.

"You're up already," she says.

"Where's Emry?" I ask.

"She's getting a scan," Jack explains.

I growl at him, tearing the last bit of tape free, leaving a red square in its place.

"Stop that," Moira pleads. "Please calm down. You'll hurt yourself."

I don't want to, but I listen to her, forcing my heart rate to slow. I'm not feeling like myself, separated from my bonded and Sebastian, needing to know they are both okay. The bond between us screams and yells, making me manic. I want to thrash at them, knock them down for being in my way, but I hold it inside. The burning of restraint feels like fire in my gut.

"Sebastian?" I bite out. "Where is he?"

"He is unconscious, but doing well," Jack says. He takes a step back with his palms raised. I don't want to scare him so I close my eyes when he speaks, counting down in my head, making myself hear his words.

"It's only been four hours since you passed out," Jack continues. "Emry is already up. She's just getting checked out. Everyone is well. Everyone is just fine. Your family is in good shape."

Emry must sense my fear, and she reaches out.

"Theo, Sebastian's fine. He's better than fine. Are you okay?"

I exhale, falling back down onto the bed.

"Emry, love. Where are you? Where's Sebastian?"

The trickle of excitement stretches between us both, knowing we are all going to be alright.

"I'm with a doctor. I'll be back soon."

"Are you talking to Emry?" Moira asks. She turns to Jack. "Is he doing the thing in his mind? I can't tell."

"I am, Moira," I tell her.

She steps toward me, her eyes wide. "Can you tell her I made pizza from scratch? Poor thing needs to eat after all of this."

"I'll let her know. She said Sebastian is doing well — better than okay."

"Yes," Jack agrees. "He's still not awake, but he won't need surgery from what we can tell. It's…"

"Magic," I offer.

Jack lets out a sigh. "It's more than that, Theo. You know we haven't seen anything like this healing agent you and Emry emit."

I'm stripping off my hospital gown while he rambles, Moira squealing and turning around.

"And to confuse matters, you aren't bonded with Sebastian."

"Yes, we are," I correct him.

"No, Theo," he argues. "You decided to spend your lives together, and that's noble of you all, but that's not a bond."

"Then why is he better?" I ask. "Why can I hear his thoughts?"

Jack's face lights up. "You can hear his thoughts?"

"Right, but he's not thinking now, so tell me where he is," I say.

"I'll take you," Moira offers, still turned around. "Once you're dressed."

I yank my pants up and spin around looking for a shirt. "Dressed," I say.

"T-Theo," Jack stutters. "This is unheard of. These developments are scientific breakthroughs, unlike anything we've ever imagined. Valuable to humanity."

Moira and I step out of the room, and Jack scurries after us.

"It's valuable to NeXus," I tell Jack.

"Well, yes," he admits. "Any company would pay dearly for a chance to examine this unique phenomenon."

Moira points to the right, and we turn when Emry's voice rings in my head.

"I'm not going back to NeXus unless they support the charity."

"Have them invest in Crowe's Crusade," I tell Jack. "They'll find out about the healing. I'm sure it's all over the news, but tell them there's more. Hold the telepathy card until they agree."

"Crowe's Crusade?" Emry's tone makes me laugh.

"What, you don't like it? I just made it up."

Her excitement makes me smile. *"I like it."*

"Crowe's Crusade?" Jack's voice raises in the question.

"What we talked about, Jack," I say. "Tell them nothing about the mind-reading we have with Sebastian. We use it as leverage to get what we want."

Jack nods and follows me, begging us to talk about this

later. We enter Sebastian's room, and a nurse smiles when we step inside.

He looks good, much better than how we found him hours before.

"He looks good, Em."

"I'll be there soon. Keep him company."

"If they fully fund it and give you their technology, will you allow testing?" Jack asks. "On the three of you? They'll want everyone."

"We'll need to negotiate everything," I say. "I think we need to do some research and discovery before going into this partnership."

"What are you talking about?"

Emry's curiosity swirls inside me, and I pull a chair up to Sebastian's side.

"Get the funding, Jack," I order. "Promise nothing to them yet. Not before talking to me first."

"The healing might be enough," Jack muses. "That supports the spectrum theory."

I lean back in the chair, keeping my eyes on Sebastian, eager for him to wake up.

"The world needs to know that Genome Theory is still around, Jack. Let's get NeXus on board so Sebastian and I can do our work."

CHAPTER 29

TWO WEEKS LATER

THEO

"This is some nice research and discovery," Sebastian says. "I expected to be stuck on a computer, taking notes like I'm in school."

Emry frowns at the comment, thinking about her job. The university is in discussions about her coming back, and I have a few favors called in to ensure it works out. She wants to teach, and we can ease their concerns about security and student attrition.

Once they understand what an attraction she will be to the school and that NeXus will cover proper safety measures, they'll beg for her to come back.

"It's just final arrangements this week, love," I tell her at the sound of her thoughts. "They'd be fools not to let you teach again."

She nods, and we walk across the vast lawn. We're a fifteen-minute walk away from meeting another bonded couple, one that has put their government money to use. A car dropped us off at the gate, informing us most guests take in the scenery on a beautiful day like today.

I didn't know what he meant, but as I pass a bright red artistic sculpture three stories high, I think I'm getting the picture.

"These people are more than wealthy. They are filthy rich."

Emry and Sebastian both nod at my thought.

A landscaper attends to a never-ending bed of flowers and a waterfall trickles in the distance. There are statues along the pathway with vines that crawl up the feet and legs of unrecognizable strangers.

"This is a lot of money and we haven't even gone into their house," Emry muses.

"You know the figures," I sigh, considering this wealth.

It's impossible not to, especially when it's right in front of us. I will partake in the testing and receive the government payments. It's part of NeXus's requirements to approve Crowe's Crusade, but I'm not taking Emry's yes just yet.

I want to be sure it won't traumatize her. She's going to therapy with Jack, and she wants to take part in the testing, but Sebastian and I think she needs more time to think it over. Even without her, it's more money than I could earn in ten lifetimes.

"Right, it's just..." she trails off.

"Audacious," Sebastian offers.

"Impressive," I try.

"Wasteful," she says, her eyes searching the property for anyone who doesn't work here.

Our hosts shouldn't be far. When the driver let us out, he said we could circle the entire property in an hour, but walking straight on the path would get us there on time. The walkway is full of interesting sights, and it gives us a moment with just us three before we meet the happy couple.

I pull the back of Emry's hand to my mouth, kissing her there and feeling her soft skin against my lips. We've already made plans with our stipend and included it in the business proposal for NeXus.

We're setting up funds for anything they won't pay for. That could be extras for the children we find, but mostly, it will be allocated for any unsavory methods to save the kidnapped kids. There aren't sculptures and waterfalls in our plans for the future.

Money talks, but NeXus needs to keep its hands clean. We don't care, and I'll use any means necessary to save a child from the pain Emry suffered. She agrees wholeheartedly, knowing that sometimes shedding blood gets results.

"We aren't here to judge them," Emry shrugs. "It just got me thinking about all that could be done. But it's not our business."

"We'll hit them up for donations," Sebastian offers. That brings a smile to Emry's lips, and it's contagious, spreading between the three of us.

Their manor comes into view, hidden behind hundreds of trees in the center of this property.

"Wow," I gasp.

I've worked with what I considered some of the richest people, owners of large companies, men and women with salaries that had more zeros than I could count, but this is a different kind of prosperity. It's generational wealth when the generations live for hundreds of years, don't need medical care, and keep their fortune in the family.

We all stop in our tracks, jaws agape at the sight.

It's a castle, several stories high, with ornate windows and archways. A row of luxury cars sits in a row on the mile-long driveway, lined up to be washed.

"Maybe we could splurge a little," Sebastian offers.

Emry shoots him a look.

"He could use a new car," I agree, reading Sebastian's thoughts.

She crosses her arms but smiles, shaking her head with a soft laugh.

A few minutes later, we timidly climb the steps to their front door, which is the height of two stories, and I'm wondering how a normal person gets it open.

Maybe keeping people out is the point.

"They're just like us," I tell Emry. "Just another bonded couple."

She's nervous, unsure of what we'll discover once inside.

"I don't know why I'm feeling uneasy," Emry admits. "I've never had a lot of friends, and I'm not really a people person. Bonding is still extremely rare, and I think, maybe, I want them to like us."

"That's normal," I tell her. "We have something important in common, and it would be great to make friends who under-stand and can give us some insight."

"It's not easy for you to trust people," Sebastian adds. "Not for any of us, but let's just see what they have to say."

We stare at each other, wondering how you knock or ring the bell, when the massive door opens and a woman in all white steps out.

She waves with a wide smile, and a man appears at her side. He's dressed casually, a juxtaposition to her traits, dark and sharp to her light and soft features.

"Come in," she says. "I'm Willa and this is Henry."

Henry shakes our hands while Willa offers hugs, Emry calming when the woman's arms wrap around her back.

We follow them through their massive entryway, a machine crank operating the door which answers that mystery, and into a sitting room that could fit hundreds of people. We take a seat on furniture that costs more than our house, and a staff member takes our drink orders.

The woman reaches out to touch us, and Henry whispers to her, "There's no need, Margery."

Her eyes narrow with the information, curious why there are two men sitting with Emry. Sebastian and I both place a hand on her, and the employee notices Sebastian's tattoo, which confuses her further.

"It's alright," Sebastian says, offering her his palm, which she touches before mentioning the drink options.

Sebastian and I order whiskey, and when Emry asks for water, Willa insists on popping champagne for this occasion. She smiles and agrees, her shoulders lowering as she grows more relaxed. The employee, Margery, casually brushes my hand, unsure who is bonded in our situation before she scurries out of the room.

"We were going to reach out," Willa says. "Or, someone would. It's just that you've had some things going on. Well, we wanted to wait until, um..."

Henry places a hand on her thigh and leans forward. "Everyone wanted to respect your privacy because of the unique situation during your bonding."

Willa lets out a long sigh, her cheeks flushing red.

"Thank you," Emry says. "We've worked past the... uniqueness."

"I see that," Henry says, his hand drifting over us in the air. "I'm happy for you three. It's a blessing to add love to the equation, is it not?"

"That's such a lovely way to put it," Emry agrees. "Thank you."

"In Nepal, polyandry was once common practice," Henry explains. "It's typically brothers, but this way of living suits so many families. I'm glad you all have each other."

"Is polyandry this?" Sebastian asks, pointing to the three of us.

"Yes, brother husbands is what it's commonly called in Nepal," Henry says.

"Sebastian and I are brothers," I say, and Henry nods, understanding my meaning.

"Henry has a flair for history," Willa remarks, looking over at him in admiration. "I mean, we have the time."

The champagne and drinks arrive on silver platters. I take in Willa and Henry, noting how he dotes on her and how she enjoys the pleasantries of living like a princess. Henry strikes me as someone who wouldn't care if his drink came in a plastic cup and this show is for her. Even so, she's a kind host, excited to meet us.

"To love," Willa says, raising her glass with the toast.

We all drink and the smooth whiskey warms my stomach.

"How did you two meet?" Emry asks Willa.

Willa's eyes light up with the question, and Henry's head falls back with a cackle.

"This should be a good story," I remark.

"Aren't all love stories good?" Willa beams.

We nod in agreement, ready to listen.

"I was in Mexico on a holiday with my mother. She's settled, and it was back when that all first started. You probably don't remember because, uh—"

"We weren't alive," I chime in.

Willa points a finger at me and grins. "Right, so, settling had just started after the big boom of the bond. The world was really divided."

Emry raises her eyebrows, holding back the comment that

we're all thinking. The world is still divided, settlers and searchers judging each other and the economy siding with those that pour every paycheck into receptions.

"I later found out she was thinking of moving us there," Willa says. "Mexico at the time was one of the first countries that tried to create a settling colony. It didn't last."

"Few did," Sebastian says.

"Oh, do you like history like my Henry? Well, anyway. I'm trying to get a drink at the bar, and the service is terrible. I mean, I waited for twenty minutes and completely lost my buzz."

I can see Henry shaking his head, and I like how it's apparent he still enjoys hearing her tell this story. "Finally, I lose my mind and just go behind the bar, getting a margarita myself. People start lining up for me to get their orders, and the bartender is nowhere to be found, so you know what?"

"You served them some terrible margaritas," Henry chimes in.

She swats at him and then continues talking with her hands. "The terrible bartender—" she says, pointing to him, "—shows up and starts yelling at me about how I can't be back there and I'm giving away all the alcohol. He grabs the tequila from me and BAM, love at first touch."

Henry leans over to give her a kiss and wraps his arm around her shoulders. "I was sick. I shouldn't have been working that day, but you know, I got better right away. Funny how that happens."

We all nod in agreement, Emry telling her how much she enjoyed hearing about their union. When Willa asks about how we met, she gives a much cleaner version that it was a meeting on the street and then changes the subject.

"Your home is beautiful," Emry tells her. "Really, I'm in awe."

"It's ridiculous," Willa says. "I know. When we first started getting the money, we just went a little nuts, but we don't waste the space."

"Oh, really," Emry says. "Is the house used for something else?"

"Yes, it's—"

Henry must say something to stop her, speaking to her without words. I see it in her face, the way it falls for a second before she retrieves her smile.

"I'll take you on a tour later, and show you," she says. "It's better that way."

Sebastian and I take another swig of our whiskey in unison, and Henry raises his eyebrows. These past two weeks, we've all become closer, finishing each other's sentences and predicting our needs, even mirroring behavior. I thought it might be strange for outsiders to see, but Willa and Henry understand.

"Before dinner, let's have a chat about your questions," Henry says.

Willa straightens, adjusting herself in her seat. She's saying something to Henry that we can't hear.

"They'll want their questions answered," he says to her out loud. "And I'd like to have an enjoyable meal together."

"Of course," she says. She drains the glass of champagne, setting it down. Someone comes over to fill it, and she whispers something to them. They nod, leave the room, and she follows, locking the door behind them.

"Seems serious."

Emry and Sebastian nod at my thought.

"We trust everyone that works for us, but it's always best to have some privacy," Henry says.

"That's understandable," I say, wishing I had gotten more whiskey before they left.

"I've kept the bottle, my friend," Henry says.

"Like he read my thoughts."

"Because I did," Henry tells me.

We all freeze, and I do my best to close the door to my mind. Emry shuts hers quickly, while Sebastian never knows when his is open. We've got a long way to go working on our gifts.

"I give you my word. I will not find my way into your mind unintentionally," Henry promises, pressing his palm to his chest. "You are new to the bond, and your frequencies are quite loud. I'm tuning myself to keep the voices silent. It will not take me long."

Willa worries her hands and bites her lip. "I'm sorry. It's been several years since we had someone new. We don't want to be rude. That's the last thing we want to do."

"It's alright," Sebastian says to her.

Red streaks appear on her neck from embarrassment, and it doesn't take long for all three of us to understand what makes Willa tick.

"You don't have a lot of friends," I say to her. My words are too blunt, but Henry just admitted to reading my thoughts, so there's no point in niceties.

Her mouth opens and closes with a loss for words, the red in her cheeks brightening.

"We don't," Henry admits. "You'll find that friendships are difficult to come by. Most bonded pairs live far from each other, desiring some level of privacy. Those you think might be new friends tend to treat you as a spectacle or a meal ticket."

"Or try to sell your private moments and secrets to the press," Willa huffs. "You three are the closest bonded to us. You're about an hour away. That is... if you don't move."

"We aren't moving," Emry tells her. "And I'm so sorry.

That's very difficult, being betrayed by someone you thought you could trust, someone you thought cared for you."

Willa wipes a tear from her cheek, and Henry tightens his arm around her, hugging her from the side.

"I heard about your mother," Willa says. "I'm so sorry. What I've been through is nothing compared to that, but I've definitely had some hurts over the years."

"I'd like to be friends," Emry says. "We'd all like that."

Willa's face brightens. "We heard you might go back to teaching at the university. Henry would love to enroll in some of your classes if that's possible."

"If it works out, I think you would be a wonderful student, Henry," Emry agrees.

Henry fills our whiskey, letting us know he has some contacts at other universities if needed. He understands the need to find purpose and explains that as much as not working sounds like a dream, the days become maddening if there isn't something to fill them.

"Sebastian, I'm having difficulty tuning you out," Henry says, his forehead creasing with effort.

"Honestly, I don't know how I'm even tuned in," Sebastian admits. "Sorry."

He shrugs, tapping a finger on the whiskey glass.

"Well, that must be part of your special," Willa beams. "That's so wonderful because the three of you are together."

"Yes," Henry agrees.

"I'm sorry, what?" I ask.

They both look at me with knowing smiles, and I lean forward, ready to talk about why we came here.

"Why can we hear Sebastian and vice versa?" I ask. "And why are we smoking like a chimney every time someone gets hurt? And what the hell... is a special?"

CHAPTER 30

"We keep some things private from the annual testing when we can," Henry explains. His calm demeanor grows more serious as he continues, occasionally looking at the door in case someone barges through the lock. "There are reports of some... exploitation when certain skills of the bonded came to light."

"Who did that?" Sebastian asks. "Was it NeXus?"

"No, no," Willa assures me. "The government performed the testing before these large research facilities were created. The government funds them now for testing, but back then, it was, oh, what do they call it?"

"The wild west," Henry says with a smile. "Complete chaos, and when specials appeared in some of the bonded, well, unsavory methods weren't far behind."

I feel my heart race, sweat pricking at the back of my neck. Theo agreed to do the annual testing, using the money for a cause I care so much about, but I can't help my physical reaction to this news.

Theo runs his hand up my thigh, sensing the unease, and I force myself to suck in a slow and even breath.

"It hasn't happened in over fifty years," Willa explains.

My breath escapes, and I count backward to myself, hoping I don't look as stiff and terrified as I feel.

"As an extra precaution, it's best to keep some things that will present themselves over time secret. That is, if you have the ability," Henry adds. "You can't do anything about the healing. That's fairly common, and the government is aware of a version of that in some sectors. Certainly not it extending beyond the bonded, but your situation is—"

"Unique," I chime in.

"Yes," Henry agrees.

"We are sorry about the media's attention to it," I say, my voice apologetic.

Henry shakes his head. "Don't be sorry. In truth, you may never know what causes a special or how to control it. It could pop out unannounced anytime. Some things are inside and easier to keep secret."

He points to his stomach, and I know what he means. It's the feeling that takes over, controlling your mind and limbs without you knowing.

"But if you figure one out, try to get control of it before the testing," Willa explains.

I down the rest of my champagne, necessary given the conversation, and Willa reaches for the bottle.

"What are your specials?" I ask her. "Is that rude to ask? I don't know the etiquette around this."

Willa fills my glass and waves her hand in response. "Oh, no," she says. "We're very open around other bonded people. There's trust between us all. I can read other bonded's minds like Henry can. Sometimes it's not clear, and I try not to lurk in other's thoughts. We also have some healing elements, although it's not as strong as yours. No chimney smoke."

We all let out a small chuckle.

"Some bonded pairs dream together in a hibernation state," she explains. "There's a couple in Africa that will sleep for months at a time creating their own world together."

"They say it helps with the heat," Henry jokes.

"Oh, let's see," Willa muses. "The oldest couple has healing, expanded telepathy like me and Henry, some shared dreaming. Everything may come to all of us over time. We don't know yet because this is still new in the scheme of things."

"Do they have telepathy with anyone else?" I ask, my eyes drifting to Sebastian.

"You mean a person outside the bond?" Henry confirms.

"Yes," I answer. "Like someone they're close with?"

Henry and Willa look at each other and then back at us.

"Some can hear other bonded couples like us, but the non-bonded..." she drifts off, looking over Sebastian. "It's new that someone not in a bond holds a special. I've never heard of that before. He's a part of your bond somehow, and that's just wonderful."

We all nod in unison.

"But no one settled has ever bonded," Henry adds. "So, you are an anomaly."

I laugh at his comment, curious if I should take it as a compliment.

"There have been cases of healing in our children and the same with others," Willa explains. "That's the most prevalent special, appearing for almost everyone at first. It's no surprise that we can pass that on somehow. Once my son broke his leg clear in half and I had it healed in about a week. Not as strong as you three, but it's something."

My mouth drops in shock, but I pick up my jaw, trying not to be someone who treats them as a spectacle. I may be bonded, but that's no excuse to be rude.

"I have a question," Theo says. "I'm not sure if you can answer or not, but I... we need to know."

"Anything," Henry says. "We are open to anything and everything. After this many years, it takes a lot to shock us."

"I know the feeling," Sebastian muses and gives me a wink.

"What happens if I die? Will Emry..." Theo trails off.

We all hold our breath, waiting for the answer. Henry leans back in his seat and slaps his hands on his thighs.

"Well, the theory has never been tested," he says. "But we believe one cannot live without the other. That's the consensus amongst the group."

"What about Sebastian?" Theo asks. That question never occurred to me. There's some piece of our bond that extends to him, but does that mean we're connected in the same way?

Henry sighs, his eyes squinting toward the ceiling, deciding how to answer. "Our children can't heal each other or share dreams, but they benefit from our specials. We've seen this in a few of them. We may even be unknowingly healing our loved ones of ailments and, therefore, extending their life. Maybe abnormal cells appear and we're killing them off with our proximity. There's a child of a bonded that's fifty years beyond normal life expectancy."

"I didn't know that," I say. "How do people not know that?"

"They faked her death," Willa says and takes a sip of champagne.

There's a moment of silence where Sebastian, Theo, and I look at each other, shocked by the admission.

"Privacy," Willa explains. "It's important to us. We give the government enough. Enough to think they are making headway on the bond, but never everything."

"Right," I say. My head swims from the information and champagne, and I set down my glass, trying to give my body a moment to catch up.

"So, I could live longer," Sebastian whispers, his voice smaller than I've ever heard before.

"You could," Henry says. "But eventually…"

"I know," Sebastian says. "Trust me. The topic has come up."

"When children die, it hurts deeply." Willa pauses, collecting herself before she continues. "But there's not a negative physical response. I think when you go, Sebastian, that it won't affect Theo and Emry."

There's a knock at the door and Willa gets up, all of us taking in everything we've learned in such a short amount of time. Willa speaks to her employee and turns around with a clap of her hands.

"Dinner's ready," she announces.

"We can continue our conversation in there," Henry says. "As long as you're okay to serve yourselves. I like my food hot and fresh."

We agree, eager to hear more about the bond.

The conversation and questions never stop, and I struggle to get bites in before I think of something else to ask. Willa and Henry know every single bonded. Everyone has spoken to each other once at the very least, but several years tick by without them seeing another bonded.

Willa's face deflates with this admission. "It's just something that happens. You have all the time in the world, so you don't make any."

I promise her that's not what we intend to do, and we schedule a time for them to come to dinner at our house in the coming months. She's warned that the presentation won't be anything like theirs, even though Sebastian is an excellent cook. When she says that doesn't bother her in the least, I believe her. This lifestyle is for them, and we don't have to be at this standard to remain friends.

We go through ten courses, and I'm still brimming with questions. The champagne flows while we talk about every bonded, and I curse myself for not making notes. When we discuss our mission, Crowe's Crusade, Henry and Willa light up.

"That's a wonderful cause," Willa says. "We'd love to help in any way we can."

"Willa's charity focuses on animal rescue," Henry says. "It would be nice to add some humans to the mix."

She swats at him again and he pretends she harmed him, buckling over in his seat in laughter.

"I didn't know you had a charity you run," I tell her. "What is it?"

"I only run one charity, but we donate to thousands anonymously," she says. "It's easier to spread it so the press doesn't catch wind. We have one employee that manages all the requests for money alone. That's her full-time job. Be prepared for that."

"We want press about this," Sebastian says. "People need to know what's happening out there. They need to hear about the lost citizens and children."

We all nod in agreement, letting a silent pause fill the dining room. There are four chandeliers above our heads, and I'm sitting in a chair that's been hand-embroidered. I'm happy to hear that Willa and Henry spend their money doing good, but this luxury isn't for us.

Sebastian needs a new car, but I doubt it would be anything with a hefty price tag. It's not something that we desire. Finding the people lost to Genome, that's where I want to spend my dollars.

The last course is finished, and I ask Willa about the rest of the house. This lifestyle may not be for me, but I'm curious to see the splendors.

Willa inhales sharply, and Henry gives her a kiss on the cheek.

"What do you think?" he asks her. "Divide up, men and women. Give you girls some alone time."

"Yes." She exhales, and her demeanor has changed, a sadness sweeping over her features. "That might be best."

CHAPTER 31

Willa and I ride the elevator to the fifth floor while she bites her lip and fidgets with her hands. I can't read people as well as Theo can, but she's nervous, worried about showing me something inside this house.

"I'm sure the rest of your home is just as beautiful," I say, confused about what we're about to see that could put her in such a state.

"It's more practical," she says. "We use the other floors for businesses and we occasionally have a school."

"A school?" I question.

"Some of the bonded's children don't go to traditional school," she explains. "They find it difficult amongst everyone. There are about a thousand kids right now who choose to attend a bonded school. Several houses provide a full class-room and they change where they have schooling every semester. When it's here, they use the third floor."

I wonder if that's some unsaid rule in this bonded society.

Is it expected that a portion of the funds go to this carousel of schools?

"Have you thought about children?" Willa asks.

"Oh, I, um, I—" I stutter.

"I'm sorry," she rushes out. "That was incredibly rude. I need to get out more and work on my manners."

I wave my hands at her as the elevator stops and the doors open. It occurs to me we should bring the topic up to Theo, and soon. He's a part of this family and even though he's going to say something about how he thought he'd be dead, so he's fine with anything, I want to know his input. So will Sebastian.

"You're fine. Sebastian and I decided it's a no for now, but that was before the bond," I sigh. "So much has happened recently, and we just haven't had time to think about it. We're still navigating the relationship between all of us."

We step out into an open room where a woman sits behind a desk. It reminds me of a reception area in the doctor's office with a dozen chairs, soft lighting, and floral artwork. There's something childlike about the paintings, and I step over to one, noticing the smudging of colors that aren't quite right.

"My grandson made that," Willa says, stepping over to the woman at the desk and asking her to get us gowns.

Gowns?

"Oh, it's lovely," I tell her.

"My grandchildren and great-grandchildren made all of these," she explains. "Their artwork is all over this floor. I had it framed."

I smile at the painting, enjoying it more now that I know it holds such sentimental value. "How many do you have?"

"Grandchildren, or great-grandchildren, or..." she drifts off. "Paintings?"

I turn to her, tilting my head as the employee brings over two hospital gowns.

"How old are you?" I regret the question once I ask, and attempt to pedal back. "I'm sorry. That's actually very rude, bonded or not."

Willa laughs and hands me a gown. "We'll need to wash up over here, and I'm about a hundred years older than you. I lose count sometimes. It was maybe a decade after Christa Sanders and Leo Thomason. They were household names back then."

"Still are," I tell her. "I mean, I talk about them in my lectures."

"That's right," she says, remembering our chat at dinner about the university. "You will certainly have an interesting class going forward. Firsthand knowledge on genetic research."

I raise my eyebrows and silently hope that I enter a lecture hall again soon. Those kids may have driven me crazy with their obsession with the bond, but I'm more understanding these days. It was never my right to judge them.

"This way," Willa says, leading me forward.

There's a washroom through the first set of doors, and my curiosity is at an all-time high. Part of me thinks I should open my mind to Theo and Sebastian, speak to them, and tell them what I'm seeing, but I'm nervous. Willa said she wanted to visit privately, and I'll respect that.

Henry may promise to stay out of our heads, but I don't know these people and Sebastian's right. I don't trust easily. Still, I'll honor her wishes until she gives me a reason not to.

"I want to introduce you to some of my family," Willa says. "Now some of them are medically fragile. They're old and we try to limit illnesses and germs."

"Of course," I say, taking a mask from her. We take our temperature, and Willa checks me over to ensure I have everything on properly.

"Okay, are you ready?" she asks.

"I think so," I answer. "I'm just not sure what for."

Willa clasps her hands at her front. "Right, well, it's hard to explain, but it's something I think you need to see. All bonded need to, really. Over the years, we've learned that."

I don't know what to say other than, "Okay, I'm ready."

She ushers us through another set of doors and the floor stretches out before us, beams of light from the ceiling funneling through. Large glass windows appear along the walls and the steady sounds of air rushing through and soft beeps come from several rooms.

It's a hospital, and there is no expense spared.

A nurse walks up, greeting Willa, and she introduces me. She eyes me with excitement, and I wonder how many strangers she meets in this line of work.

"I think it's a good day to see Thomas," Willa says.

The nurse's face falls, and she looks down at her tablet. "Not much time left."

"We're lucky to have as long as it's been," Willa tells her, resting a hand on her shoulder. She hooks her arm into mine. "Come on, now, Emry. Let's meet my eighth-born son."

I have to hold back the gasp that threatens to escape, fearful I'll offend her with the shock. We walk through the hospital equipped with everything from X-ray machines to a small cafeteria and a full staff.

"We treat only our family and families of other bonded," Willa explains. "But it's a full house. I had twelve children before I just couldn't anymore."

"Oh, do you mean? Well, is that because of, um," I ramble, unsure of what I'm asking.

We don't age like other people, but is there a biological clock for the bonded? Will Theo, Sebastian, and I need to make decisions sooner rather than later?

Willa takes in a shuddered breath, and we stop in front of a door. Cards are taped to the front, and I notice one reads *We love you, Thomas*, written in marker in a child's handwriting.

"I just couldn't do it anymore emotionally," she admits. "When I got pregnant with my twelfth child, my oldest was nearing a hundred, and she didn't have a lot of time left. She never got to meet her youngest brother."

Willa's eyes well with tears, and I'm hit with another hurt that may happen to our family. Parents are supposed to die first, but that's not the case for the bonded.

"It hurt too much. Watching her go felt so wrong, and I had a hard time with the rest of my pregnancy. It was a terrible situation," Willa continues. "And Henry and I decided it was best to stop."

Her words hit me in the gut, wrecking my insides. This is why she didn't want to tell me before dinner about this part of the house. I need to see this to understand.

"Is this a type of initiation?" I ask her.

She lets go of my arm, placing a hand on the door, ready to push inside.

"It's a warning," she corrects me. "My children, grandchildren, and on and on, they give me so much purpose, but nothing can prepare you for the cemetery of loved ones you'll bury. I want you to know everything before you make any decisions. We all do."

The door opens, and an elderly man rests in a hospital bed. There's a large birdcage in the corner, and a macaw rests on his stomach, its neon blue feathers taking me by surprise.

"Oh, wow," I say, stepping to Thomas's bedside. He's asleep, peacefully resting while Willa pulls up a chair for herself and takes his hand.

"This is Thomas. And this," she motions to the bird with a look of disgust, "is Porty."

I sputter out a laugh. "Porty? Well, it's a beautiful bird."

"How about another lesson, Emry," Willa warns. "These birds live for over fifty years, so if one of your children gets one when they're nearing ninety years old, you're volunteered to be the god-parent."

She mimics putting her finger in her throat and making a vomit sound. The bird squeaks an inaudible word at her.

"Oh, my," I say. "I'll take that to heart."

I sit down on the other side of Thomas, watching the slow breaths of this man that she and Henry created. My heart hangs heavy in my chest knowing even if we decide never to have children, this will be something I'll need to suffer through.

There's nothing more beautiful than a place like this to spend your last days, but that doesn't take away the sorrow.

"Willa, if I have any family that..." I trail off, the question catching in the back of my throat.

"Sebastian would be welcome to come here anytime," she says. "But we also have portable medical beds and nurses. Your family will always be well taken care of."

"Thank you," I manage to get out.

"Of course," she says. "You're a part of the bonded family now. And I think, well, I'd like to say that so are the children."

"The children?" I ask, confused.

"Genome Theory, if they are still out there, as you say, they'll have lots of lost little souls," she sighs, recalling our conversation from dinner. "They're welcome here if they need medical care."

"That's so generous," I say, and with her offer, I make my decision about children.

One that will change our lives.

One that I know is right.

CHAPTER 32

"They want to do a ninety-day trial run," Jack explains.

"Trial run for what?" I argue, opening the file emailed to us all.

We ended up staying with Willa and Henry for a few days, enjoying their palace hidden in the woods. It was easy to turn off phone notifications and talk openly with people who understand and are wise beyond our years. Now we're back home, going over the business plan for Crowe's Crusade.

"There's still a lot of doubt that Genome Theory has the stronghold you're proposing," Jack explains. "They don't want to fully fund this project until they have a news story they can run that will help their reputational status, boost their numbers, and prove this is a non-profit that won't be challenged."

I scoff at his answer, flipping through the pages of their documents.

"It's just business," Jack explains. "You, out of everyone in this room, should understand that."

He's right. I'm a business person through and through, or I was not long ago.

Everything is different since the bond. The way I see the world changed, and I won't waste an opportunity to do something with my extra time on this earth. It doesn't matter that I have hundreds of years. I have a life to live and lives to save, and we need to get started.

"Without their funding, we still have enough to do this. NeXus isn't the deciding factor," Sebastian reminds me. He's right that we'll have money. Everyone signed the testing agreements while we were with Willa and Henry.

They assured us we could go together and get comfortable with the process for the first few years. Even with that stipend, we need NeXus to succeed. They have technology that will change the game and get us to Genome's underground hideouts faster.

"Monday morning, we get to work. Ninety days is plenty of time, especially with everything you've already uncovered," Jack says, taking the tablet from me and turning it off. "Leave all this for tomorrow. You have a big day with some exciting stuff, I hear."

Moira's been talking, but I can't blame her. She's almost as excited as I am.

"Are you coming with us?" I ask him.

"Moira and I had some plans, but I'm happy to cancel," Jack offers.

I shrug and lean back in my chair. "No worries. I know it's last minute. We don't want anything leaked, and we're lucky we got it approved."

"I understand," Jack says. "Best to strike when the iron's hot, as they say."

Sebastian nudges Jack on the arm, almost sending him out of his chair. "When's it your turn, Jack?" he asks him.

He smiles and shrugs his shoulders, not giving anything away. If he hurts Moira, I may murder him, which would be too bad because I like the guy.

Alison and Emry skip into the room, both dressed from Emry's closet. Emry's wearing a green floor-length gown that hugs her curves in all the right ways. I remember it from a shared vision when I first came to the house, and my cheeks flush with heat at the sight of her. I can't get over how beautiful this woman is, inside and out.

"You going fishing?" I ask her.

Alison's face twists in confusion, and her mouth opens in question. Emry giggles, swaying the bottom of her dress back and forth.

Sebastian and I are dressed and ready except for our suit jackets, which hang by the door. Alison is bouncing on her toes with excitement while Emry is calm, at peace with what the day brings.

It's surprising, considering this is our first trip out into the city since we bonded. She's been to the hospital and NeXus, but today we are going together for the settlement ceremony, and people will recognize us.

"Lucas is here," Alison says, looking down at her phone. "We were wondering if you wanted to go to dinner after. Your choice, but he says his friend has a restaurant and they can give us a private room to celebrate."

I open my mouth to object, but Emry cuts me off. "That would be lovely. Don't you think?"

She looks at me and Sebastian and we both nod, our eyes still glued to how gorgeous she looks in that damn dress.

She and Willa spent almost every waking moment

together, and in that time, something in Emry soothed when it came to her place with the bonded and out in the world.

I knew she needed time to accept everything, but I never expected it would happen so fast. I can't see anything in her mind that flipped the switch with such assuredness, but I don't want to ask her and risk upsetting our bliss.

We see Jack and Moira out, all piling into a car together before it hits me.

I'm getting married today.

I don't hide my thoughts from Emry and Sebastian, who both turn to me with bright smiles.

"Yes we are," Emry says. "I can't wait to be your wife, too."

"Have we decided on a name for us?" Sebastian asks.

"Brother-husbands," Emry answers. "Like Henry mentioned."

Sebastian adjusts his suit jacket, and I can tell he's uncomfortable wearing something so confining. It's kind of him to do it for us.

"I like that. Works for me," he agrees, fidgeting with the collar of his shirt.

"So, just to double-check," Alison says. "We are not going fishing, right? I'm not dressed for that."

Emry lets out a cackle, and we head out, Alison's question unanswered.

The drive through the city is uneventful, and when the Tattoo Emporium comes into view, the crowds thin to only a few passersby. It's not a busy place. Beautiful, but quiet, and I let out a sigh of relief.

Henry and Willa were kind enough to confirm the laws with us regarding settling. It doesn't state that it must be between just two people. The verbiage speaks as if it is a couple, meaning only two, but everything has a loophole.

Those in the bonded community have some of the best

attorneys in the world, and within hours, we had an approved marriage between the three of us. It helped we hadn't signed the testing agreement yet. We held a carrot out for the government and a piece of paper with a tattoo wasn't a big price to pay.

It was everything to us, though.

Everything to me.

I worried that word would get out and we would arrive to find a crowd of onlookers, but only a few people walk along the street. Emry goes to open the door, and I stop her.

"Do you want to wait for those people to walk on?" I ask. "Keep this private?"

"It's going to get out eventually," she shrugs. "I'm proud of you, of us. And any time anyone talks to me, all I'm going to talk about is Crowe's Crusade, so a little publicity can't hurt."

She flashes a wide smile before she pops out of the car, the green fabric flowing behind her. She's a goddess, confident and sure of what we're here for today. I've never felt her so happy, and it bleeds into me, almost making me jump for joy.

It doesn't hurt that the university agreed to allow her to resume her classes on Monday. The students have been on pause, so she'll need to work hard to expedite the lesson plan and extend it to the summer for those who don't want to drop, but I can tell she's up for the challenge.

We walk together past another bridal party, ready for the big day. No one seems to recognize our faces as we go into the shop, and the manager greets us with a strong handshake. We've had some email exchanges, so none of this is a shock to him, and he signed the nondisclosure agreement without hesitation, citing that love is love.

I like him immediately.

The tattoo artist comes by to say hello and look at the design. She's dressed up as well, which is tradition, but it's another reminder that this is happening. We're going to have a ceremony, and I'm getting tattooed with the Crowe name.

She inspects Sebastian and Emry's wrists, taking a stencil of one and excusing herself to draw before the person performing the ceremony comes over with the paperwork.

"This is happening," Alison squeals as we all step onto a podium. Lucas lets out a chuckle and shakes his head, still confused about this situation, but supportive nonetheless.

The three of us don't need every detail of our future figured out to know what we want — what we need. This family is what's most important, and I'm desperate to get that ink on my skin.

"We're ready," Emry announces.

"Right," the man says, handing over the paperwork. "Really, you don't need me to do more than witness. You, um, know your vows?"

We all nod.

"Okay, well, after you say them to each other, you'll sign. Then Trish will be ready to add the name."

This feels simple and right, and I'm taken aback that we made it all the way here. After every trial along the way, I'm standing with the two most important people in the world, about to promise them forever.

"Ready?" Emry asks, taking our hands. We face each other in a circle, Sebastian and I both nodding. Alison starts to cry and blows her nose, elated for her friend and maybe considering this ceremony for herself and Lucas.

"Let's say them together," Sebastian offers.

"Yes," Emry and I say in unison.

We count down in our heads and say the vows together out loud.

This vow I make to you of my own free will, to never separate

or stray. Our bond of mind and spirit will forever unite us as one. I will honor our commitment for all the days to come, from this day forward, until death do us part.

"Is that it?" Alison asks through her sobs.

"That's it," Sebastian answers her.

"That's everything," Emry chokes out.

The tattoo artist steps forward and offers me her hand, leading me to the chair. Sebastian and Emry sit on either side, her head resting on my shoulder, watching as they prep my wrist.

The needle starts slightly pinching, but the pain is minimal. That doesn't stop a faint mist that pours from Emry, seeping into the wound. The woman pauses, her eyes flicking up to me.

"It's okay," I tell her. "Keep going."

She smirks. "I saw the, um, story about your..." She trails off, unsure what to call them.

"Was there just one?" Emry asks, half-joking.

The artist shakes her head and chuckles. "You three are all anyone can talk about."

The C comes to life on my wrist, and I feel a lump form in the back of my throat. My dad would be proud, and not because I'm settled or bonded. He would find happiness in my joy, peace that I found love, and a family.

"He would be thrilled for us."

Emry's thought makes it difficult to keep it together, but I suck in a breath and square my jaw, not wanting anything to delay the letters from forming on my wrist.

"Are you sure we want to go to dinner?" Sebastian asks us. "Sounds like we'll be a topic of conversation."

Emry shrugs. "We need to eat."

Alison stands in the doorway, and Emry pops her head up.

The tattoo is almost complete, outlined, and ready for the fill-in.

"It's up to you if you want to go," Alison says. "He's holding the room."

"How about I go, and you and Emry head back home," Sebastian offers.

I jerk my head around and find Emry narrowing her eyes at him.

"What?" we both ask, ready to argue.

He can't wipe the grin from his face when he says, "It's your wedding night."

CHAPTER 33

They finish Theo's tattoo, and the offer hangs in the air between all of us. Theo stares at it while we talk, in awe that we're all together this way. It doesn't take much convincing to accept time alone with him, and something about the wedding changes things.

We've made vows that no one intends to break. Not even the bond split Sebastian and me, so a solo night with Theo doesn't feel like a problem.

Before I know it, we're taking a separate car home. I run my thumb across Theo's wrist, already healed thanks to our special.

He's pensive, his thoughts bouncing between our future, the wedding, and everything he wants to do in our bed.

I'm flushed from head to toe, almost dripping down my legs by the time we make it home.

Theo and I get dropped off at the front door, the driver pulling away when we step inside.

The house is dark, with only a small light from the kitchen illuminating the front entrance.

I almost trip over some shoes left out by Alison, ones she changed four times back and forth before we left. A heel gets tangled up in the fabric of my dress, and I shake the skirt, hoping I'm not ripping the fabric to get it free.

The door shuts behind Theo, and the lock clicks into place as the heel tumbles to the wooden floor.

It's quiet, too quiet. Only our uneven breaths make any noise inside the house.

Sebastian and I talked about this at Willa and Henry's. We discussed the idea of Theo and me being alone for the first time.

The two men aren't attracted to each other, enjoying instead watching me find pleasure with the other. I don't know if that will change.

All I know is in the future we'll share intimacy between the three of us, but this first time will be private.

Sebastian said he wanted it that way, but standing alone with Theo in the dark, I'm not sure of anything. After endless discussions about this night, I'm no more ready for it to be time.

The bond between us knows, and it's impossible to ignore. My skin is on fire with angst while my heart pounds so hard in my chest that I'm sure Theo hears its rhythm.

Through the shadows, I watch him unbutton his jacket with shaking fingers, hanging it on the wall by the door. I take off my shoes, letting them fall by all the pairs Alison left behind.

We're still standing by the front door in near darkness, half undressed, about to give in to the bond that's been screaming for this moment since that fateful day in front of Moira's shop.

I reach around and unzip the back of the dress, letting it

slip to my shoulders and hang loose at my chest. Theo's excitement won't stop gushing from him. His rapid pulse floods my ears, and the euphoric thrill of what's coming bounces back and forth between us.

Say something.

I can't make myself speak, and neither can he.

The wall in my mind is down, and I'm nervous, but it will stay that way.

I've considered this for days, curious if it would be too much, but when Alison pointed out the benefits far outweigh the disadvantages, I realized knowing everything the other is thinking and feeling would help us both.

"He would have a user's manual to your body," she said. "A play-by-play of your thoughts."

"I know," I argued with her. "That sounds mortifying."

"Does it? Remember your first time with Sebastian? I know he's great, but you can't tell me that was perfect," she scoffed. "There's a learning curve with sex, and you could skip all of that. Everywhere you want to be touched, speed, positions..."

"Okay, I get it," I relented.

She was right, and as nervous as it makes me, I'll let him see inside my thoughts and give him everything he needs to make this right.

Theo groans, a hand slapping the wall to keep him steady while the other reaches for his throbbing cock.

"We don't..." He pauses, catching his breath. "We don't have to. Only if... if you're ready."

"Theo, I think we are both past ready," I say. "Can you please just—"

His mouth finds mine in the dark, hot and wet, the pressure taking me by surprise. I trip over the mess of shoes, and he catches me, hoisting me into the air, my legs wrapping around his waist. The ripping sound of my dress only fuels our fire.

We feel our way to the bedroom with a few shoulder and hip bumps along the wall until I'm thrown onto the bed, the front of my dress falling to my waist. His shirt opens with the pop of buttons, and I sit up, reaching for the waistband of his pants, fumbling with the clasps.

I can't tell anymore what fabric is tearing and flying, Theo's pants or my dress. All I know is we're both naked in record time, and I'm staring at his waiting cock that glistens at the tip.

"Are you—"

"If you ask me if I'm sure or ready one more time, I'll lose it, Theo," I bark. My words are commanding, desperate for him to be inside me.

He smiles, his chest expanding with a deep inhale of breath. Our bond riots inside us, pulling us together like magnets. His face strains with the struggle, and I understand. Neither of us wants anything quick, but we can't fight this anymore.

"I want this to last but..."

His thoughts mimic my own.

"Don't worry about that. We've got... forever."

My legs open as he crawls over me, his lips, chest, and hips meeting with mine. All of his worries and fears rush through, and I kiss him, sending him assurances it will be alright.

"It will be good because we love each other. Trust me."

His lips trail along the sensitive part of my neck.

"I trust you. Tell me what feels good, love."

I'm dripping onto the sheets as his tip lines up with my entrance, my fingernails digging into his back.

Kisses line my collarbone as he inches inside. "I love you," he says out loud, as he pushes in to the hilt.

His first thrust sends sparks through my body that settle at my core and swirl with pleasure. With his second, the feeling amplifies, something new and foreign making me cry out.

"Do you feel that, Theo?"

He moves his face to mine, our lips barely touching. "Are you serious with that question?" he rushes out.

Another thrust, and I scream, "Oh, fuck!" The magnitude of what we're doing rushes into my body, sending waves of ecstasy into every place Theo touches.

He groans, his arms wrapping around my back, almost lifting me off of the bed. His movements become steady and controlled, but urgent, pushing in and out of me. Each time he fills me up, the seal of our bond grows and morphs into something about to explode.

It's like I'm floating out of my body, overtaken with pleasure, unable to control my movements or thoughts. I never want him to stop, and it occurs to me he won't. We're married, and this moment can happen over and over for as long as we both need, for as long as we want.

The darkness fades in the room, a band of colorful light trickling around us both.

"Do you see that?"

My thoughts are on him, the rapture of his body, the way his cock fits perfectly inside, but I can't help that I notice it looks like someone turned on a holiday tree inside our room.

"All I see is you, Emry."

I whimper at his words, my body taking more of him, deeper and harder. My climax inches closer with every movement, touch, and kiss. I see him clearly in the bright lights, bands of color that whip around our bodies, illuminating his face.

His head falls back in ecstasy, his jaw falling slack. He sits up, never separating our bodies, and lowers his hands to my waist.

Holding me there, his steady thrusts make my back slide on the sheets as our eyes meet. His thighs slide under mine, my hips lifted at the perfect angle that exposes my clit for his every stroke.

The muscles in his chest and arms flex as he drives into me, and I cling to the sheets, pulling them from the sides of the bed.

I'm not sure what I expected, but this surpasses anything my imagination has created.

He can read my mind, which is no doubt how we ended up in my favorite position, his cock buried deep and my back arched off the bed. His wide hands keep my most sensitive areas against him, the pressure and angle so perfect I'm struggling to hold back my orgasm.

I'm whimpering with every push and pull of our bodies, the light brightening until I'm forced to close my eyes.

I don't want to shut them.

I want to see him when he comes.

"Emry," he gasps, his thrusts coming faster. "I'm about to."

The climax hits and I lose control, my hands clawing at his body as I lift myself until I'm sitting in his lap, my arms wrapped around his neck. The sound of us coming together echoes in my ears. Our bare chests touch, my sensitive nipples grazing across his skin. My lips find his by touch, both of us still blinded by the streaks of color we see beyond our closed eyelids.

I'm straddling him, taking control as my orgasm peaks, and I scream into his mouth. Nails scratch into each other's skin, hearts pound in time with one another, and we move together until I feel him explode inside me.

He pulls his mouth away with a roar, the bed rocking with us, threatening to collapse. His heat fills me, and I tremble as the waves of our climax ricochet between us both.

I'm crying and moaning, my lips against his neck, holding on with weak limbs with his final push inside before he moves one hand to the bed, lowering us both back to the tangled sheets.

We don't speak, still dealing with the aftershocks of our orgasms that ping back and forth while we hold each other.

"I love you, too," I say, realizing I never said it back.

He lets out a soft chuckle, our breathing slowing, the multi-colored lights fading around us so we can open our eyes.

"Wow," he whispers, his grip around me loosening.

"I know, I—"

Knock. Knock. Knock.

We both jolt from the sound of the door, the light fading to a darkened room with the break in our focus.

Knock. Knock. Knock.

A voice calls from the door, but I can't make out the words.

"I bet it's the guards," Theo says.

I slap my palm against my forehead in awareness. Maybe they heard us during sex, not to mention we projected beams of light from inside this room. I'm terrified to check if the blinds are closed.

Theo rises, heading to the bathroom before he goes to the door. "I'm coming," he yells, throwing on a pair of pants when they knock again.

A creak sounds through the room, and I sit up, knowing what's about to happen.

"Get off the—" Theo blurts out, but it's too late.

The bed crashes to the floor, sending me bouncing on the mattress.

The romantic moment ends with a literal thud.

CHAPTER 34

THEO

"It was Milo," I tell Emry. She's buried herself underneath the covers on the lopsided bed, her face in her hands.

"I'm mortified," she says. "Don't tell me what he said."

"Okay," I agree, but she hears my thoughts. I can't help letting them seep through.

She groans and shivers at the idea of Milo checking in to make sure everyone's okay. The comical smile on his face and the laughter in his tone are unmistakable. I would guess all the guards dared him to go up to the house, and he did so as a joke because he had a good excuse.

"Let's just fix this," Emry whines, but she's smiling when she says the words. She almost tumbles off one side of the broken bed, making a ta-da motion with her hands when she gets to her feet.

We are almost finished when Sebastian arrives home earlier than expected, and we call out to him when we hear the front door open.

"So, you won't believe what happened," I say nervously as he steps inside the bedroom. We're sitting on the floor with an open toolkit, reinforcing the bed. I don't want there to be any competition in the bedroom between us. Emry and I haven't discussed their sex life much, only that it's equally amazing, and I'm not going to brag about a broken bed. It's best to make fun of ourselves for this.

He rushes to the closet before I can explain, seeming unbothered that the bedroom is a construction site.

"Are you alright?" I ask. I can't pinpoint Sebastian's feelings, but something is off.

"Yeah, I'm just, well, Alison is out there," he says, yanking clothing from drawers. "She'll tell you all about it. Can't fucking wait."

"Brave of her to come in," Emry jokes. "What if we were... you know."

"Oh, she knows you're done," Sebastian bites out and slams a dresser drawer.

I look at Emry, both of us sharing the same confusion. We can't hear Sebastian's thoughts, which is terrible timing because we have no idea what he's talking about.

I hear Alison laughing from our living room, and I shake the side of the bed again, testing that the bolt I put in makes it secure enough. Knowing what Sebastian and I can do to Emry in here, it may need to be made out of steel. I strongly consider that and throw the wrench into the toolbox. The other side can wait until we deal with whatever happened during dinner.

"Did you break the bed?" Sebastian asks with a lopsided smirk.

Emry skips out into the living room to talk with Alison, and I grab the toolbox to put it to the side.

"Yes," I answer with a shrug.

Sebastian throws his clothes in the hamper and responds, "Nice."

"What's up? Why are you so agitated?" I ask him.

He puts his hands on his hips and looks to the floor, tapping his foot and sucking in a harsh breath.

"And why are you back so early?" I continue. "Did something happen at dinner?"

"Yeah," Sebastian says. "Something happened at dinner."

We stand in silence, Sebastian staring at his shoes as I try to see inside his mind. That would be easier, and at some point, I'd like to go back to Henry and Willa's and ask if they have any more guidance about our specials.

Emry lets out a squeal of laughter from the living room and then silences herself. Muffled giggles make their way into the room, and without speaking a word, it comes to me.

I understand what happened to Sebastian at dinner.

"You know," I sigh, shoving the toolbox to the side with my foot and stepping closer to Sebastian. "When Jack took me to NeXus that first day, I got there before you and Emry. You two were still at home. Do you remember what you were doing?"

Sebastian looks up at me, head tilted in thought. One side of his mouth rises in a smile when he recalls that day.

"Jack had to pull over because I was... feeling the effects of it," I admit.

"Tell me more," Sebastian demands.

"We had to stop the car because I came in my pants," I admit.

Sebastian does not look at all surprised, which confirms my suspicions.

"I used my shirt to clean up. I thought I would get my suitcase when we got there, but they took it before we got out of the car, and no one at NeXus offered me any clothes until I got to my room. I carried around a semen-soaked shirt while I met all the scientists."

"And you didn't think to tell me about this," Sebastian deadpans.

"Not until this exact moment," I sigh. "Sorry about that."

"I spewed just after drinks hit the table," Sebastian groans. He runs his hands through his hair, shaking his head. "Lucas will never, and I fucking mean never, let me live this down."

"Good thing you had a private room in the restaurant," I say, giving him a few friendly pats on the shoulder. He looks me in the eye, and I try my best not to burst into laughter.

Sebastian takes in a deep breath. "Payback's a bitch, I guess."

I squeeze his shoulder and shake my head. "You know I wouldn't wish that on you. I never thought it would go both ways or I would have told you. Actually, I think I blocked that moment out until just now."

"Right, well, I'm hungry," Sebastian says. "Help me make some dinner while you go tell my brother that this happened to you, too. I refuse to be the only one mocked for eternity about this."

"No problem, man," I say. "And while we're on the topic, I don't think we should be with Emry alone. Like that, I mean, without knowing where each other is."

Sebastian nods and raises his eyebrows. "Could you imagine being at work? We need to keep tabs on each other. Spontaneity is good and all, but imagine the headlines if it happened in the wrong place."

We both widen our eyes at the thought, and I get a flush of second-hand embarrassment for Sebastian's situation. It was lucky they had a private room, and no one spotted him in the city.

"Maybe in the future, we can control it more, just like

everything," I add. "This isn't something I want to ask another bonded about just yet, so we'll have to work on it on our own but... together. Are you comfortable with that?"

"We've already been with Emry together," Sebastian points out.

"Not like this," I say. "Not sex."

"Sex with Emry," Sebastian adds, and I can't tell if he's asking a question or not.

My jaw opens and closes, but I can't bring myself to find out for sure.

Sebastian shoves his hands in his pockets, rocking back on his heels. He pauses, thinking over what to say, and I'm a little frustrated he can close his mind to me even though he's not trying.

"I mean, we're all married," Sebastian says.

"But you and I aren't—"

"Yeah, I know," Sebastian stops me. He lets out a cough, rolling his eyes at himself because we're both avoiding the thing that's left unsaid, the topic we should discuss.

"I don't feel attracted to you," Sebastian admits. "But I'm turned on when you're with Emry."

"Same," I agree. "Very turned on. I mean, you look good, I can admit that. I like to look at you."

"Same," Sebastian says.

"For now," I draw out my words, feeling more unsure than uncomfortable.

I know I can talk to Sebastian about this, and we've danced around the topic many times. My hesitation, and maybe his, is that I'm in fear of ever losing our friendship or doing anything that would put a wall between us.

"For now, that's enough," I tell him. "But if anything changes and we want more..."

I take a step back, and I'm not sure why. Maybe I'm

protecting myself, my heart. Sebastian steps forward, a smile on his face, and he brings one hand to his chest, placing his palm across his heart.

"Hey, if either of us wants more, want to experiment in any way, let's just say it," he says. "A no is just that. It doesn't change what we have."

"Right," I agree, letting out an exhale of relief. "And if it's a yes that we decide later is a no, that's also okay."

He opens his arms to give me a hug, and we both embrace as Emry bursts through the door. She runs up, wrapping her arms around us.

"Did you hear that?" I ask, pulling back and giving her a kiss on the cheek.

"Maybe," she admits.

Lucas and Alison let out another howl of laughter from the living room, and Sebastian glares in my direction.

"Go tell them about the ride with Jack," he orders. "Now."

Apparently, Emry wasn't listening to everything because she crumples her face in confusion.

"What ride with Jack?"

CHAPTER 35

"Welcome back to evolutionary biogenetics. I'm Professor Emry Crowe. I'm so glad to see so many of you are still here."

My words, full of false confidence, fall flat. I'm a terrible liar, pretending I'm not nervous about standing in front of my students after all that's happened, and so much of it in the public eye. My hands are sweaty and my heart beats so hard I'm afraid it will leap out of my chest.

"I appreciate you all being so flexible," I continue. "Please understand with the delay in classes, this course will spread into the summer months. Your patience while I dealt with a personal matter is undeserved. I plan to make it up to you by devoting extra time to anyone who requires private study. I'll be holding a Saturday morning session to go over notes and questions, which will include test prep."

The students' faces soften, and a few sit up in their seats, anticipating an easy A. I won't be soft with them, but I will help them get up to speed while restoring my credibility at this university. Rolling my shoulders back, I flash a smile and step forward toward the first row.

I don't think I'm spreading myself too thin like Alison says. It's important I stay busy, especially with Crowe's Crusade in full swing already. The guys are traveling this weekend to a site hundreds of miles away, and the thought of sitting alone in that house doing nothing but waiting for them makes me want to vomit.

This university is giving me a second chance to do what I love, and I've accepted my teachings align with my bond. Speaking about my home life isn't something I've ever enjoyed, but it does give me a chance to bring up our non-profit and encourage students to keep themselves safe.

The students adjust themselves in their seats as I walk through the rows, eager to hear any news about my *personal matter* that is still blasted on every news outlet every day. Several of them stare at my wrist, their eyes glued to the Crowe scrawled across my skin. Alison warned me of this, and so did the administration many times before today. I had a formal email explaining their concerns, then a more personal message over the weekend, followed up by a visit with the board this morning.

"Students will need their curiosity squelched, Ms. Crowe," one said. "We need them focused on their studies, not here to visit a sideshow."

"We all know you're private," another offered. "But please address the elephant in the room and get on with teaching."

I must admit, the walk on campus this morning felt odd. Replacing the constant unwanted touches was a barrage of stares and phones pointed in my direction.

The trade-off wasn't any better.

Impossible to ignore, and coming off that dreadful meeting with the board, I decided to delay my expedited lesson plan, just for one more day, to deal with their curiosity.

I reviewed the printout of the student roster on my desk this morning, surprised by what I saw.

"Only fourteen of you dropped since I took my leave," I say. "If you recall, on our first day, I gave you several lectures about the drop date, even letting you all test for the bond right away so you could walk out if needed."

A series of wide eyes and a few nods fill the seats.

"Today, we can talk about my bond. If I don't want to answer a question, I will say so, and that subject is off-limits. But I will try." I let out a heavy sigh, rolling my eyes, and a few giggles bubble up. "If after this discussion you decide to drop, there will not be a negative mark on your record. Does everyone understand?"

The call buttons on my remote light up in agreement, and I reset it before I continue. "This is a class about how species, primarily humans, change and grow over time. There is natural selection and historical implications, and we can tie that directly to your lifetime because it's happening at a rapid pace. I understand I'm one of the few who has experienced the bond, an event that drives our society and it's worth discussing."

Smiles beam back at me, the lights from their desks blinking again, ready to be called on for questions.

"For educational purposes, I suppose," I huff, and another round of giggles echoes in the room. The sound relaxes me, my heart rate slowing, and I wipe my palms down the front of my pants.

"Please, I implore you," I continue. "Ask me things that may have some small thread that ties to evolutionary biogenetics. I'm resetting your call buttons again. So, hit them only if you can make it about the science."

Just as many lights blink, and I resist the urge to groan when I hit the first button.

A young girl stands from her chair. She's small, and I would guess her to be the youngest in the classroom. Her familiar features spark a memory from earlier this year as a timid girl, but astute in her responses.

She lifts her chin before she asks her question. "Do you agree that your bond with Theodore Lorwerth was a genetic response? Do you find that to be true, scientifically?"

A tattoo of black letters on her wrist flash in my line of vision. They loop in a name she chose with a partner, and I wonder if I've let her down. Did she think of me as someone to aspire to, evidence that settling is possible?

"Yes. It's an auto-response. Somewhat controllable, but in truth, complete restraint is, um, impossible. The genetics of it is not like a predisposition. Someone can have an inclination to be an alcoholic but easily abstain. This is more of a—"

I struggle with the best way to describe the situation, not wanting to shed a negative light on my bonding.

"I want to say disorder, but please note, I'm thankful for my bonding. It's like migraines. Incurable, unstoppable. You can take preventative measures, but you cannot avoid their onset forever."

I let out an awkward cough, holding my hands behind my back. "In my scientific opinion."

"For scientific purposes." She holds back the smile that's threatening to break through. "Are you still with Sebastian Owens, or Crowe?"

"Crowe, and yes," I respond. I sense the room is hanging on my every word, holding their breath and waiting for her next question. There have been countless articles and news stories about me, all contradicting one another, each one looking to grab someone's attention. The only way to know the truth is to ask me.

"We are genetically pre-disposed to survive. Sorry, I know I'm repeating what you know, I just want to set up the question," she says.

"Don't apologize. Continue."

"That hasn't changed across all species for billions of years," she affirms. "We are wired to survive. Does your relationship with Sebastian Crowe ensure your survival? Is that marriage a... genetic response?"

"No," I say with certainty, forcing myself to answer without bias. "There isn't an internal predisposition or disorder that creates that union. It's a voluntary bond."

"So, what is superseding a genetic response?" she asks. "What could contradict the basics of biology?"

She's the same girl from the Friday before I met Theo, the day we had free-form teaching. I'm sure of it now.

"Love," I say. "It's cliche and boring, unscientific if you want to argue the point, but I find it factual if I'm used as a specimen of study."

I step forward, ascending the stairs of the classroom through the crowd of students. They look me up and down, curiosities brimming on their lips, wanting to know more than I'm sure I'll tell them. It feels right because, for the first time, I don't think I'm fighting against the societal norm because there is no fight. Everyone has a right to seek out their own happiness, no matter what that looks like.

"Our descendants might have more bonded. Possibly less. We're no closer to finding the key to the bond," I say. "Those shifts in our ancestry are what we will study in this classroom, but there is one thing that has remained the same since our earliest records in history."

I reach the girl, and we stare at each other. Her eyes are

kind and, up close, I can tell she's not judging my decisions, only curious. There's an understanding between us, and my eyes flash to the tattoo on her wrist. It's beautiful and so is she.

"In ancient civilizations, we find entombed couples holding one another. Animals pair off not only to parent but for companionship. The bond doesn't change a basic human instinct."

"Love," the young girl says.

"Yes, that's right," I respond.

I want to tell her that love may be why we healed Sebastian, why we can speak to him with our thoughts, but I didn't put magic in this year's lesson plan.

She runs her fingertips along her tattoo, takes her seat, and I hit my remote for the next question.

"How was class?" Alison asks. We're standing in front of the university coffee makers while I pour my third cup of the morning. It's difficult to get back into the swing of things, but I'm enjoying the chaos.

"It was good," I say. "A bit intrusive."

"So you took the board's suggestion? Gave away all the gossip."

"Not all," I whisper into my cup, letting the steam warm my face.

She leans closer, hooking her arm into mine. "So you didn't tell them how you can make one of your men spontaneously come on demand?"

I push her away with a sputtered laugh, almost spilling my precious coffee in the process. "You stop. You whisper yell. You're like a child with that."

Someone brushes by us, touching us without thought, and

I shudder. I don't expect everyone to recognize me or stop their habits, and I'm grateful the unwanted caresses of skin slowed, but it still makes me uncomfortable.

We take a seat at a table hidden from view, hopeful no one will step over to touch me or Alison.

"How are things with Lucas? You making him come on demand?" I mock.

"Every damn day," Alison says with a smirk.

She hasn't been back to her apartment, and I doubt she'll renew the lease. Sebastian is impossible to get information from, so I have to give him specific questions to ask Lucas and half the time he forgets. The fact that he doesn't care shocks me, but men miss details when it doesn't directly affect their lives.

"Are you nervous about this weekend?" Alison asks. "Lucas was talking to Sebastian, and I didn't get any details, but I got the impression they're going out of town. Does that mean what I think it does?"

I nod, knowing I can't tell her much, but it would be nice to have some support. "They'll be away with Crowe's Crusade, and it's the first, you know, big mission."

Her forehead creases with worry. "Seems soon."

"Well, tracking down Genome wasn't as hard as we thought," I shrug. "Turns out no one was looking because all anyone cares about is—"

"The bond," Alison interrupts. "I know, I know. Hey, I was right there with them. It's terrible that it's happening, but amazing you're doing something about it."

She reaches her hand across the table and grabs mine.

"I'm proud of you. Do you want to hang out this weekend after your study sessions?"

"Are you free?" I ask her. "I heard there's a reception only an hour away, a legitimate one."

She lets go of my hand and waves it at me. "I'm done with all that."

I almost spit out my coffee and ruin another one of my shirts. It seems Alison abandoned her closet and my wardrobe is all that's keeping her dressed. "I'm sorry, what?"

Her eyes drift to the hallway, watching as people brush by each other, making sure to touch.

"It was very lonely," she admits. "I was always around people, always in direct contact, but I never felt seen. Lucas, he sees me. That's so fucking corny I'm going to make myself sick, but it's true."

"Sebastian and Theo do the same. I understand. Once you have that kind of companionship, it's hard to give up. Do you think you'll settle?"

She shrugs her shoulders. "All I know right now is I don't want to search anymore. I'm more at peace than ever before because I know I don't have to keep up the charade."

"What if Lucas asks you to settle?" I ask her. "You know that's what he wants. You may have to make that choice."

She turns back to me, her eyebrows drawn together. "Not really. If I settle with him, I can still bond."

"Well, I guess, but that doesn't mean you aren't choosing to settle."

"Doesn't it," she argues. "I know you don't read headlines, Emry, but you are really out of the loop."

"What does that mean?"

Alison brings up her phone, scrolling through a few screens before she turns it to me. Another headline about me, but this time, it's not just gossip.

Have it all. Why marriage licenses have skyrocketed since the Crowe bond.

"Knowing that someone could stay in a marriage after bonded, well, that changes everything," Alison remarks. "You've created another option. I've been invited to three settling ceremonies next month."

I lean back in my seat, eyes wide.

"So you think if you settled with Lucas, and he bonded with another woman, you'd stay?" I ask.

She nods and bites her lip. "Sounds kinda hot," she says, wiggling her eyebrows.

"It sounds like you've made your decision about choosing."

"I guess in a way," she admits. "I think it doesn't have to be all or nothing anymore. That's the door that you've opened. The bond doesn't take away your free will to love someone, and that takes away all the fear."

"Just tell me when the ceremony is," I say. "I expect to be there."

Alison laughs to herself. "You'd have to be. What would I wear if it didn't come from your closet?"

CHAPTER 36

ONE MONTH LATER

THEO

It's only our second trip to a Genome facility, but we're already in sync and going through what feels like familiar motions. It helps that Sebastian and I hear each other's thoughts with little effort. Turning those thoughts off from one another remains a struggle, but we don't work at it much. It's not a necessity or something we worry about. When I'm hungry, he pulls over without asking. If I'm anxious or nervous, he stops, puts his hands on my shoulders, and calms me down.

This connection between us isn't one I'm eager to break.

Emry keeps her mind closed when we get to this point of the mission. We can't have any distractions that could negatively impact saving these lives, and everything about Emry is a distraction.

I look over the notes again, speaking them to Sebastian

without words. "*Eight expected abducted. All under the age of ten. Four guards at the entrance with cameras and motion sensors. This one will be tricky.*"

Sebastian nods, gripping the steering wheel while he speeds through traffic and a call comes through. He flicks a button to answer, and Jack greets us with a good morning.

"Do you have an insider yet?" Sebastian asks, getting right to the point.

"Excellent news," Jack answers, seemingly unbothered by Sebastian's tone. He knows the pressure we're under and doesn't react to his terseness. "First, Moira is delivering two new recipes to your house this week. I've gained ten pounds so I can no longer be her taste tester, but you're young and still have a metabolism."

Sebastian fights his smile, but I hear him think about how much he wants a home-cooked meal. "And?"

"Two employees have accepted our payoffs. One of them is a guard stationed at an entryway."

"*Perfect.*"

I mirror Sebastian's thought and pull up the schematics of the entrance once more.

"Which one?" I ask. "Do you know their post?"

"First checkpoint," Jack says.

That is great news. We can get this person to guide us past every guard, or if things go like they did last time, through them. I'm not shy about doing what is needed to get to the people captured and tortured. It sends a message to others, and with time, Genome will disband.

It won't be quick or easy. Even with the uptrend in settling, people are still desperate to find the fountain of youth. The latest news talks all about the updated vows, settlers promising they'll remain together even if one of the couple bonds. Things are easing. Reception attendance was at a record low last week, but Genome won't go down without a fight.

"Where's the other employee?" Sebastian asks.

"They manage the nursery," Jack says.

I suck in a breath of air between my teeth, disgust settling into my stomach, and I fight back the rage I feel. If it's too much, Emry will open her mind, afraid of what's going on, and I don't want her to worry.

"Piece of shit bastards," Sebastian mutters.

"Do not kill our informants," Jack orders. "They need to be let go. That's the terms of the agreement. Remember, if word gets out that you've killed those you made promises of safety to—"

"I know," Sebastian barks. "As much as they deserve to be held accountable for their crimes, I get it. Means to an end and all that shit."

He's spitting every word, disgusted with this deal, but we don't have a choice. Soon we hope to find someone on the inside who will stay with us, giving us intel along the way, but we don't have that person yet. We won't ever have that person if we kill everyone.

Our phones ding with a message from Jack. "I've sent over the guard's location. You're five minutes away from him."

"He's that far from the facility?" I ask, knowing we still have another fifteen minutes before we get there.

"Yes, they are watching for incoming cars, reporting the information back," Jack tells us. "Having someone at the first post will give you a chance to have the upper hand all the way to Genome."

I open the message, going over the new details. We knew this was another underground facility using a factory as a front. The business is real, but the workers don't know that there are passageways that lead to Genome's newest site.

A reception service that popped up in the past decade runs the building, and I don't doubt it all ties back to Genome. Easier to steal people when it's your reception with your guards. With enough information, we will expose them. I have a plan to get Adherence onboard as well, and I don't doubt they jump at an opportunity to put their competition out of business.

"Good luck, gentlemen," Jack says.

"Hey, Jack." Sebastian stops him before he hangs up.

"I'll check in on Emry," Jack says without having to be asked. "Heading there now."

We end the call, solely focused on the mission ahead.

"The guard is in a white vehicle with blacked-out windows," I tell Sebastian. "Should come into view—"

"Now," he says, pointing at the side of the road. Sure enough, there's the vehicle in Jack's write-up, just on time. A man steps out of the driver's seat, hands in his pockets and head hanging low when we pull over.

We wave to each other cautiously, Sebastian radioing his crew to drive around wide enough to see with their scopes but to remain out of sight. NeXus's technology takes away a lot of the risk, but not all of it, and I fight the nerves that jump around in my stomach.

"Bruce," I say. I'm doing my best businessperson act, pretending this is all an arrangement in a meeting room instead of ripping the man's throat out. Sebastian lets out a low growl at my thought.

"Yeah, and you are?" Bruce asks.

"You spoke to our counterpart, Jack—" I begin.

Sebastian speaks up over me. "Someone that will kill you in an instant if I need to, so let's get a few things out of the way."

Sebastian meets him toe-to-toe and Bruce struggles not to

run. He takes a few steps back, looking to me for help, which I don't offer.

"I don't care about you," Sebastian seethes. "I think you're garbage. I'll murder you for what's happening to the babies over there. You don't need to know my name or his, and if you speak a word of this to anyone, I'll rip out every one of your teeth and pull out your fingernails before I give in to your crying and begging and allow you to die."

"I've seen him do the teeth thing, so I wouldn't try anything," I tell Bruce.

Bruce gulps and nods. He points a shaking finger toward the roof of a building in the distance. "Genome keeps them under the plant. I was given this post a week ago, and I knew it was wrong. I know I'm scum. Just let me try to make this right."

There's more to it than Bruce is letting on, and I press him further. "Where did you find this job?"

He shoves his fists deeper into his pockets. "It sort of found me."

I tilt my chin up and step forward, placing a hand on Sebastian's shoulder to pull him back. This man won't tell us anything with the threat of Sebastian's fist inches from his face.

"Explain," I order.

"I don't know." Bruce shakes his head. "I worked at the plant. Word got around about triple wages to stand around, and I need the money."

"Did they tell you what it was for?"

Bruce's eyes meet mine and I see the shame in them. It makes me hate him a little less, but only a little.

"I saw what it was for," he explains. "They had me guarding the, um, the kids."

I fly in front of Bruce before Sebastian takes a swing, his anger flooding his better senses.

"What's going on?" Emry speaks to us.

She's unable to stay away, feeling the rush coming from me and possibly noticing Sebastian's fury.

"Emry, please close off. We're fine."

I don't want to order her away, but we can't work if she's listening. Knowing we're safe and understanding the importance of that, she tells us she loves us and closes the door to her mind. After pacing for a few minutes, and everyone taking the time to cool off, we continue.

Bruce explains there are two guards at the entrance of the facility, which is gated. We come up with a plan to use a NeXus employee as a pawn.

Bruce will escort them to the gate in handcuffs and tell the guards his radio doesn't work. He'll accuse the NeXus employee of asking questions about Genome as a cover for Sebastian and me to slip inside undetected.

Milo's ready to volunteer as the cover, walking up as Sebastian breaks the radio in such a way Genome won't notice at first glance. We collect Bruce's credentials and explain he'll need to go into hiding after this, and NeXus will help him in creating a new identity. This pleases him, and he offers to do more to help if there is anything in the future. I don't know how much good someone with one week of information will do, but it's a start.

"You know what to do," Sebastian tells Milo, and he nods. There's complete trust between the two men. Milo knows we'll come back for him, and if needed, he can free himself from the cuffs Sebastian puts on his wrists. Milo's a professional, and I trust he can take care of himself.

We hide in the back of the large vehicle, Milo bound in the middle seat behind Bruce as we arrive at the plant. It smells like chemicals, and when I inhale, it burns my lungs and stings my eyes. The metallic taste sours my gut and only hastens my need to get underground.

Bruce gets out, dragging Milo along with him. Everything in our line of sight is empty, everyone working deeper inside. We see our entry point before we get out of the vehicle, knowing the clock starts as soon as we exit the car.

There are likely cameras everywhere, and if the right person notices something is amiss, it's over. True to his promise, Bruce creates a scene, distracting anyone who is observing the video footage.

He yells at the other guards as Milo fakes an attempted escape, and we slip into a side door that leads underground. Bruce's badge clicks it open, and we're through. No one is around to stop us as we make our way down the dim hallway dug into the earth.

"Smells just as bad in here."

I nod, agreeing with Sebastian, and we jog forward. The passage mimics an old mining tunnel from hundreds of years ago, with dirt walls and flickering lights overhead. When we see the signs of technology develop, we know we're close.

Sure enough, the first guard appears in the distance. He doesn't get an opportunity to inform anyone. Sebastian takes him out with the help of a silencer. We don't kill if we don't have to, but we wouldn't have gotten to him in time, and I remind Sebastian of that when we pass his lifeless body.

"They have a nursery here, man. We don't have a choice."

We take his badge and weapon and keep going. Sebastian swallows hard and thinks of those inside, his guilt lessening as we approach a steel door.

We use the credentials of the dead guard and step through to another world. The money it takes to create this, and only for a temporary amount of time, has to come from deep pockets. Bile rises in my throat at the thought, knowing it's the reception company that owns the plant over our heads.

People pay to find their bond, and that money funnels down to the bowels of this place, but we will stop them. One by one, this ends.

"People this way."

Sebastian's warning rips me from my anger, and I'm focused on the mission. We speak to each other in silence, grateful the bond helps us with our purpose.

"Let's get NeXus," I urge Sebastian.

"Not yet. We have to make sure we have hands on the victims."

This is a point of contention between us. Sebastian wants to ensure Genome doesn't flee with who we're trying to save. If they realize NeXus has infiltrated, they'll run, and while I think we have enough manpower to block off any exits, Sebastian doesn't agree.

It comes down to my trust in him. When he leads, I'll follow. We check the notes again, reviewing the detailed schematic Jack provided.

"Nursery is likely past that group of four," I muse and show Sebastian the drawing. *"Guns or what?"*

I spin the silencer on my weapon and peer out to look at the four men wearing white lab coats.

"No choice," Sebastian agrees and we move forward, swiftly taking out the threat.

It's quick, and when they fall to the ground, I think about the visions Emry showed me these past few weeks. Men and women like them poked and prodded at her, never looking her in the eye. It helps me when I take a life or ten. I need reminding that these aren't people, they're monsters.

In the quiet, we hear the stirring of babies.

Soft cries at the end of the hall.

We jog toward the sound and there's a window, but I don't

see anyone inside. It's only plastic cribs and monitors, but it's too late anyway to avoid being seen. Someone's watching and we've left a bloody mess not far behind.

I call in NeXus, Sebastian and I both knowing it's time, and we go into the nursery, guns drawn just in case. The second guard that took the payoff is long gone, and there's no one in sight.

They've left the babies here alone, and only a few of them cry. The others must have nothing left, knowing their tears won't bring anyone that will hold them. The baskets are separated by boys and girls, eight of them in total.

"Do you think this is all of them?" I wonder. *"Only infants this time?"*

Sebastian brings his hand to his hips and shakes his head. There's a rustle at the doorway, someone opening the door, and he turns, raising his gun and firing before the other person can get a shot off.

Another lab coat falls to the floor with a splat, their weapon slipping from their hands. I fight the urge to go over and kick them in the gut.

We circle the room for a few minutes, the wide eyes of babies following our every step. They squirm in their plastic cribs, and I'm not sure what to do except wait.

My phone rings, and I answer to hear Jack on the line, letting us know NeXus is in the underground tunnel and coming our way.

Sebastian picks up one baby that cries. Stickers cover his or her thin body, ribs sticking out and eyes bulging from malnourishment. *"They're so small. Are you sure we can do this?"*

"I'm sure Willa is sending over every nurse in her arsenal."

It's the only argument I have because I don't know if we can do this. I've never even held a baby, and I wonder if Sebastian has either the way he's fumbling with the tiny infant.

Its whining stops when he cradles the baby in his arms, and I look over to a girl who screams in her crib. Reaching inside, I mimic Sebastian's movements, noticing how the baby falls silent once shown some attention and love.

Maybe we could do this. It's what Emry wants, what she decided that first weekend with Willa and Henry. We haven't decided on biological children, but Sebastian told me it was off the table before I came around.

Was this how it was supposed to be?

We go from zero to eight children in our first few months together.

There are sure to be challenges, but we'll raise them with the help of nurses and nannies. No one else would understand what they've been through and with love and time, we'll try to undo that hurt.

"It's just Milo," Sebastian warns. I jerk my head up to see a face in the room's window.

"Well, look at you two," Milo says, stepping into the room.

"Are there any others?" I ask him.

"So far, a set of twins, five years old."

I reach out to Emry, letting her know what we'll need. The sooner she has the information, the easier for her to set up the kids' rooms and order enough supplies. We've built a makeshift hospital in less than a week, but without knowing exactly how many children and how fast they'll come in, it's chaotic to get their rooms set up.

Milo goes over to Sebastian, tickles the baby's belly, and it giggles. It's an odd sight, considering Milo's shirt is covered in blood from someone who got in his way.

"What's their name?" he asks.

We look at the plastic containers but know the truth without searching very long. Genome didn't bother to give these children anything of their own, not even a name.

The radio in Milo's ear goes off, and he touches it with one hand, listening to the information. A few seconds later, he lets out a hoot and laughs.

I tilt my head in question, and another baby cries.

"Tell us what's got you laughing and pick up that baby," I tell Milo, my voice muffled by the infant's sudden screams.

Milo takes the baby in his arms, more adept than us at how to swaddle and hold the infant.

"Well, look at you," Sebastian jokes with him. "You're an expert."

"And you'll need my help," Milo says. "They just found three more kids, all under the age of ten. Congrats daddies, you're parents to a baker's dozen."

CHAPTER 37

EMRY

The ding sounds through the house from the guard at the gate. Sebastian and Theo are finally home. There are days when I think this security might be overkill, people following me around campus and walking our grounds non-stop. Then I remember Genome is still out there, ready and waiting for me.

It's not only Genome that could pose a problem. We're wealthy with the government stipends, Theo and I going through with our testing solely to have extra funding for Crowe's Crusade. But outsiders don't know or don't believe where our money goes, and that makes us a target.

My heart jumps in my throat, excitement building as I see their car in the distance. I busy myself as much as I can when they're gone, but I only had one class to teach today, the day they were due back. There's only so much cleaning and time-wasting a person can do.

They've been gone for almost a week, and I count every

hour, laying in bed at night alone waiting for them to return. I know this is a life we chose, but it doesn't make it any easier.

Their car pulls up on the property, driving entirely too fast, but I don't care. Both doors fly open, and I can't help how I run toward them, Theo allowing Sebastian to grab me first. He saunters behind with a grin and calls out, "Honey, we're home."

I go to jump into Sebastian's arms, and he flings me over his shoulder instead, slapping my ass and laughing.

"It's good to be home," he says. I lean forward and give Theo a kiss while I bob along. A guard walking the property stops in his tracks at the sight of us, and I wave, showing off my Crowe tattoo. They all signed non-disclosure agreements, but that doesn't stop them from gawking.

Sebastian ducks through our doorway so I don't bump my head. "You can put me down now," I say, not really meaning the words.

Knowing what's on everyone's mind, he stomps over to the bedroom, Theo at his heels.

"Hey, big guy, before you get any ideas..."

"Oh, we have more than ideas," Theo says. "We have drawn out plans with a play-by-play. We haven't touched you in six days."

Sebastian playfully tosses me on the bed, and I bounce, pretending to kick him away. "Play-by-play? You two really need to join that rugby team with your sports talk."

"Fuck," Sebastian growls, ripping his shirt off over his head. "You know what I need."

Theo's slipping out of his shoes while Sebastian unbuttons his jeans, and they both freeze, staring at each other, the argument so loud in their minds that no one can block it out.

"Wait, are you?"

"I thought I was... and then you."

"*I drove the whole way, man.*"

"*The car drives itself. You wanted to drive.*"

I cackle a laugh at their silent back-and-forth argument, and they turn to look at me, both wearing a frown.

We've had some time to explore this relationship, all of us figuring it out as we go along. As much as they love to say we can talk about our intimacy, it's a lot of fumbling through the dark and then making sure everyone is okay before going forward.

Sex only happens when we are all in the house, at least for now. The other person can't control the feelings that ricochet and that can get embarrassing. The last thing we need is one of us arrested for indecency because they orgasm in public.

There are things we do one-on-one, and sometimes we take part together. It's all new and fresh and exciting, and so far, no one's been upset or hurt. We like to test the boundaries and see what feels right. If someone's uncomfortable, they'll say so, and no one will question why.

Although that's yet to happen.

Our most intimate moment, one that I hope to repeat, happened the night before they left. I haven't been able to stop thinking about it since. They begged me to shut them out while they were gone because it infiltrated my thoughts so much.

I sat Theo down in a chair after undressing him. I wore something better than old gray pajamas, and they both took notice. Sebastian sat on the edge of the bed and watched, his eyes darkening when he realized what I had planned.

Moving myself between Theo's legs, I dropped to my knees and watched as his breath hitched and his cock lengthened. I kissed him for several minutes, our mouths ravenous for one another, massaging my hands up his thighs and almost touching where he wanted, teasing him until he was begging.

I trailed my lips down his chest, grabbed his cock, and pumped slow strokes from the base to the tip until finally, my mouth closed around his flesh. When I took him down my throat, the groan from Sebastian watching sparked everyone's flame of excitement. My hand dipped between my legs, and I felt how wet I was from pleasing both of them at once.

Until that point, sex was only between two of us, the other person close by and enjoying the show. When I felt Sebastian's hands on my hips, I knew that was about to change. He untied the ribbon on the lace gown I wore, letting it fall down my chest and legs until it hit the ground.

Our thoughts ran together, everyone focused on each other's pleasure, but I paused when Sebastian's proposition to Theo spoke louder than the others.

"I want to fuck her from behind while your cock is down her throat."

My whimper vibrated my lips that were wrapped snugly around Theo's thick cock, his hands combing through my hair and pulling me further down onto him.

"Do it, brother. Fuck. I would love to see that."

Theo pulled me up by my hair, strong enough to pinch, but not enough to hurt. I've let him in on all my secret wants and desires, and he's a good listener. His length fell out of my mouth with a pop. Our eyes met, and I clawed my fingernails into his thighs.

"Do you want that, love? Would that feel good?"

I nodded, telling them yes without words.

Sebastian leaned over me, his chest resting hot on my back with his lips to my ear. "I want to hear you say it."

"I want that," I rushed out, my voice pleading.

Sebastian went to his knees behind me, his fingers digging into my hips while his slick tip teased my entrance.

"Want what?" he asked. "Say it. Describe it."

I fought the hold Theo had on my hair, wanting to suck him again, feel him glide into my mouth and make him feel good.

"I want you to fuck me from behind while I choke on Theo's cock," I said without pause. The words sounded foreign to my ears. Some other woman desperate with need would say something like that, but it was me speaking, me begging for their attention.

Sebastian thrust forward and filled me to the hilt just as Theo pressed down on the back of my head, his cock sliding down my throat. Both of them inside me at once almost made me peak, but I held it back, wanted to draw this moment out as long as possible.

The thoughts and emotions that ran between us amplified, and the struggle to hold back everyone's orgasms was all that filled our minds.

I heard Theo's thoughts to Sebastian. "*I don't want this to end.*"

"*Me neither. She feels too good.*"

Sebastian mirrored his want, but couldn't help how close he was getting.

I clenched every time I felt Sebastian's hips against my bare ass, and he groaned, sounding almost pained. My fingernails dug into Theo's thighs, threatening to draw blood, but still, his pleasure grew.

"*I'm coming,*" Theo warned us.

Sebastian slammed himself deep while Theo came in my mouth, his heat spilling down my throat while Sebastian's dripped down my thighs and brought me to climax.

The colors that sparked inside our bedroom grew so bright, I couldn't see, only feel.

I felt them both take me, the orgasms that ripped

through us all, and the bliss of both cocks drained all because of me.

I'm theirs and they're mine.

"Did you not want to share today?" I ask, looking at them both half-dressed at the end of the bed. I'm thinking about that night, and they know it, both of them getting turned on with the images flashing through my mind. "Because last time we—"

"It's not that," Theo says. "We both want things we can't get at the same time."

"So, it's who goes first," Sebastian explains.

Oh.

Sebastian's pants hit the floor, and Theo senses a race, his shirt almost ripping when he tears it off his body, and I join in on the fun, stripping my clothes as fast as possible.

In seconds we're on the bed together, our breaths quick and excitement roaring between the three of us.

They're fighting over me in a playful way, one of them kissing on my neck while the other cups my sex, whispering dirty things into my mind.

"You want one cock in your mouth and the other in this pussy again? On your back this time. I want to see your tits shake while I pump into you."

I'm already close without anyone inside me, but that changes when I'm thrown onto my back, Sebastian moving toward my head while Theo spreads my legs.

I take Sebastian's cock in my hand and turn my head, guiding it to my mouth, moaning in pleasure when Theo teases my opening with his tongue. He licks at my clit, and I lose focus, unable to stroke Sebastian the way I want when the orgasm hits me, sending sprays of colorful light around the room.

"It's always good to know when you come," Sebastian says. He's pumping the base of his cock while I lick the tip, my tongue gliding along the smooth surface.

Theo gives me a languid lick, his arms wrapped around my thighs. "The visual is one way to make sure you never fake it." He rises and lines up his cock at my entrance. "Fuck, you're wet."

Sebastian groans, and I take more of him into my mouth, whimpering as it stretches my lips and hits the back of my throat. Theo pushes inside, and I feel his pleasure course through my veins, lighting me on fire and restarting my climb to another climax.

"We were fighting over who would go down on your first, love," Theo says.

Sebastian tilts his hips, gently rocking himself in and out of my waiting mouth. "But we can share, baby."

Theo's head tilts back as he moves faster, and the need in my core grows. I'm whimpering with every thrust, and Sebastian reaches for my hard nipples, pulling at one until it hurts just enough to bring me close to the edge.

"*You want me to come on her stomach so you can lick her clit, man?*"

Sebastian's cum leaks into my mouth as he gets ready to release, and I reach for his cock, wrapping my fingers around the base.

Sebastian shakes his head at Theo's offer. "*I don't care about that.*"

The realization that his cum will be inside my pussy, and Sebastian will lap it up shortly after, sends Theo crashing over the edge. His orgasm hits so fast and hard that it sends an earthquake of ecstasy outward, and we all come at once.

I'm screaming with Sebastian's cock flooding my mouth, my free hand digging into Theo's shoulder until my fingers hurt.

They both pull out of me, and I'm limp, my body spent after the most intense orgasm of my life. I can't move or think, unable to leave this spot until my strength returns.

That is until Sebastian yanks me by my legs to the edge of the bed, nestles his face between my thighs, and licks the length of my dripping pussy.

CHAPTER 38

"I'd like to talk about the visit," Jack says. "If it's too soon to have this conversation today, that's fine, but it's important we don't let it fester for long."

I cringe at his use of the word fester.

It sounds worse than dead, making me imagine my mother rotting away in her cell, drowning in her own demise.

She's been waiting in that prison, hoping I would come to her rescue. I did show up, but it was only to tell her goodbye. It felt so important at the time, like something I had to do, but when I got there, the meaning behind it was gone.

Theo and Sebastian chirped in my ear until I told them to stay quiet. I didn't shut them out, afraid I'd lose my nerve without them there. They offered to go with me, but I needed to face her myself.

"We can talk about it now," I say, scooting forward in my chair. It's still the same worn leather from years before, but this office is new.

Jack sees me for therapy at NeXus, and it's easier that way. Our foundation is here, and I'm not afraid anymore. Vera meets me for coffee and makes dry jokes about how my genome doesn't cooperate with their testing modules. She's funny in a robotic way, full of sarcasm and wit. I'm thinking about setting her up with Robin. They would be the perfect match.

Jack's brought over that clock from his old office. It sits in the corner and ticks too loud even after all these years. He's made tea without asking, not wanting to hear me grumble about its lack of caffeine. The coffee cart had a line a mile long, so I swig it down and pray it does something.

I can heal myself and others and live for hundreds of years, but I can't wake up in the morning. It might be a placebo, but I'll never give up the java.

"I saw her a few days ago," I say. "She looked different."

"Different how?" he asks.

I bite my bottom lip, wanting to use words that are more accurate than insulting. It's a difficult task when I talk about Blaire Crawford.

"She's less delusional, I suppose. Less confident. She seems to understand the gravity of her situation, but she still doesn't accept how she got to where she is."

He nods, not speaking or writing anything down.

I offer him more hot water for his tea and he nods. After another silent minute, I realize he's wanting more. This would be easier if I could read his mind.

"She's scared, but still making excuses for herself. She doesn't think she did anything wrong, but knows she's in trouble."

"How is she making excuses?"

I huff out a breath, remembering the words she said, the way her face went blank as she spoke them.

"She told me that the bond was important for everyone,

and if she were in my place, she would have volunteered to go back to Genome because they could uncover the key faster than anyone else."

I toss a heaping tablespoon of sugar into my cup and stir, hoping it will somehow convert the drink to coffee.

"She claims that she never knew Gilbert would be back, and they promised this time they wouldn't perform any painful techniques. I tuned her out after that."

"Did you really?" Jack asks. "You stopped listening."

"I did, mostly. I just started listening to Theo and Seb," I admit. "It's kind of nice having a call in progress that nobody knows about. I let her carry on and talked to them."

Jack leans forward and places his elbows on his knees, his hands resting in prayer. "Did you get what you needed from her? Did her reasoning give you any finality to the relationship? You don't need to love someone just because you feel empathy for them."

"Or even care about them," I joke.

"You may care about the hurt someone caused, all while discarding the person," Jack says. "Your pain is valid, and it's there, no matter what she told you."

"She lied. It doesn't matter all the reasons she offered up. She just... lied."

"Yes," Jack says. "She did. She will continue to lie."

"I thought I would feel some regret when I saw her. This time was so different. She couldn't say they tricked her like when I was fourteen. On the way, I thought about what it would be like if she apologized. You know she's never said she loves me. I can't remember it—ever."

Jack crosses his legs, watching me intently, understanding I'm working something out.

I take a sip of hot sugary water and curl my legs under myself in the chair. "She didn't have any emotion, just answers to questions I initiated. That's because she doesn't care about me. She doesn't love me or hate me. There's just... nothing."

It's my turn to be silent, knowing that's all I can manage to say about Blaire Crawford for this hour. Every word takes too much effort, but I know in time it will get better.

Jack, sensing that I'm waning from the topic, asks me one more question. "How did you leave the conversation? What was the last thing you said?"

I tap a fingernail on the cup and shrug. "I told her I'm making it my mission to save every kidnapped person from Genome, and if she cares about me, she'll give up any information she has to help. Then I left."

The clock ticks for a solid minute before I speak again.

"She sent a message that her attorney advised her not to speak on the matter. Then I had her and her attorney blocked. It all goes through our lawyers now. I don't have to talk to her ever again."

"If you do," Jack says. "I'm here to talk about it."

I raise my eyebrows and tilt my head. "But I shouldn't?"

Jack smiles, not answering. The side of him that's my friend wants to tell me no, but the doctor sitting across from me can't. That's a decision I need to make for myself, but she's not going anywhere, not ever with the evidence stacked against her.

"Have you been meditating like we talked about?"

"I've been sitting in silence wondering if that's meditating," I admit. "Does that count for something?"

"Counts for a lot."

Jack sips his tea and looks at me with affection. He's done so much for me and my family, and the least I can do is fail at meditating.

"And not to throw another curveball at you—" he starts.

I roll my eyes. "You men and the sports lingo."

"I want to touch on the housing transition for the kids," he says. "I got a very detailed email from someone named Willa."

"Well, you are on the board for Crowe's Crusade, Jack," I say with a smile.

He puffs out his chest in a dramatic gesture. "Yes, I'm very important—"

I almost spit out my tea. Jack isn't one to make many jokes, but ever since he moved in with Moira, there's a quickness to him. It may have always been there, but when your day is full of science and patients, it's difficult to get out.

"And when reviewing this important correspondence, I noticed all the medical interventions taking place at your property. You've added a few buildings to the land, I see."

I've been listening to hammering and saws for weeks, but it's worth it to give these kids a home. When we started, I had no idea we could create additional houses in a few weeks' time. They almost grew overnight, but obscene amounts of money grease the wheels better than anything else.

"We have a small on-site hospital for the two nurses that will help with medical needs," I explain. "Privacy is a big deal to us, but if we need to go to the city, we absolutely will."

"No, I think that's wonderful," Jack adds. "But what about the therapeutic resources for these children? They've been through trauma, and as much help as you will be to them, I think they will need regular therapy. I'm not trying to tell you how to parent, just giving you my professional opinion."

"I'm not their parent," I correct him.

"Based on Willa's documentation for expedited adoption, you will be soon."

"That's just legalities," I explain. "To protect them—get them access to our resources and the trust if anything happens."

I know I'm lying when the words leave my lips, a heaviness

settling into my heart and my voice cracking a few times when I speak.

"Emry, please," Jack says. "Let's try again. I want a therapist at your home for these children. That's all I'm getting at."

"Okay, done. Could you email Willa any recommendations and we'll hire someone before they arrive in a few days?"

The paperwork to get these kids has been a nightmare, and we've had to wait for what feels like forever to bring them home. It's red tape that I can't even cut through with fame and dollars, but they're coming. They'll be ours soon.

"And regarding you as the parental figure for the children," Jack sighs. "Perhaps we should discuss that later."

"Right, doc. Time's almost up. Any other words of wisdom before you send me out into the world?"

"Just to enjoy your evening. I hope you liked Moira's dishes." He slaps his stomach which has grown since he met her. "I'm missing out."

Moira noticed how gluttony was not suiting Jack, and she's been trying a raw diet with him. He's miserable, but I'm not complaining about all the extra food from her shop that finds its way to our doorstep.

"You know we are, especially Theo. I think Sebastian might even be a little jealous. His cooking skills are getting rusty with everything she brings over."

I set down my tea and stand, noticing a picture of me and Moira hugging on Jack's desk.

"Will you and Moira come over for dinner this week?" I ask. "She might give you a night away from raw vegetables if there is an occasion."

"We would love that." Jack stands and gives me a friendly shove on one shoulder. "You know I'm proud of you, kid."

"Thank you." I blush at his compliment. "You should end all your sessions with praise."

He laughs and goes to open the door so I can escape the tea-filled psychoanalysis.

His desk is full of pictures, and there's one of Moira and her daughter. I've never met her, but I've heard what Theo did for their family, and I know she'll come to visit soon. She and Moira look so happy with their arms wrapped around each other.

"Jack." I stop him and he turns on his heel while I keep staring at the photograph. I don't know what it's like to be a mother. I've never had what Moira does, and the thought of a child smiling in a picture like that with me seems impossible.

"I'm scared is all," I admit. "That's why I'm being defensive about the parent thing."

"I know," he says. "Might I say something in a... non-medical opinion?"

"As a friend?" I laugh at his wording and nod. "Yes, please do. The hour's up, anyway."

Jack steps forward, placing his hands on my shoulders.

"You will be a fantastic mother."

CHAPTER 39

"I really should have paid more attention to that diaper changing class."

Emry and Sebastian chuckle at my thought, both of them shaking their heads. Emry grabs my hand while Sebastian pats me on the shoulder.

A black van pulls up in our driveway, and we walk over to the nursery to meet Willa. She's come for the occasion and so have four full-time nurses because I'm convinced I'm not capable of keeping a baby alive.

"You'll do fine," Emry promises, and Sebastian nods at the thought. *"It's a hands-on thing. We just need to learn the ropes and before we know it, we'll be experts."*

She might be trying to convince herself, but I relax, reaching for her hand before we all greet Willa.

"They're here!" Willa squeals.

Her excitement makes my nerves spike, and I take in a deep

breath of air, Emry kissing the back of my hand and sending calming assurances my way.

This is exciting, and the idea of expanding our family is wonderful, but I'm also terrified. Babies are small and fragile and have to be fed constantly, and we'll have so many.

"It's going to be fine," Emry promises. *"All we need to do is love them."*

Two of the nurses go up to the van, and the door slides open. We are getting four of the children today. Two boys and two girls. The rest won't be far behind, and I'm relieved it's not over a dozen at once, especially because we leave for another mission in a few weeks.

Emry feels confident, and we have hired more help than we probably need, but Sebastian and I hate to leave her in the throes of chaos.

A nurse steps over with one baby swaddled in her arms, and Emry reaches out her hands. Right behind her, another nurse places the next baby against my chest, and then Sebastian. Willa takes the last little boy and turns on her heel into the nursery.

The three of us stand in a circle, all of us staring at the tiny sleeping creatures. They're plumper than when Sebastian and I rescued them, their skin bright and smooth. Small, heart-shaped mouths occasionally pucker into a suckling motion.

"Are you coming?" Willa asks.

We trail after her, and the nurses follow until we're doing the same thing, but only inside a nursery.

None of us have a clue what to do with these children.

"No one knows what to do at first," Willa says.

"Get out of our head, Willa," Sebastian jokes.

"Sorry, but you're so loud, Sebastian."

I'm not sure what she means, but there's something in her

special that struggles to tune him out. It doesn't help that we're all thinking the same thing.

"What now?"

"Now you put them in their cribs or hold them or do whatever you like. You could sit in one of these beautiful rocking chairs and cuddle them." She plops down in one. "Aren't these gorgeous? Perfect for loving and feeding. Best of the best."

"Thank you for the rocking chairs," Emry says. "They are wonderful."

Willa brushes her off, and Emry goes to sit down next to Willa, resting the baby girl on her chest and trailing her fingers down her back. Sebastian and I follow suit, taking a seat and slowly rocking while the babies sleep.

A nurse steps forward with a clipboard in her hand. "They are due to wake up in about an hour and then we will eat, play, and then go back to sleep. The team and I are going to prep some bottles for the day and night and finish working on some things. If you want us to take over, just say the word."

"Thank you, Lucy," Emry says. "We'll be depending on you a lot in the next few months, years... lifetime."

Both women laugh, and Lucy turns back to her crew, busying herself with the million tasks on her list.

"Have you decided on names?" Willa asks.

I feel the drop in Emry's heart and watch as she bites her lip before she answers. This part is hard, but it's what she wants, and I understand. They didn't give these babies names at all, and it's important to us we give them ones with meaning.

Emry tries to answer a few times and chokes on her words. Sebastian reaches over and takes her hand, silently telling her he's happy to tell Willa. She nods and plants a kiss on the baby girl's head that snoozes on her chest.

"We received an email from someone imprisoned by Genome several years ago. Emry didn't know her well, but they had met a few times. When they first rescued everyone, they tried group therapy," Sebastian explains. "Some survivors got close, made friends with others that suffered the way they did."

"Present company excluded," Emry chimes in and shrugs.

Sebastian offers her a smile before he continues. "The woman was best friends with another victim who didn't make it."

Willa's face crumples in confusion. "Make it?"

"She committed suicide," Sebastian says. "Some survivors struggled with life, and others suffered some aftereffects of what Genome did to them. They died prematurely. Not everyone got a happy ending."

"Oh, I'm so sorry," Willa says, but I'm not sure to whom. Maybe she's speaking to the universe, feeling the sorrow we all do about how those kids weren't properly treated when they got out. A stack of cash doesn't take away the pain or miraculously heal someone. A wave of gratefulness passes between Sebastian and me that Emry is thriving and sitting with us today.

"The email asked we name one baby after her friend," Sebastian says. "And I think it's a good idea. We all do."

All of us nod in unison.

"But then more emails came. And now we have a list of about thirty, and we promised we would make sure their names were spoken again, and tell the kids about those that came before them."

"If there are older children that might remember their name or want to pick their own, we're going to give them that opportunity," I add. "But for the babies, this is a good way to honor the others."

"That's wonderful," Willa says. "Might I make a suggestion?"

"Of course," I reply.

"Get to know these babies a little first. You said you have thirty names. Let them tell you who they are. It will come to you."

"I like that idea," I say and feel how Sebastian and Emry agree. The tiny thing in my arms wiggles against my warmth, and I stroke my thumb against his cheek, curious what name he wants.

We spend the next hour relaxing and rocking, followed by the shock of uniform screaming when they're all ready to be fed at once. It's not difficult with all the help, and Lucy flutters around, making sure we burp them regularly and hold them at the right angle.

It strikes me that this is more difficult than infiltrating a Genome facility, and Sebastian laughs at my thought.

The sun is down by the time we leave the nursery, Lucy changing the shift and introducing us to the overnight staff. We head out together and enter our house to the wonderful aroma of something Moira dropped off.

"Perfect," Emry thinks as her stomach grumbles, and we file into the kitchen. We're scooping heaps of pasta onto plates, ready to devour the goodness.

Emry pops up on the counter to eat while Sebastian and I stretch out in the chairs. We're exhausted for no apparent reason, but happy to find ourselves so tired. Tomorrow will be more of the same, and I can't wait.

Sebastian pops a beer for me and slides it across the table, and when he leans forward, the light catches in his hair. I sit up straighter to get a better look, and he notices me gawking at something and asks me what's wrong.

"Do I have spaghetti on my face?" He wipes his jaw before taking another bite.

Emry slides off the counter and her fingers dip into his thick hair, combing through and catching what I noticed.

Her finger strums across the few grays I saw, and she takes in a shuddered breath.

My stomach drops at the sight of those gray hairs. It's physical proof of his aging while we do not. I prayed that something in this bond might keep him with us, help him age so slowly, that maybe—just maybe—we wouldn't be without him for long.

Sebastian takes her wrist and pulls her into his lap. He hears her inner worry, both of our worries that flood forward. We can't help it, and as much as I don't want to ruin this perfect day, a wave of premature grief hits me.

"I'm so happy," Sebastian says.

His words are simple and perfect and I sputter a laugh.

"I was a minute ago," I admit.

"All we have is this second," Sebastian tells us. "That's it. Those babies will be one day older tomorrow. They'll grow up and leave, die someday. Jack and Moira, Alison and Luke. Even the both of you. We're all temporary fixtures in each other's lives."

"You're not helping me feel better," Emry says.

"Don't feel better. Be in this moment with me. Eat these carbs and drink a beer and talk to me about which baby you want to name because I know you already have one picked out. Feel everything. All the sad and happy. Feel it."

"I don't want to lose you," I say, somewhat surprised at the pathetic words that come out of my mouth.

"But you will, and I won't spend the rest of my life counting down my days. We're going to live in the now, and that's all that matters. No more talk about my getting older, and you know what, I want birthday parties every year. Big ones. I want to celebrate every year I get with the people I love more than anything."

Sebastian reaches his hand across the table, and I take it. His other arm wraps tightly around Emry, and she rests her head on his shoulder.

"Can we let Alison plan it?" she asks. "She isn't going to receptions, and I can tell she's desperate for a party."

Sebastian laughs and nods. "Absolutely. Tell her to make it a huge event. I want to celebrate my time here."

I wrap both hands around Sebastian's, twisting his wrist up and staring at our Crowe tattoos. "Okay, then. We'll just live and enjoy our time together."

I'm promising this to myself, telling myself to do this even if it feels impossible.

"And have big birthday parties for you, old man," I add.

Emry gives him a kiss and wraps her arms around his neck.

I loosen my grip on his hand, but he doesn't let me go, his eyes meeting mine for a moment.

"You know I love you, brother," he says.

I might hate the reality that we can't have a full bond with Sebastian, but I'll take anything I can get. I'll cherish every second, minute, day, and year with my best friend.

"Yeah, man. I love you, too."

CHAPTER 40

EMRY

"Tell me about my great-grandmother," Andrew says.

I don't have a favorite child, but the one he asks about has a special way of melting my heart. Andrew's smiling at me with huge brown eyes that resemble hers down to the last detail. Streaks of gold slice through the copper and long dark lashes that everyone envies blink up at me.

I remember her looking at me like this when she asked a question.

I remember all of them.

I'm curled into one end of the couch, a book in my hand that I've read a hundred times before, but it never gets old. Andrew's running his fingers over the projection of his schoolwork: a tree with hundreds of branches glowing in the center of the sitting room. It flickers with the movement, names flashing in and out of focus.

"Your great–great–great grandmother," I correct him, my eyes growing wider with each great.

He giggles and points to a branch. "There she is."

"Yes," I sigh, looking over all the twinkling lines of the branches. There are too many to count, but I know them all. They're a part of us and our family. "And there is her partner, Beck."

Andrew taps on Beck's name. Several facts appear about eye color, height, jobs, and children–things people ask at dinner parties or when you're first getting to know someone. I know how Beck was allergic to shellfish and what they wore on their wedding day. Those things don't make it into a family tree, but they should.

"Mr. Frank said great–great–great grandmother is in our history book," Andrew says. "So I need to write down something new to tell my class, not the boring stuff already in there."

"History isn't boring," I object, but his face falls, and I giggle, knowing to him, anything that isn't playing outside is horribly dull.

I set my book down and open my arms. Andrew crawls into my lap with a smile. He's all elbows and knobby knees and smells like the outside—like Sebastian.

Theo opens the door, packages overflowing in his hands. He smiles at Andrew and looks over at the wall chart, surprised again about which child visits today. He's always losing track, but we've all been preoccupied lately, lost in our thoughts and worries.

"You don't have to write it down. Just listen in here." I touch his chest where his heart beats. "You remember better when you feel it."

It's true. I have records and logs of all the children over the years. Their favorite things and gifts they gave me, but all I have to do is close my eyes and think of them, and the memories flood back.

A group of us sit on the grass, passing out peanut butter and jelly sandwiches.

Sebastian and Theo running around pouring milk into sippy cups while the nannies scoop up children to bathe or change.

Sebastian's counting heads before we leave for an event while Theo checks seat belts for the tenth time and I run back into the house to get something else we forgot.

I'm with Andrew's great–great–great-grandmother, holding her hand on that first day while she watches her brothers play swords with fallen branches.

Andrew wiggles in my arms, heavy for a six-year-old, but I enjoy feeling the weight of him. They're only this little for so long.

"Her name was Nova, which she picked for herself. Did you know she picked her own name?" I ask him. I know the answer, but it's fun to let him chime in and tell the story from his perspective.

He nods, his hair tickling my chin. "She didn't remember her name because she was so little when she dispapeered."

I don't correct him, silently chuckling at his attempt at a big-boy word. "That's right. Some little children disappeared," I draw out the word so he understands, "when they were too little to know their own name. When we found Nova, she was three, and old enough to pick. Do you remember why she picked Nova?"

Andrew beams, staring up at the skylight in our ceiling and points. "Because pa-pa Theo showed her the stars."

"That's right," I tell him, combing through his brown hair with my fingers. Theo steps over, his hands free of the packages, and gives us both a kiss on the head.

"And a Nova is an exploding star," Theo says. "She thought it was so funny that a star could explode, and she named herself Nova."

"Is that in the history books, Andrew?" I ask him.

"I don't think so, but tell me something else."

"Well, Nova had four brothers who lived with her. When we found her, they all came to be a part of our family."

"She was in the dark place," Andrew adds, his voice low.

I bring my lips to his ear and whisper softly to remind him. "There are no more dark places."

Andrew turns his head, squinting his eyes at me. "I know ma-ma Em."

"Well, okay, then," I say, scratching at his head. He giggles and I continue. "She had four brothers, and they all were more interested in playing outside instead of picking their names. Sounds like someone else I know."

I tickle his stomach, and he laughs again.

"They'd never seen the outside before," I sigh. "Not that they could remember, anyway."

I take a deep breath, remembering the way they looked up at the sky for months and months. Theo built a skylight when the on-call therapist mentioned how much it would help to always have the sun and moon within sight. "Her brothers were a little older and told Nova she could pick their names. It was very nice of them."

Andrew jerks his tiny body up, his fists digging into my ribs.

"After stars!" he yells, a forgotten memory surfacing. His bedtime stories are full of tales from the past, and this isn't the first time I've told him about Nova and her wild brothers.

"Yes," I say.

He smiles wide, his chubby cheeks making his eyes squint. "That's not in my history book."

"Well, that," I tell him, nudging my nose to his, "is something I will write down for you if you insist."

"I inspits," Andrew agrees, and I chuckle at his cuteness.

"Dinner's set out on the table," Theo tells us. He looks at Andrew. "Your mom's here. She's going to eat with you and take you home."

Andrew crawls off of me and frowns at the thought of leaving.

"Your puppy misses you," Theo adds, and Andrew's frown flips into a bright smile.

"Did you meet him?" Andrew asks Theo, his voice drifting as they walk into the kitchen.

"Oh, I never miss a chance to meet a puppy," Theo says, and then they're gone.

It's quiet, and now that Andrew's mother is back, I head out of the guest house. It's one of several we have on the property, full of everything someone might need and the latest advances in technology, but it's not home.

That's where I'm going and where I belong, back toward the same walls that have stood for over one hundred and fifty years. Walls I want to come back to every day, and I wonder if that will change soon. It might be too much for me, for us, to face the place that holds so many memories, knowing we can't make any new ones.

My feet move faster, and I hear the door of the guest house

shut, Theo no doubt catching up behind me. I don't turn back, bursting into my home more breathless than I should be, but I'm eager to see Sebastian.

Willa's cooking in my kitchen, which might be the first time it's been used in a month. The smell hits me when I step inside, making my stomach grumble. I can't remember the last time I ate, and she knows that. She may not mean to, but she digs into my mind when she worries.

"The nurse is still here," Willa says, her voice timid and low. "Just in case."

"Well, she doesn't need to be," I bite out.

I don't mean my words. I'm a wild animal these days, sometimes hiding my tears, other times lashing out. I threw a set of dishes in a rage last week while Willa watched. She waited a few minutes before getting us both brooms. We cleaned up in silence, letting it all sink in and knowing there was nothing we could do to feel better.

We have to feel it.

All of it.

I toss my bag on the couch and look back out the window. Theo was following behind me, but a few guests had him stopped in a conversation.

"What I mean is, you can send the nurse home," I tell her. "We can handle his pain. There's no need."

Willa's crying, a soft sound that echoes in the kitchen, and I know I'm responsible.

"I'm sorry," I call out, trailing my hand against the wall as I walk toward her. My sadness is too great to keep away, pounding at the door of her gift, forcing its way through.

"It's not just you," she admits, chopping vegetables as she cries over the produce. "We're all going through this together."

She sets down the knife and wipes her eyes.

"I just never thought."

I rush up to her and wrap my arms around her shoulders, holding my friend tight. "You can go. I can take care of myself, and being here is asking a lot of you."

Her head falls on my shoulder the way Alison's used to, and my sadness grows. There are times when I think the gift of the bond is too much, but I remind myself that everyone loses people they love. I'm lucky to have had so many to lose.

"He's always taken care of you both," she says. "My dear, I'm afraid you'll starve to death without him. The first bonded to wither away to nothing."

We both sputter out a laugh at the truth of it because I have worried in the night's silence, when I'm alone by his bedside, if I might not survive this. People die from grief, don't they? Another unexplained phenomenon similar to the bond.

A light blinks on my watch, and my heart jumps.

"Got to go," I tell Willa, kissing her on the cheek. "Thank you for being here."

She nods and waves to Theo as he steps through the door.

"He's up," Theo says, pointing to his watch.

He holds me for a moment before we go in, and wipes away my tears.

"I'd tell you none of that, but it's impossible," he admits, his eyes welling up the same as mine.

We head down the hallway, the wood beneath our feet worn with decades of use, and step into our bedroom.

"Hey, babe," I say, rushing over to Sebastian.

He makes a sound I can't make out, but I know what he wants to tell me. I hear the whisper in my soul, his voice still youthful when he speaks to me this way.

"Hello, my darling. It's time."

CHAPTER 41

My best friend doesn't have many days left. He may not even have hours. Henry thinks I've gone mad, and maybe I have a little. My actions aren't rational, and I know people are worried, talking in whispers everywhere I go. They worry I'll break or worse, fall into some depression I can't escape. I may have already. Emry's the only thing that will keep me going, and she's not doing well herself.

It would be like this, we knew, but the reality of it is a different thing. Talking about something horrible in the future in no way prepares you for living through it, and it certainly doesn't make it easier.

In some sort of act of desperation, when they couldn't level the land for Sebastian's headstone in time, I decided to dig it myself. Another irrational action that got everyone talking. I swear Henry put a guard out here just to watch me and report back that I'm not trying to hurt myself.

I've spent countless hours building a mausoleum, having

granite shipped in, creating the perfect burial place. I considered etching the stone by hand and setting up weekly flower deliveries.

I'm spiraling, trying to control the situation.

Willa and Henry arrived weeks ago, and no matter how good I am at shutting off my mind, they found a way inside and realized what was happening. The look on their faces sent my panic into overdrive.

They hear the things I refuse to admit.

Sebastian's ticking clock is about to run out, and there's nothing I can do about it.

A few years ago, when we knew his time was running short, I tried to convince him to visit receptions. Maybe then he could bond and live forever and never leave us.

"They're different these days," I had told him. "Well-organized, affordable now that so many settle. We have the resources. My god, why didn't we do this before? You'd be young again in an instant."

"I don't want to spend my last years with strangers. I want to be here. With you and Emry," he insisted. "I've lived my life. I'm ready to go."

When Emry caught me trying to bring the receptions here, funding them with a business model I threw together with hope and denial, they sat me down, and Sebastian set some boundaries.

We argued, and I cried like a child. I'm ashamed of letting him see me in so much pain when he had no choice in the matter of dying. I tried to manipulate his last wishes, and I hated myself for that.

I still do.

Days later, when the subject came up again, I listened. It broke my heart, but I let him speak without arguing my point. I forced myself to hear the words and let them sink in, every syllable a torturous reminder of what I couldn't control.

"I'm ready to die," he said. It was direct and harsh, and exactly what I needed to hear. "I've known I would have to prepare myself for death ever since I laid Lucas to rest in our cemetery. I knew then the burden you and Emry would carry, watching everyone you love age and wither away, and I'm sorry for that, Theo. I truly am."

He was right that we grieve everyone who leaves us, but for some reason, I never thought he would join the others buried in the earth. Lucas's death stabbed us all in the heart, and less than a year later, we buried Alison by his side.

Every time we attended a funeral or a birth, every time I would have coffee with Sebastian and see the signs of him growing older, it broke me a little. The passage of time came slower than most for him, but wrinkles and gray hair appeared before my eyes while I never changed.

The bond extended Sebastian's life, and I'm grateful, but it's not enough.

His apology shocked me, and I reached out and hugged him, accepting what our future held.

"Don't ever be sorry for letting me love you — for being in this family," I said. "I would do it all over again for us."

The words crack, barely audible, but I had to get them out. He needed to hear me say it.

Arms that almost crushed me in his youth, hugged me back softly. "We have had... an amazing life together," he had said.

I don't know how we can keep going without him.

"I don't want to die in the bonded hospital," he told us. "I want to die here, at home, and I want you to bury me with the rest of the family. Don't make a big fuss about it."

I can always argue that we have different versions of what a big fuss entails. The mausoleum sort of happened, and he saw it growing out of control, allowing me to focus my efforts on something I thought might help.

It's a fool's errand trying to fix this with cement and fancy stained glass windows in our backyard. I'll never recover from the loss of Sebastian, and when I hear Emry's thoughts, they mirror mine.

She's broken like me, and this is an ache even the bond can't fix.

My watch chimes with an alert, a delivery man at our gate. I've seen him hundreds of times before, and I buzz him in, heading to the drive to meet him halfway. They come every day for something. With all the family that comes in and out, it's food or presents, or something to add to this fucking mausoleum.

"How are you today, Theo?" the delivery man says, handing me a few packages.

I shake my head, my jaw clamped tight, fearful I'll be unintentionally rude.

He notices how I tense and sighs.

"You know we're all very sorry." He pauses, his head hanging low. "We're just so upset about Mr. Sebastian. Me especially. I wouldn't be here if it wasn't for the both of you."

I try my best to give a thank you, but something breathy and inaudible comes out.

He tips his hat, and heads back into his van, turning it around to leave while I collect myself.

Everyone who kept roots close by has a tie to Crowe's Crusade and all the children rescued. We adopted every kid we could instead of having biological children. No one could be a better mother than Emry. She knew how they felt and what they went through.

There are people who say, "I understand," but they don't. Unless they suffered the same pain, it's foreign to them. Even I, who can share Emry's thoughts and emotions, can't truly understand what those children endured.

That first decade was chaos and the best kind. We hired dozens of nannies. The first guesthouse was for Lucas and Alison, both of them jumping in to help.

They rest in the cemetery beside Jack and Moira, the impromptu grandparents we so desperately needed.

I turn back to the cemetery and stare out at the headstones that line the dirt. They're distant enough to go unnoticed most days, but now they're all I see when I walk the property.

Sebastian is right. There's peace in letting go and joining the ones you love.

All those kids we rescued grew up, had their own, and so on. Our delivery driver is someone's relative, just like so many others, and even though new life spurts up at every turn, nothing replaces what we've lost.

Nothing can fill the void of losing Sebastian.

I recognize Andrew's mom, who pulls up to the guesthouse where these packages need to go, and she waves to me as she goes in through the back. It's dinnertime, and six-year-olds don't like to wait to eat.

I find Andrew curled up on Emry when I get inside, talking about Nova, one of the first we rescued. That child made me and Sebastian camp outside for a week staring at the stars.

We loved every minute of it.

I wish we could go back.

Willa knocks on the door of my mind, and I try to push her out. She's probably just asking what to make us for food, but I don't want her to fall into a depression when she hears my thoughts.

Emry tells Andrew that the first children picked their own name, something comical given that they later chose their last name as well. So many we found decided to settle, and more than ever before do so each day.

Something about our relationship changed things in the minds of searchers. You don't have to leave the person you choose to love because of the bond. Relationships shift and change, and they have the power to grow into something new.

Life is meant to be lived and love is meant to be had. So far, forty other bonded were already married when they found their fated person. Thirty-seven chose a life together, and I know our story had something to do with that. We keep in touch, knowing that it isn't always easy, but that doesn't mean it's not worth going through the rough parts.

"And a Nova is an exploding star," I say to Andrew, keeping my voice light. He's so innocent, and I don't want him to know how much we are hurting. "She thought it was so funny that a star could explode and named herself Nova."

I take the packages to the kitchen, telling his mom I'll bring him in to eat. Andrew later comes with me, disappointed to leave but excited about the new puppy we got him. His mother had reservations, but I bargained with her that adoption always brought us joy, and she relented.

By the time I'm back in the sitting room, Emry is heading home to Sebastian, and I'm right on her heels.

A few people interrupt me on my way, and I do my best to be polite while rushing them along. They know where I'm going and don't keep me.

Everyone knows.

Every news outlet leads with the story of Sebastian Crowe, sending love and kindness to our family. No doubt one of those packages was full of gifts and letters for us. He did something amazing with his life, and that meant something. Dying with that kind of legacy is wonderful, but it doesn't change that it hurts so damn bad.

My watch blinks with his vitals, telling me he's awake. I burst into our house, smelling the food Willa has going on the stove. Emry is so small, and she needs to eat. I notice how my watch hangs off of my wrist and realize I need to follow the same advice.

"He's awake," I tell Emry, holding her and kissing her on the head before we go to him.

We open our minds to each other, making sure Sebastian can get through. He can't speak anymore, and beyond that, the telepathy is spotty.

Sometimes we don't hear words but see pictures, memories of our lives together.

All of us sitting on the patio with coffee.

Tents strewn around the yard for camp-outs.

Emry smiling across the dinner table, sipping on a glass of wine.

Me sleeping in on a long weekend, Sebastian setting a plate of bacon by the bed.

These things aren't extravagant or especially memorable to anyone else, but it's all the little moments that make up our lives together.

We had over a hundred years full of those joyous moments.

The bond may have been the reason we came together, but Sebastian is the reason we were a family.

I'll love him forever.

CHAPTER 42

EMRY

"You sound good today."

I curl up into the bed next to Sebastian, resting my hand on his chest. There's only a small health meter that clings to his skin, giving us his vitals. No more medication or life-saving measures.

He wants to go.

"I love you both."

He struggles to speak to us even with his mind, but he's told us every day he loves us, going back to our first year together. He can't talk anymore, so we lay in this room and have entire conversations without a word spoken between us.

Theo crawls into the other side of the oversized hospital bed, a gift from Willa.

Sebastian's hands shake a little when he turns them both upward, and I rest my palm inside his, Theo doing the same.

"Who today? Kids?" Sebastian asks.

I smile at his question, remembering last week when this

room was packed to the brim with visitors and children. There were lines across the property while people waited to say their goodbyes.

"It was Andrew today. He has a school project on the family tree," I tell him.

"Emry was telling him about how Nova and her brothers got their name," Theo adds.

There's a flash of memory from Sebastian. It's a moment where I'm holding Nova on my hip, trying to save another dessert I've ruined with my terrible baking skills. We've given up, and she's eating sprinkles from the can while I frown at the mess of chocolate.

"Willa's doing a lot of cooking, and people can live without dessert," Theo says. His voice in our heads is full of giggles from the memory.

"What people?" I argue. *"I need coffee and dessert with every meal and in that order."*

There's a small squeeze from Sebastian's hand, and Theo feels the same. We squeeze back, and I move closer to him, wanting to hold him tight but afraid I might hurt him.

He's over one hundred and forty years old, and even though his face and body have changed, all I see when I look at him is the same man who saved me all those years ago.

Theo pictures us all on the patio, the image in his mind reaching out between us. It was Sebastian's fiftieth birthday, and all he wanted was to stay home and watch the snow fall on the trees around us. After years of wild birthday parties full of guests, fireworks, and dancing, we needed a respite year.

We were sharing one of our favorite meals together while Theo told us a story about a mishap from one of their missions. Sebastian laughed so hard his face was red and his eyes were watering.

I'm doubled over, unable to control my laughter while

Theo stands, acting out the tale that has us all smiling until our faces hurt.

"That was a good day," I say. *"One of many good days."*

Our watches beep with the drop in Sebastian's vitals, and Theo reaches over to turn mine off. He removes it from my wrist and then does the same with his, tossing them to the edge of the bed.

My breaths are shallow and quick, my eyes blurring with tears. Theo wipes his face with his sleeve and lays back down, gripping Sebastian's hand.

"We're ready," Theo says. *"Whenever you need to go, we're ready."*

I wrap Sebastian's arm around me, and curl into him, resting my head on his chest. *"We'll be fine, Seb. We love you. Thank you for spending your life with us."*

The rhythm of his heart beats against my ear, and it slows with every thud. He struggles to breathe in gasps of air, his chest tensing with every inhale.

"We love you so much," I repeat. *"I'll never stop loving you."*

Sebastian doesn't speak, but I feel the frustration of his trying. His thoughts jumble in his head, images of our past and present mixing together. I know that he's leaving. Something inside him gives me the signal that these are his last moments —his last breaths.

"Okay, my dear husband. It's time then. We're here and we aren't going anywhere."

"We love you," Theo says. Even in his thoughts, his words are stricken with tears.

Reaching for Theo, I see a dark mist that rises from his hand. I turn my palm up and notice the same black smoke wafting from my fingertips.

It swirls around us and dips into Sebastian's chest, disappearing as he takes it into his body.

Sebastian breathes in, deep and smooth, and I feel the wave of relaxation that hits him, followed by a hundred pictures that flash through his mind. They're all so clear. Perfect images with bright colors and smells that flood us with a million emotions.

Theo feels it too, and he makes a sharp gasp, followed by a hushed cry.

It's a countless barrage of Sebastian's memories, ones I've never seen before or knew existed.

Running through the woods with Lucas.

His mother teaching him how to cook.

His first day working at NeXus.

The moment he found me when I was a teenager.

Him meeting Jack.

Our first date.

Our first kiss.

Our first time.

Buying our house.

Me studying on the living room floor.

My first day of teaching.

Meeting Theo in the hospital.

Breakfast with Theo at NeXus.

The first baby he ever held.

Painting a child's bedroom.

Taking a dozen girls to dance practice.

Saying goodbye to Jack.

Making love to me.

Watching me make love to Theo.

Taking pictures at a graduation.

Teaching our kids how to make bacon.

Sleeping outside in tents.

Saying goodbye to Lucas.

Our son's broken arm.

Dinners on the patio.

Visits with Henry and Willa.

Grandchildren.

Birthday parties.

Weddings.

Great-grandchildren.

Watching me sleep.

Theo teaching the kids to fish.

Watching Theo work on his burial plot.

Holding our hands in this bed, while he lets go.

We hold our breath, letting every memory flow between us.

"Goodbye, Sebastian."

I want to keep each memory with me forever, reach out and grab it somehow, as if they were pictures I could put in a box. I won't forget them, but I'll never see them like this again.

I'll never get to feel this level of emotion that Sebastian shares with us as he remembers a kiss, a hug, or a death. This is the most precious and most terrible moment of my life.

And I wouldn't change a thing about our family or the here and now.

All the pain is worth every bit of love.

Sebastian's heart slows until, finally, it stops.

The End

ALSO BY LIZ HAMBLETON

For other works and signed paperback copies visit www. lizhambletonbooks.com and read below.

The Storm Series is a completed trilogy. It follows Rowan as she navigates a post-apocalyptic future with her twin nephews. She stumbles across an unconscious man, and they create a family together in the chaos of this new world.

The first book in the series is The Third Storm.

The Center Duet is a romance set in a dystopian future where marriage is only promised for ten years at a time before you are forced to renew or find a new partner.

The first book in the Duet is The Discovery Center.

Affluence is a dark romance standalone about a woman who comes back to her island job ten years later to seek revenge and come face to face with the man she still loves.

Keep in Touch is a contemporary second-chance romance standalone about a woman who moves to another country. She wants to connect with a pen pal she's kept since childhood, but an unexpected romance blossoms along the way.